MURDER ON STILETTOS

A Detective Joe Ezell Mystery

Book Four

P.J. Conn

Book and cover design by eBook Prep
www.ebookprep.com

October, 2018
ISBN: 978-1-947833-95-1

ePublishing Works!
www.epublishingworks.com

CHAPTER 1

Los Angeles, October, 1947

Bloody footprints surrounded the body in dancing steps. Joe Ezell had come across a more gruesome murder scene only once, and he'd done his best to forget it. He bent down to get a closer look at the tracks, and the sickening stench of freshly spilled blood instantly straightened his spine.

There was no sign of a fight, so the deceased must not have seen the first blow coming, and had had no chance to mount a defense. Blood splattered the wall in a sweeping arc, spoiling the pristine décor. The once beautiful apartment had been a serene mix of black and white, making the bright red splash doubly jarring.

Not wanting to smear whatever incriminating fingerprints might have been left behind, Joe knocked at the neighbor's door and a slim blonde answered. "I'm Joe Ezell, a private detective. There's been a murder, and I need you to call the police."

"Oh no." She gasped and grabbed the doorknob to steady herself. Dressed in a tightly belted pink satin robe and feathered mules, she appeared to be getting a very late start on the day. She glanced down the hallway to the door Joe had left standing ajar. She raised her hand to her throat. Her beautifully manicured nails were painted a bright red.

"I've never called the police. What should I say?"

"Give them your name and address and tell them there has been a murder in apartment eight. They'll take it from there."

"All right, I can handle that." She closed her door, and then yanked it open. "I'm sorry, but I'm not dressed and can't invite you in."

"I'd prefer to wait out here in the hallway. Please hurry and make the call. Then it would be a good idea for you to find some street clothes."

"Oh yes, right away." She closed her door and this time left it shut.

Twenty minutes later, LAPD Detective Jacob Lynch stepped out of the elevator. As always immaculately dressed in a well-tailored suit, he took one look at Joe, winced, and swore under his breath.

"Have you recently moved into this building, Mr. Ezell? If so, this is quite a step up for you."

Lynch knew where Joe lived because there had been a murder in his apartment building. Joe regarded the comparison between his modest home and this high-priced address rude in the extreme. He had never liked Lynch anyway. In fact, he could barely stand the man.

"No, I haven't moved. I was in the neighborhood working on a case."

"Really? You've shown a rare talent for showing up at murder scenes."

Joe nodded. "Yeah, I'm lucky that way."

When he'd been hired, he'd expected the usual follow and photograph work, and wondered how he could have been so badly mistaken.

Earlier in the week
Office of Discreet Investigations

During World War II, Joe Ezell had served in the Coast Guard on the Greenland patrol forecasting weather for Europe to aid the Allies in strategic planning. In his spare time, he'd read Dashiell Hammett's mystery novels and developed a deep admiration for his detective, Sam Spade.

With few jobs available for weather forecasters at the end of the war, he had studied a manual written by a former Pinkerton detective. After passing the California exam for a private investigator's license, he had proudly opened Discreet Investigations.

He had recently purchased a colorful painting of a California desert scene to give his small office some class. This morning he planned to again visit the Salvation Army thrift store in search of a rug. Interrupted by a ringing telephone, he counted to three before answering to appear busier than he actually was.

"Discreet Investigations."

A woman inquired in a hushed voice, "Are you really discreet?"

Joe muffled a totally inappropriate snort. "Indeed I am. You can be confident I'll take your secrets to my grave."

"My own secrets don't concern me. I need to speak with you in person. Do you have an opening this morning?"

He had no appointments for the day, and the purchase of a second hand rug could wait. "I have eleven o'clock free."

"I'll see you then. I'm Constance Remson."

"I'll look forward to meeting you, Miss Remson." He assumed a woman was unmarried, and let her correct him if she had a husband. Miss Remson hung up without comment, so apparently she was single.

He made a fresh pot of coffee, and took out a new manila folder and a yellow legal pad to make notes on her case. Another quick trip to the restroom at the end of the hallway provided water for the philodendron atop the file cabinet.

Its glossy green leaves had barely begun to droop, but he wasn't taking any chances.

Constance Remson arrived precisely at 11:00. Her glossy brown hair floated over her shoulders in a free-flowing pageboy cut, and not a strand lay out of place. Her eyes were a deep brown, and her thick black lashes left faint shadows on her cheeks. Her man-tailored white shirt was tucked into the waistband of a slim black skirt, but there was nothing masculine about her.

She had a wealthy woman's tall, slender body, and a wide gold bangle on her right wrist. She took a chair opposite Joe's desk, crossed her long, shapely legs, and bounced a black stiletto heel on her toe.

Joe didn't recognize her cloying perfume, but she smelled like trouble. He planned to marry soon, however, and needed every dollar he could honestly earn. He welcomed her with his most charming smile.

"Tell me about your problem, Miss Remson, and I'll do my best to solve it."

"Do you know Matteo da Milano?"

"Sorry, we're not acquainted. Would you care for a cup of coffee?"

She cast a dismissive glance toward the coffee pot sharing space with the potted plant on the filing cabinet and shook her head. "No, thank you. I should have asked if you knew of Matteo. He's the featured cellist with the Los Angeles Philharmonic. I'm a patron of the orchestra, and we met at a party following a concert. He's a musical genius, very charming, devilishly handsome, and known to be a lady's man."

She pulled a small photo from her purse. "You can keep this. We've been seeing each other for several months. He swears he adores me, but he may have several other women on the side. I won't abide it."

"Nor should you." She spoke with the crisp diction of a voice coach, and he readily understood how little patience she would have for a man with straying affections.

The photograph appeared to be a publicity pose showing Matteo with his cello. His dark hair had a slight curl, his brown eyes held a teasing sparkle, and his features were as perfect as a Greek god's. Women undoubtedly found the slight quirk to his smile doubly appealing.

"Would you like me to follow him for a week or so to gauge how deep his regard for you might actually run? I'll supply photographs whenever possible."

"Yes, proof is exactly what I need. I refuse to engage in childish arguments. If you find Matteo is seeing other women, I'll hand him the incriminating photos, and tell him good-bye before he has time to realize he's been caught in an unforgivable lie."

Joe asked for her address and telephone number for his file, as well as Matteo's information. He also added twenty dollars to his usual retainer, and she paid it without a single bat of her remarkable eyelashes.

"I brought a copy of the LA Philharmonic's schedule, and the address where they rehearse. He's there most days, but the hours vary."

He laid them on his desk. "I'll begin this afternoon, and call you when I have something to report." He stood as she rose from her chair and walked her to the door. He closed it behind her, and waited a moment to be certain she wouldn't return before opening the window to let in some much needed fresh air.

Cleotis Cotton, the building custodian, knocked on Joe's door and looked in. "I saw your new client. I swear it was like watching money slink down the stairs. Can't say I care much for her perfume though. Would you like me to bring in a fan?"

"Yes, that's a great idea, CC." Before beginning his surveillance of Matteo da Milano, Joe would have time to get a quick lunch at the counter in the drug store downstairs. The telephone rang while he was placing Constance Remson's file in his desk drawer.

"Discreet Investigations."

"I must speak with the owner, please," a woman responded in a breathless rush.

"This is Joe Ezell. How may I help you?"

"I'm Paloma Val Verde, and I need to see you today about a romantic matter that simply can't be delayed. I can be there in ten minutes."

"Fine. I'll see you then."

Paloma Val Verde was as exotic a creature as her name. Her curly black hair was knotted atop her head and decorated with ribbons and fresh red roses. Upswept eyelashes framed her hazel eyes. The bodice of her flowing aqua dress was heavily embroidered with colorful flowers and looked to be from Olvera Street, a historic plaza and tourist attraction located near Union Station. The shops there sold colorful clothing and crafts celebrating Los Angeles's Spanish heritage. Authentic down to her toes, Paloma wore Mexican huaraches.

She took a chair and arranged her dress in neat folds across her lap. Silver bracelets circled her wrists, and provided a faint musical accompaniment as she accented her words with graceful gestures. Her nails were polished a pale pink, her only subdued note.

"Thank you for finding time to see me. You must hear more than your share of women complaining about unfaithful men."

Joe hadn't kept track. "And vice versa."

"Yes, of course, but I'll bet most of your clients are women. We seek answers for our problems while men tend to hope their troubles will disappear on their own. Pathetic creatures most of the them, present company excepted, of course." She giggled, as though she'd meant her comment in fun.

"Thank you, but this is Discreet Investigations, and I never share client information with anyone."

"I'm delighted to hear it. I'm an artist, Mr. Ezell, and a great admirer of the celebrated Mexican painter, Frida Kahlo. Perhaps you've heard of her?"

"Yes, I have." He'd seen a photograph of her in a magazine, and recalled her intense gaze and flower-bedecked hair.

"She paints extraordinary self-portraits, while I'm concentrating on colorful birdhouses. I build them from scraps of wood to have models for my paintings. I'm becoming popular with those who collect art, although I don't pretend to have even a particle of Frida Kahlo's talent.

"But I digress. I met Matteo da Milano at an art show last spring. Have you heard of him?"

Joe's clients astonished him so often he had become adept at masking his surprise. "The principal cellist with the LA Philharmonic?"

"Yes, that's Matteo. He's become a dear friend, much more I should say. He may soon propose, and I want to be certain he's not seeing anyone else before I accept."

Perplexed to have a second inquiry about the same man in a single day, Joe wasn't sure how to respond. "It's natural such a talented man would be popular."

"Believe me, he'd be popular playing the harmonica on a street corner." She giggled again. Paloma was a pretty young woman and clearly knew how to use her looks to a saucy advantage. She handed him the same publicity photograph Constance had given him.

Joe studied it as though he'd not already seen it that morning. "You're right, he's a very handsome man." It was difficult to believe the famed cellist could have been attracted to someone as aloof as Constance Remson, as well as this adorable artist.

"I'll make a point of attending a LA Philharmonic concert someday soon. Has Mr. da Milano done something to make you suspicious of his intentions?"

She pursed her lips and gave his question a moment's thought. "No, he's wonderfully attentive, but he does have a reputation for womanizing. Artists are known to be free spirits, Mr. Ezell, but it pays to be sensible when the situation demands it."

"I couldn't agree more." Hoping a professional way to serve both clients would soon come to him, he accepted a retainer, and she provided Matteo's home address and the LA Philharmonic performance schedule. "I'll call as soon as I have something to report."

"Please do. Now I must get back to my work." She rose, gave her dress a quick swish so it fell gracefully into place around her ankles, and slipped the strap of a tooled leather handbag over her shoulder. "It's been a pleasure to meet you, Mr. Ezell. I was afraid you'd be as gruff as Humphrey Bogart is in his films."

"He's playing a character," Joe reminded her. "He's probably very pleasant in person."

"I shall hope so for Laurel Bacall's sake."

He opened the door for her, and remembered too late that he'd neglected to ask if she'd care for a cup of coffee. He received few compliments on the brew, but still, it provided a gracious welcome to his office.

Joe dined that evening with his fiancée, Mary Margaret McBride, a nurse who worked at the West Los Angeles Veteran's Hospital. In addition to being a fabulous cook, she was a sensible young woman, who gave insightful advice.

"Two women came to see me today about the same man. Before I could voice a coherent, ethical objection to taking the second woman's money, she'd already paid me and left."

Mary Margaret was a petite redhead with a musical laugh. "Oh, Joe, when woman number two came in, you had the answer to both women's concerns."

He finished a bite of a savory pork chop before he answered. "I realized it at the time, but I run Discreet Investigations remember, and can't divulge one client's complaint to another. It also occurred to me that if a man is seeing two women, he might also be seeing a third."

"Good point, and you can report on woman number three to both clients without telling them about each other."

"While I've serious misgivings about the case, it's worth a try. The second young woman gave me a different home address for the man. That struck me as odd."

"Some people do have more than one home."

"Within two blocks of each other?"

"You're right. That is odd. Are they nice places?"

"Yes, they are in well-appointed apartment buildings in West LA. He might have some movie star neighbors. I checked the mailboxes, and he uses initials on one, and his last name only on the other. He's a musician, and it's possible he uses one place as a rehearsal studio."

Unimpressed, her gaze took on a skeptical gleam. "Are you making excuses for him?"

"Certainly not. I'm merely considering all the possibilities. He's something of a public figure, so if he had a wife and family, both women would know."

They often discussed his cases, without names, of course, and she loved a good story as much as he did. "How do you plan to approach the case tomorrow?"

"I'll park near apartment number one in the morning and follow him if he appears. I know where he'll be later in the day, and I can follow him from there if need be. I doubt the case will take long."

She nodded thoughtfully. "Whatever cases you have, please remember to keep time open in December for our wedding and honeymoon."

He leaned close to kiss her. "Of course. How much rain is there in Seattle at that time of year?"

"A lot, so we won't plan a garden wedding. I know what you're thinking, it will be beautiful here where all our friends live, but my family lives in rainy Seattle."

Joe would have preferred to get married at the courthouse and be done with it, but she deserved to have a beautiful wedding to create cherished memories. "What do you hear from your mother?"

She rose to gather their dishes and carried them to the kitchen. Her cottage was small, so it was no more than a few steps. Joe followed to help. "Is it bad news?" he asked.

"Not exactly, but she is disappointed she won't have an opportunity to meet you before we arrive for the wedding. Two trips would be too costly for us, she understands that."

He slid his arms around her narrow waist and hugged her tight. She was the dream girl he'd never thought he'd have, and he loved her desperately. "I promise to be so charming she'll welcome me into the family with open arms."

She leaned against him. "That might take some practice. We should probably begin tonight."

"If you insist," he whispered against her ear, and the dishes were promptly forgotten.

Early the following morning, Joe parked his Chevrolet sedan across the street from Matteo da Milano's Almont Drive apartment house. Built after the war in the Moderne style with curved balconies and a flat roof, the three story building's pale gray exterior was brightened with red doors and window trim. Matteo's second residence was in a sandstone building reminiscent of the country estates featured in English movies.

Joe had brought along the morning's copy of the *Los Angeles Times* to read and put up as a shield if necessary. He looked up often, and recognized Matteo from his photo as he left his building with a beautiful companion. Surprised, Joe sat up straight.

He had met Lily Montell, an exotic dancer, or striptease artist in plain language, on his last murder case. She used an elegant 1920's Art Deco costume for her act, and often wore gowns of lily-patterned fabric. He lifted his camera and got a quick photograph of them kissing good-bye before they left in separate taxicabs.

He'd hoped Matteo would be involved with a third woman, but Lily Montell hadn't been what he'd had in mind. He liked her, and didn't want to involve her in a case complicated by too many women. In addition to being a superb musician, Matteo must also possess the skills of a disappearing artist to keep them from bumping into each other.

Joe stopped for breakfast at Herbert's Drive-In on the southeast corner of Beverly Blvd. and Fairfax. The bacon and eggs were good, but he failed to come up with any strategy to satisfy his two current clients other than the hope Matteo might be involved with a fourth woman. He hadn't been in his office long when the phone rang.

"Discreet Investigations."

"Hi, Joe, this is Lily Montell. Were you parked on Almont Avenue this morning?"

He took a deep breath and released it slowly. "Nice to hear from you, Lily. I never discuss my jobs, but I might have been in the neighborhood."

"I don't have to ask why you were there. Are you free to see me before noon?"

"Of course. Come on over."

Lily wore a form-fitting lavender silk dress splashed with a bold lily print. Black stiletto heels boosted her height above her natural five foot four inches. She kept her hair short and styled in the neat waves fashionable in the 1920s. It was perfect for her act, and gave her delicate features a lovely frame, but her expressive dark eyes held a hint of sorrow.

"I've ended the affair with my married beau, and I miss him terribly. We were doomed from the beginning, so I've no one to blame but myself for the predictable sadness now. Matteo da Milano and I met only a few weeks ago, and he's definitely single. He's also an ardent lover."

She paused to study Joe's reaction. "Am I embarrassing you?"

He had done his best not to squirm in his chair. "No, certainly not. I can appreciate a sophisticated young woman's tastes as well as the next private detective. Go on, tell me more."

"I've probably already said too much, but if another woman has hired you to follow Matteo, there has to be competition for his affections. You can say yes or no to that, can't you?"

"First tell me why you believe Matteo's affections aren't sincere."

"You slipped a copy of the LA Philharmonic's schedule into your desk when I came in. That's certainly a tipoff. The group travels to present concerts in other cities. Matteo is also a featured guest with the New York Philharmonic. I'm never sure whether or not he's in town, and it's disconcerting."

"He doesn't give you a copy of his schedule?"

"No, and I haven't asked for one other than the one for the LA Philharmonic's concerts in town. He calls me when he has a free evening. That's a bad sign, isn't it?"

Joe shrugged. "It's difficult to say."

She laughed at his continued effort at discretion. "Fine, I saw you keeping an eye on Matteo's building, and that's all I really need to know. Stay safe, Joe."

"You too, Lily." He walked her to the door and waited a moment to close it. She was too perceptive a young woman to fall for the noncommittal responses he'd given, but he hadn't betrayed his clients' confidence. Being ethical meant a great deal to him.

Later than morning, Marty Streech peeked in his door. "Are you busy?"

A reporter with the *Los Angeles Examiner*, they had met while Joe was working on a murder case last summer. Marty appeared slightly disheveled, as though he'd been too caught up in a story to go home, shower, and change clothes.

Joe closed the folder on his desk to hide the crossword puzzle. "Come on in. What's up, Marty?"

He slumped into a chair and assumed his usual careless pose. "I've been covering the death on the movie set at MGM. You must have heard about it."

"I have. A couple of extras got into a tussle, a set collapsed, and one ended up dead."

"That's the one. Thalia Dupré was set to star in the film, some South Seas adventure titled *Flamingo Lane*. Now she's refused to appear in it unless the film has a new script and title. Apparently she's the superstitious sort."

"I thought all theatre people were."

"That's what I've heard too, but apparently the set wall was so poorly constructed it was bound to fall on someone. Thalia could have been the original target."

"That might be difficult to prove, Marty."

He grinned. "True, but it will make for a good story. The carpenter who built the fallen wall disappeared the day before the accident. The police are looking for him, but I hope to find him first. I just came by to see if you were working on anything worthy of a column."

"Just the usual follow and photograph jobs. No new clues on the Black Dahlia murder?"

"No, the police are flummoxed, which happens too often. I just don't want another pretty young woman found sprawled in a field in two bloodless halves."

"I agree. One such grisly death was too many."

Marty rose and adjusted the cuffs on his wrinkled jacket. "Give me a call when you're working on something meriting reporting."

"Will do." Joe let him go without offering a cup of coffee. Marty was ambitious, and a good source when a mention in the *Examiner* might help solve a case, but Joe didn't regard him as a friend. He doubted Marty would call him one either.

That afternoon, Joe followed Matteo da Milano's taxi home from the rehearsal hall to his apartment on Almont Drive. The cellist entered the starkly modern building carrying a black cello case. With the man's fondness for women, Joe doubted he would stay in for the evening, and he planned to follow him wherever he might be bound.

A woman wearing a fur coat and stiletto heels came around the corner and approached Mateo's building. Her face was hidden by a fur hat pulled low over her brow.

"What do we have here?" Joe brought up his camera for a quick photo seconds before she passed through the apartment's glass entry doors. Maybe she was a resident returning from an errand, but a woman that well-dressed would most likely arrive in a taxi, unless she asked to be let off down the block so no one could place her as having been there.

Matteo successfully juggled three women, and this might be the lady number four Joe had hoped to find. Unfortunately, she would be difficult to identify bundled in furs and a face-shading hat.

Joe still held his camera when less than five minutes later the fur-wrapped woman exited the building and hurried down the sidewalk in the direction she had come. He got another couple of photos, mainly of her back, but she'd been nearly sprinting in her stilettos, which was no mean trick.

Something was definitely off. He left his Chevrolet to cross the street. When he found bloody footprints on the sidewalk, he tracked them until they grew faint and disappeared at the corner. The woman was nowhere in sight. She had either had a car or taxi waiting, which meant she hadn't planned to stay long.

He jogged back to Matteo's building, yanked open a glass door, and followed the gory footprints up the stairs. They led to apartment eight, Matteo's residence, and the door had been left unlatched.

"Mr. da Milano?" he called. When there was no answer, he gave the door a gentle push, and it swung open to reveal the cellist lying in a pool of blood.

Detective Lynch yanked Joe's attention to the present. The detective held the small notebook he carried with his pen poised to write. "Did the case you were investigating involve Mr. da Milano?"

"Clients rely on my discretion. I never discuss my cases with a third party."

"Don't become tiresome, Ezell, or I'll take you downtown where you'll have plenty of time to reconsider your answer."

Lynch was too serious an individual to make idle threats, and Joe didn't doubt him. "Since you insist, I was following the cellist, but not for just one client, for two women who doubted his affections. Clearly he was also involved with several more."

"One woman is difficult enough. How did he manage it?" Keen to hear the details, the detective peered closely at Joe.

"Not well, obviously." He gestured toward the cluster of bloody footprints. "Did you notice the shoeprints are all from the left shoe?"

"Of course. The murderer appears to have hopped around Mr. da Milano as she delivered killer blows with her right shoe. A stiletto heel made for a vicious weapon. The first blow to the back of the head must have killed him."

Joe nodded thoughtfully. "He could have opened his door, and turned away as he welcomed his guest inside. He wouldn't have seen death coming."

"Marvelous insight." A dry, sarcastic edge flavored Lynch's observation. "If he'd recognized her intentions, he wouldn't have stood there and allowed her to pummel him with her shoe without fighting back. Bring the photographs of the women he was seeing to me as quickly as you can."

"I don't photograph my clients. I do have one of da Milano with Lily Montell, but she wasn't the woman I photographed today entering and quickly exiting this building."

"The stripper?"

"Yes, she's a lovely young woman when you get to know her."

The detective shook his head. "Undoubtedly, I want the names of your clients, and Lily's photo along with the other woman's."

"I'll have prints made for you, but the woman who appears to be the murderess was so bundled in furs it will take a close friend to identify her."

"It's a start, Ezell."

"That's true," Joe agreed, but he doubted the detective would know what to do with it.

After the detective returned to apartment eight, Joe lingered in the hallway. He kept out of the way as the LAPD crime scene photographer arrived carrying his 4x5 Speed Graphic camera. Two men with Coroner stenciled in white on the back of their navy blue windbreakers left the elevator with a stretcher.

The young woman who had called the police peeked out her door. She'd dressed in tan slacks and a white sweater. "Is it Matteo who's dead?" she whispered.

"Was there someone else who also lived in number eight?" Joe asked.

She took a step into the hallway. "No, but he often entertained company."

"Did he host noisy parties?"

"Oh no, sometimes he played music, but it was the dreamy classical kind, not anything fun for a party and dancing."

Jacob Lynch regarded Joe with a dismissive glance as he joined them. He again had his notebook and pen ready. "I need your name, miss."

"Tanya Olson. I don't actually live here. This is Linda Skye's place, and I'm looking after her apartment while she's working in London for a couple of months. I barely knew Mr. da Milano. He was friendly, but I leave early for modeling assignments, and seldom saw him. I've no idea who could have killed him, if that was your next question."

"It wasn't." He asked for her telephone number. "I'll give you a call if there are any further questions. Please return to your apartment so you won't be in our way."

"Of course. I wouldn't want to impede your investigation." She regarded him with a dazzling smile before turning toward her door.

Miss Olson had clearly been impressed by Jacob Lynch, and Joe bit his tongue rather than laugh. It must have been the detective's bespoke suit that had caught her eye, because Lynch sure hadn't flirted with her. Some women were drawn to the strong, silent type, and it looked as though Tanya Olson might be one. He hurried away before the detective could order him to go.

He dropped off the film at Pete's Cameras. "I need these for the police as soon as possible, and I need copies for myself as well."

"I'll rush them through tonight, and have them for you in the morning. If the police are involved, it must be an important case."

Pete had red hair and freckles, and a friendly, helpful manner. Joe didn't confide in him, however. "You could say that. I'll see you in the morning." He always tipped Pete for fast service, but this time, the need was truly urgent. If he had a photo of the murderess, he hoped Detective Lynch would put it to good use, but that was probably unwarranted optimism.

CHAPTER 2

"I'm afraid it's ended in the worst way possible."

"Oh no, has someone died?"

"Yes, the man with multiple girlfriends. Apparently one young woman took violent exception to his wandering affections and beat him to death with a stiletto heel."

She clasped both hands over her mouth to silence a most inappropriate giggle. "You don't mean it."

"I do. The case was assigned to Detective Lynch, and he was as charming as always."

"Which is not at all?"

"Exactly. He demanded names of my clients who were interested in the man, and copies of any photos I'd taken, so he did take me seriously, for once. Unfortunately, the woman I saw hurriedly leaving the dead man's building was so swathed in furs, she won't be easily identified."

"Today wasn't really cold enough for a fur coat," Mary Margaret observed.

"You're right. It was a balmy day. The furs may have been a disguise. She was in and out of the building in under five minutes."

"That's hardly long enough to begin a murderous argument, let alone end one. Could she have gone there intent on murder?"

"It seems likely."

"Wait a minute," she cautioned. "What if the woman you saw fleeing the scene was married, and always disguised herself for a rendezvous with her lover? She might have happened upon his body, and rather than call the police, bolted to protect her reputation."

Joe sat back and took a sip of coffee while he considered the idea. "She was the only one I saw entering the building after the man came home."

"Someone who lives in his building could have been lying in wait and killed him."

Tanya Olson had come to the door in her robe. Had she slipped it on after discarding her bloodstained clothes? After this many hours, she would have gotten rid of whatever incriminating evidence Lynch might have found had he searched her apartment that afternoon.

"You're right. I met one woman who lives in the building, and there are twelve occupied units, if I still count Matteo, who won't be coming home again. I'm not sure how many are rented by women. I'll have to check."

"Don't discount married couples," she warned. "A jealous husband could be the murderer. Isn't there a rear door to the building he could have used?"

"There must be." Her insightful questions made him feel as inept as Jacob Lynch. "It's been a long day."

"Yes, it has." She stood, and he helped her on with her jacket and placed a quick teasing kiss behind her ear.

She took his hand, and murmured a not so subtle suggestion they talk about something other than murder.

Joe was happy to oblige, but he sure hoped it wouldn't be their upcoming wedding.

First thing Thursday morning, Joe picked up the two copies of the photos he'd taken at the Almont apartment, and dropped one set off for Detective Lynch. Fortunately, the man hadn't come in yet, which Joe considered a great start for the day.

Once at the office, he needed to call Paloma Val Verde and Constance Remson to let them know Matteo had died. He could also report the popular cellist had been seeing other women, which would only add to their sorrow. He doubted either would want to fund a private murder investigation, but he was sure he'd seen the murderess, and he couldn't let it go.

He began with Constance Remson, but there was no answer at her number. He was surprised a maid didn't respond to take messages when she was out. He dialed Paloma Val Verde's number next.

"Good morning, Miss Val Verde, it's Joe Ezell. I'm afraid I have awful news about Matteo."

She sniffed loudly. "I heard it on the radio and read all about it in the *LA Times* this morning. I can't believe someone so full of life is dead."

He was relieved not to be the first to tell her of the tragedy. "Yes, it's a terrible shame. However, I do have a report for you." The instant he said the words, they struck him as totally inappropriate.

"No, please, keep the retainer, but I don't want to know if Matteo saw other women. I'd rather pretend he loved only me. Is that a silly thing to do?"

"Of course, not. You're entitled to cherish your memories of him."

"Thank you, you make me feel better. I'll keep your card in case I ever need a detective again."

He sought a way to add another important point without revealing anything she didn't wish to know. "The detective covering Matteo's death may call you. We spoke at the scene, and he insisted upon having the name of anyone concerned with the case."

She stifled a choked gasp. "You mean I'm a suspect?"

There was no telling what Lynch might dream up, so he couldn't promise she wasn't. "He'll probably simply be gathering information about Matteo's friends and habits. Please don't fret over it."

"All right, but I can't talk about Matteo without crying. He meant the world to me."

Joe spent a while longer offering what comfort he could before telling her good-bye. He tried Constance's number again, but there was still no answer.

When his office telephone rang, he hoped for a new case that wouldn't involve murder. "Discreet Investigations."

"Hi Joe, it's Hal." An insurance executive and former client, Hal Marten was Joe's golf buddy. "We spoke a while ago about your working on insurance fraud cases for California West. Are you still interested?"

"Sure. Tell me what you need."

"Let's meet at noon for lunch." Hal named a café near his office building.

"I know the place." Joe got there a few minutes early and found secretaries and women out shopping also ate there as well as successful businessmen whose suits cost more than he would spend in a year on his wardrobe. Detective work required him to fit in rather than stand out, and he made no effort to be as sharp a dresser as Hal Marten.

Hal was five foot ten with fair hair and blue eyes. He had a lean build, but there was nothing boyish about him. He'd served in the Quartermaster Corps during the war and, like Joe, had not seen combat, but he was proud to be a veteran. He slid into the seat opposite Joe and picked up the menu.

"Let's eat and then talk," Hal suggested.

"Fine with me." Joe loved bacon, lettuce, and tomato sandwiches, and the café served an exceptionally fine one. The quality of the bacon made all the difference, and he ate every crumb. When Hal finished his sandwich, Joe took out his notebook and pen.

"Emily MacNaughton and her husband, Daniel, have been insured by California West for nearly twenty years. She claims her two carat diamond engagement ring has been stolen. She usually wore only her wedding band and saved the diamond ring for special occasions. She wanted to wear it for a lunch date with a friend, but when she opened her jewelry box, it had disappeared."

"Did she report the loss to the police?"

"That very morning, but nothing else was missing from her home, and there was no sign of a break-in. She's had the same cleaning woman and gardener for years, and insists a stranger must have entered her home and stolen the ring on a day both she and her husband were out."

"Why wouldn't a thief have taken everything in her jewelry box, or the box itself?" Joe asked.

"My thoughts exactly. Daniel is recently retired, and he's in and out of the house as well as his wife, but one or the other is usually at home."

"So with no date for the loss, or evidence of a break-in, you suspect fraud?" Joe asked.

"That's the question I want you to answer." Hal handed Joe a California West Insurance identification card. "Will you talk to the couple and give me your opinion on them? We'll double your usual fee, plus a bonus if you locate the ring."

Joe would gratefully add it to the wedding fund. "I'll be happy to speak with them. If the man is retired, he might be short of money and could have pawned the ring without telling his wife."

"Or maybe just sold it, but California West isn't paying their claim without being certain it's an actual loss." He pulled the couple's contact information from his breast pocket. "Your visit might be enough to inspire them to tell the truth. Threaten jail time for fraud if you need to." There was no mistaking the seriousness of Hal's mood.

"I hope I won't have to go that far."

"So do I. On a lighter note, how are the wedding plans coming along?"

"Mary Margaret is such a terrific gal. I adore her, but planning a wedding in Seattle is way beyond me."

Hal rose with him. "Let her handle everything. All a groom has to do is show up on time."

If the ceremony were going to be in Los Angeles, Joe would have asked Hal to be his best man. He supposed he'd have to ask one of Mary Margaret's brothers. She'd choose one to escort her down the aisle, and he hoped the other one would be gracious about being his best man. He'd hate for their marriage to begin with trouble between her brothers, but not having met them, he couldn't help but fear the worst.

Once back at his office, Joe called the MacNaughtons and introduced himself as an investigator with California West. He made an appointment to see them that afternoon at four o'clock. They lived in a quiet West Los Angeles neighborhood in a brick home with sparkling white shutters and window trim. The lawn was a verdant green and the flowerbeds filled with yellow chrysanthemums in full-bloom. Joe strode up the walk, and rang the doorbell.

Emily came to the door. She was a petite woman who stared up at him through her glasses with an inquisitive owl-like glance. "Mr. Ezell? I'm so pleased to meet you. I miss my ring terribly, and hope to replace it soon."

Daniel waited for them in the living room. He extended his hand, but dropped Joe's after a perfunctory shake. The room was comfortably furnished in greens of varying hues, and Joe chose a leather armchair. Emily and Daniel sat together on the sofa. She moved close and clutched her husband's arm.

Emily repeated the same story Hal had told him. She impressed Joe as being sincere, while Daniel stared at the rug. He was a chubby fellow with thinning gray hair, and let his wife do all the talking.

"I'll check with the police for reports of robberies in the area. Have any of your neighbors mentioned suffering any losses?"

Emily glanced at Daniel, who shrugged. "No, but I've been too embarrassed to tell anyone my ring is gone. That it was in a jewelry box that doesn't even have a lock makes it seem as though I'm careless with my things, which I assure you isn't the case."

"You don't recall coming home and finding a window open or a door unlocked that you were certain you had locked when you left?" Joe asked.

"No, not even once. What about you, honey?" she asked.

Daniel shook his head. "No. We're careful and don't leave a key under the doormat like many people do."

"That's good," Joe replied. He trusted his instincts, and while Emily projected a concerned innocence, Daniel had difficulty meeting his eye. He wouldn't admit anything in front of his wife, however.

"Mr. MacNaughton, would you please walk with me around the exterior of the house? We might see something that's been missed."

A flash of alarm crossed Daniel's expression before he leaped to his feet. "Sure. Whatever you think we need to do."

Joe ushered him out the front door before Emily could join them. He took a few steps on the lawn and looked up at the house. "This is a beautiful home."

"Yes, we've been very happy here."

Turning to face him, Joe lowered his voice, "Valuables don't just disappear. Is your wife the type who might have left the ring on the counter in the kitchen where it could have been inadvertently swept into the trash?"

Daniel concentrated on the chrysanthemums while he answered. "Oh no, never. She's not a careless woman, and she didn't wear the ring while working in the kitchen."

Guilt nearly dripped off the man. "What did you do with the ring, Mr. MacNaughton? Did you need money and sell it without telling your wife?"

Daniel took a staggering backwards step. "You've no proof of that," he stammered.

"I soon will. Insurance fraud is a serious crime, and California West will insist you're prosecuted to the full extent of the law. Drop the claim now, and we'll erase it, or you can risk prosecution if you so choose."

"I'd never meant for things to get so badly out of hand." Daniel pulled his handkerchief from his back pocket and blew his nose. "Do you ever go to Hollywood Park or Santa Anita for the racing?" he asked.

"I've been to both places. Did you bet money on horses you couldn't afford to lose?"

Tears filled Daniel's eyes, and he reached out to clutch Joe's arm. "You won't tell my wife? She doesn't have to know, does she?"

"Tell me the truth first, and then I'll decide." Joe could be tough when he had to be, but he felt sorry for the poor guy.

"Emily believes we're comfortably well-off, and to some extent we are, but we need to watch our expenses. She can't seem to understand that."

"Blaming the mess you've gotten yourself into on your wife won't impress anyone at California West," Joe warned. It certainly didn't impress him.

"Oh no, I'm not blaming her," he insisted. "I just thought if I won money at the track, we'd have more of a cushion."

"And not surprisingly, you were wrong?"

"Yes, I don't know how I could have been such a fool. I won quite a bit the first time I went to Hollywood Park, but then fell into a losing streak. I took Emily's ring to a jeweler, and asked him to replace the stone with one of lesser quality. I sold him the flawless stone to make up for what was missing from our savings. I didn't think Emily would ever notice."

The matter was predictably appalling, and Joe shook his head. "But Emily discovered the ring was missing before you could return it to her jewelry box?"

Sweating now, Daniel folded his handkerchief to wipe his forehead. "She didn't wait for me to get home before she called California West and the police. I didn't know what to do other than to go along with the robbery story. I'm sorry. I didn't mean to cheat California West. I know it's a crime."

Joe wasn't fond of sniveling. "You ought to explain what you did to your wife."

"Oh no, I could never do that. Her father was a gambler, and she'd never forgive me for risking our savings betting on horses."

"Where is her ring?" Joe asked.

"It's upstairs in my dresser. It's so beautiful, she'd never have noticed the stone had been replaced."

As Joe saw it, he'd saved California West the cost of replacing a diamond ring, which is what the job required. He couldn't walk off, however. "Go get it. When you come back, you're going to pretend you found the ring under a window where the 'thief' dropped it as he hurried away."

Daniel's face brightened with hope. "You think it will work?"

"It's worth a try if you're opposed to the truth, which is what I really recommend."

Daniel hurried around to the rear of the house to enter and returned in under a minute. "The powder room on the first floor has a window that's often left open. A thief might have used it to come and go. Let's find it there."

Joe walked with him to the side of the house where a low hedge bordered the lawn. "If the ring had been dropped in the dirt, it would have been easily recovered before the man sprinted away. Let's say a glimmer of gold caught your attention. You leaned over to investigate, and found the ring in the hedge."

"Yes! That's believable." He looked into the hedge and placed the ring on a small branch. He stepped back to make certain it could still be seen. "I'll say I found it right there should Emily want to come out and see the exact spot."

"Before you speak with her, I'd like your promise you won't do something this foolish ever again."

Daniel raised his hand. "I swear it. I'll insist we make a budget and stick to it."

"Set some money aside for taking your wife out for dinner and the movies. She also ought to have a clothing allowance."

"Entertainment, of course, I'll include it, and she loves new clothes. I'll make certain she understands we need to be more frugal now that I'm retired."

Joe followed him inside and stood back as Daniel showed Emily the ring. He was so excited to escape an insurance fraud charge every word rang true. "I'd never have found it had Mr. Ezell not suggested we check the area around the first floor windows. He deserves all the credit!"

Emily slipped the ring on her finger, hugged her husband, and then Joe. "Thank you so much, Mr. Ezell. I was so afraid my ring was lost forever. What do we do now? Are there papers to sign to withdraw the claim?"

Joe thought there must be. "I'll turn in my report, and you'll hear from California West. In the future, it would be a good idea to make certain the powder room window is closed and locked before you leave home."

"It won't be overlooked ever again," Daniel promised.

Joe walked out feeling he'd handled the job to everyone's satisfaction. Now would be a good time to visit Matteo da Milano's apartment building when residents would be getting home from work.

Streetlights coming on in the gathering dusk gave the twelve unit building on Almont Drive a pale, iridescent sparkle. Lamps brightened the windows in ten of the apartments. Joe checked the mailboxes for names. Number one had only Manager neatly printed on the card in the slot. He began there.

A tall, thin man with thick, dark hair answered the door. There was an odd twist to his mouth, as though he preferred a sneer to a smile. Joe introduced himself and handed him his business card. "I represent clients concerned with Matteo da Milano's death." He showed him the photo of the woman swathed in furs. "Does she look familiar, Mr.?"

"Perkins," he replied, and his voice held an odd hollow ring as though it echoed from his toes. "Never saw her."

"You were aware Mr. da Milano frequently had female visitors?"

"So?"

What was required was the dental approach, because getting anything worthwhile out of Perkins would be like pulling teeth. Unfortunately, Joe had yet to perfect such a useful technique. "One of those women may have killed him. That a murder happened here isn't a plus for the building."

"There's a long waiting list," Perkins replied.

"I'm sure the owners are pleased." Joe responded. "Good evening."

Perkins hesitated before closing his door. "If any of the tenants complain you're ruining their evening, I'm calling the cops."

"That would be excellent work on your part." Joe turned away, but waited until he'd heard Perkins lock his front door before he knocked at number two. The resident was listed as Winifred Lacewell, and he couldn't wait to meet her.

"Miss Lacewell?" he asked when she opened her door. He introduced himself and handed her his card.

She was a petite woman with snowy white hair, and showed charming dimples when she smiled. "It's Mrs. Lacewell, and I've no need for a detective, young man."

He explained his purpose and showed her the photo. She studied it carefully before handing it back. "I wish you luck with your investigation, but her own mother wouldn't recognize her under all those furs. I loved Matteo's music and attend the philharmonic concerts whenever I can. He'll truly be missed."

"I'm sure he will be. Keep my card. Something relevant may occur to you in a day or two." He bid her a good evening and went on to apartment three. "Mr. Ambrose?"

"Don," he corrected. "My wife and I are realtors, and we like to get to know everyone on a first name basis."

Joe explained his purpose and showed Don the photo. "She doesn't look familiar. Let me ask my wife. Sylvia, will you come here for a minute?"

Sylvia came to the door wearing an apron. "Hello, I'm Sylvia Ambrose. How do you do?"

They were a charming couple, or at least pretended to be to sell real estate. Joe waited while she studied the photo. She bit her lip and looked as though she might be some help, but then shook her head.

"I'm sorry. We meet so many people in our work, and most faces fade from memory before suppertime."

Joe left his card, thanked them, and moved on before they could quiz him on his housing needs. A Robert Galindo lived in apartment four, and he yanked open his door with an absolute vengeance. Joe nearly ducked before he caught himself. He gave his usual introduction and handed him his card.

"Have you ever seen this woman here?"

Galindo gave the photo a quick glance. "No, I'm an attorney and spend more time at my office than I do here. I'm preparing for a trial and have no time to chat about Matteo. I do love the Philharmonic orchestra when I have time to go, however. Good night."

Joe used the stairs to reach the second floor. Michael Campbell lived in apartment five. Of average height with brown hair and eyes, his lime green shirt and brightly patterned tie made him instantly memorable. Unlike his neighbors, he welcomed Joe into his home. A large modern painting hung above the fireplace. The near-blinding bright splashes of color threatened to give Joe a migraine, but he smiled as though he admired it greatly.

Michael followed Joe's glance. "I'm an interior designer and purchase art for my clients. I'm not sure about this piece yet, but it's beginning to grow on me. Have you been in Matteo's apartment? That's my work. I did his other apartment too. He requested a traditional style there. Ho-hum in my opinion, but my work has to please my client, or I won't be paid."

"I have the very same problem. I'm sorry I haven't seen more than the entryway of Matteo's apartment. Do you know why he bore the expense of having two places so close together?"

"He wished to accommodate visitors from back east, and didn't want them underfoot. I just tell visiting family and friends to rent a hotel room." He laughed and then sighed. "I can't believe Matteo is dead. He was such an attractive man. Creative energy rolled off of him in torrents, and he inspired everyone he met."

"Apparently one person disagreed," Joe reminded him. "Have you ever seen this woman here?"

Michael carried the photo to a floor lamp for better light. "Looks like someone from New York to me. They drape themselves with furs there, and you don't see women wearing them nearly as often here in our warmer climate."

"Thank you, that's an excellent point. Please contact me if you recall something relevant."

"Of course I will. Matteo was popular with the ladies, but I'm often at my design studio until late, and don't remember sharing the elevator with any of his dates."

Sofia Ragland had apartment six. She was a tall, no nonsense type in a navy blue suit. She looked to be in her fifties, and pushed her glasses up her nose to get a better look at him. He introduced himself and showed her the photo.

She peered at it closely. "Odd outfit for California."

"Yes, others have also mentioned it. Does she look familiar in any way?"

"No one I know wears fur coats." She gave him the photo. "Good luck, every murderer ought to be caught."

"Amen to that. Thank you."

Tanya Olson, whom he'd met the day of the murder, lived in number seven. "Thank you again for calling the police. I'm checking with everyone in the building. Do you recognize the woman in this photo?"

"Did she kill Matteo?" Tanya asked, her pretty blue eyes wide.

He thought better of describing the trail of bloody shoeprints the mystery woman had left on the sidewalk. "She entered the building near the time of the murder."

"So she's a witness?"

"Maybe." Tanya was again dressed in slacks and a sweater. She was such a pretty girl, he wondered if she hadn't been among Matteo's many conquests. "Did you ever go out with Matteo?"

"Me?" She blushed. "No, I think he preferred brunettes. His loss, as my mother used to say."

"Wise woman. Keep my card and call me if you remember anything more."

"I sure will."

Joe was both tired and hungry and decided to visit the four residents living on the third floor another night. If the woman in furs had been a guest from New York, then according to Michael Campbell, she would have stayed at Matteo's other apartment. That meant he might have better luck showing her photo there. Of course, if the furs had been part of an elaborate disguise, then no one would recognize her there either.

CHAPTER 3

Friday morning, Joe went downtown to see Hal Marten at California West Insurance to turn in his report on the MacNaughtons. Hal's spacious office was beautifully furnished, which reminded Joe he still needed to pick up a used rug for his.

"There wasn't much to type," Joe explained. He described how quickly Daniel MacNaughton had confessed to replacing the diamond in the ring to cover gambling loses. His wife was unaware of the scheme. That was the sum of his report, even if there were more to their story.

"I don't know how one of your company adjusters would have handled the case, but we led Emily to believe the 'thief' had dropped the ring as he climbed out of the powder room window, and that Daniel had found it in the hedge."

Hal stared at him a long moment. "Mr. MacNaughton admitted to submitting a fraudulent claim, and you stayed to help him invent a story so he could return the ring, which hadn't actually been stolen, to his wife?"

"That's what I said," Joe responded. "She truly believed there had been a theft. You can tear up the claim, and Mrs. MacNaughton has her ring back. Everyone should be happy. I'm just charging you for my time, I don't expect a percentage of the value of the ring. That's simply too much when the issue was resolved so quickly."

Hal leaned back in his chair. "No, you deserve ten percent for solving the issue to California West's advantage. That's our standard policy. I'm sure we'll have other cases for you, but please don't make it a habit to help crooks cover their crimes."

"Mr. MacNaughton can't really be described as a garden variety crook, or I wouldn't have helped him." Joe took the check Hal offered, but he couldn't promise not to help the next poor fool who thought he could get away with making a fraudulent claim.

"There's a breakfast meeting scheduled for executives this Saturday morning, so I won't be able to play golf with you and Gilbert Werner. Maybe you two will still want to play."

"Let's all take Saturday off. I'll call Gilbert and let him know. See you next Saturday."

"I'm looking forward to it. Meetings that last more than fifteen minutes usually put me to sleep. On Saturday, that means there will be a real danger I might doze off and smother in my scrambled eggs."

"Take care that you don't. One of the benefits of being my own boss is that I never have to sit through tedious meetings, and I make Employee of the Month every time."

After depositing the generous California West check in the bank, Joe went to Sears and treated himself to a new rug. CC helped him carry it up the stairs to his office.

"This is a right pretty shade, Mr. Ezell. It brings out the colors in your painting."

"I'd hoped it would. Terra cotta I believe it's called." They rolled it out in the front half of his office, made sure it was straight, and placed the client chairs on it. "All right, the oak clothes tree and desk came with the office. I've added a file cabinet, coffee pot, a philodendron, an impressive California landscape, and a fine rug. Am I missing anything?"

CC surveyed the office with an appreciative glance. "Looks perfect to me. When you're ready to hire a secretary, you'll need to move into a larger space though."

"If I moved into a larger office, I couldn't afford a secretary. Mike Hammer, Mickey Spilane's detective, has a secretary but an author can makeup anything for a book."

"I like his stories. Anything else you need while I'm here?"

"Thank you again, CC, that's all for now." After the custodian left, Joe sat down at his desk, took 3x5 inch cards from the top drawer, and got to work creating a suspect map on the bulletin board he hung on the wall behind his desk.

Matteo da Milano's name went into the center. He wrote Paloma Val Verde and Constance Remson's names on two more cards. He added Lily Montell's card. They might not have had anything to do with the murder, but they belonged on the edge of the investigation. The woman dressed in furs had a card, but there still had to be a lot of people missing.

As for the residents of the Altmont apartments, Miss Lacewell and Sofia Ragland wouldn't have appealed to Matteo. Mrs. Ambrose was also outside the age range he preferred, so it was doubtful jealousy would have prompted her husband to murder.

Tanya Olson had said she hadn't dated the cellist, but that might not be true. That she'd greeted him in a dressing gown still disturbed him, and he put her name on a card to keep her in mind.

After having no success reaching Constance Remson, Joe was surprised when she entered his office without bothering to knock. He quickly removed the bulletin board and turned it toward the wall before she had a chance to see a card with her name. He stood to greet her, but with her strange perfume, he should have smelled her coming. She was dressed in a tailored gray blouse, a darker gray skirt, and the same pair of black stiletto heels.

"Miss Remson, I called several times, and was sorry not to find you at home."

Before taking a chair, she gave the new rug a fleeting bit of attention. "I see you're dressing up the place."

"Thank you for noticing," he remarked, although he doubted her comment had been a sincere compliment. He returned to his desk chair and rolled it into place. "You've heard about Mr. da Milano?"

"Of course, that's why I'm here. A Detective Lynch called me this morning to ask if I had an alibi for Wednesday afternoon when Matteo died. Fortunately, I was surrounded by friends at a birthday luncheon, that lasted well into the cocktail hour."

After a glance at the colorful landscape, she sighed. "Would you care to tell me how he happened to have my name?"

She didn't look pleased, but he doubted she ever did. He described meeting Lynch at the scene of Matteo's murder. "I was there following up on your case, and he insisted upon having your name, and any photographs I'd taken." He handed her the photo of the mystery woman. "Do you know her?"

Constance studied it closely. "That's Matteo's apartment building, that's all I recognize. Who is she?"

"No one seems to know, but she may have killed Matteo."

Reacting as though the photo had seared her fingers, she tossed it back to him. "So he was seeing other women."

It wasn't a question, but clearly she wanted confirmation. "Your suspicions proved correct." He'd not reveal her rivals' names, however, or how he'd happened upon the murder scene. That a woman would kill a man wielding a deadly stiletto heel didn't sound real anyway. Not that many women wore stiletto heels, something he should have considered earlier.

"This may appear to be an absurd question, but bear with me. Where did you buy the heels you're wearing?" he asked.

She responded with a strained smile. "It's certainly a quirky inquiry. These were custom made by Luigi Albano.

He also makes men's shoes, and Matteo wore them. Once you own a pair of Luigi's shoes, you'll no longer hunt for a perfect fit in any shoe store. They are pricey, of course, but they'll last much longer than your average shoe, and with his classic designs, they won't go out of style."

"Where is his shop?"

"It's on Vine Street in Hollywood, near the Brown Derby. Let me see the photo of the woman in the fur coat again." Joe handed it to her, and she studied it closely. "She is wearing stiletto heels, and they may have come from Luigi Albano, and maybe not. It's impossible to say."

Joe made a note of Luigi Albano's location. "Where else would a woman with a fur coat buy stilettos?"

"The high end department stores, Bullock's Wilshire, or I. Magnin must have them. Frederick's of Hollywood probably has some at a much lower price. From what I've heard, they sell enticing lingerie and other provocative clothing. Stilettos heels fall into that category."

He'd heard of Frederick's, and knew the average woman didn't shop there. "Thank you. With those leads, I might find someone who knows the woman."

"You're welcome." After a lingering glance at the colorful landscape, she sighed softly and straightened her already erect posture. "I want you to continue working for me to find who killed Matteo. Let's go to the funeral together tomorrow afternoon. It will give you a chance point out the other women Matteo was seeing."

It was an astonishing request, and one he couldn't condone. "I'll agree to work on Matteo's murder, but I won't identify those women. You wouldn't want to create a scene at the funeral. Let's go to watch for the woman in furs."

Displeased, her gaze narrowed slightly. "All right, I'll accept your terms rather than go through the hassle of hiring someone new. As for the woman in your photo, we've enjoyed mild weather this autumn, and she wouldn't have needed to wrap herself in furs. Would she show up again dressed for the North Pole?"

"She might. The police have the photograph I showed you, but they didn't release it to the press, so she wouldn't know she'd been seen leaving Matteo's building."

"Maybe she's an eccentric soul who always dresses that way."

"Let's hope so. I have a dark suit, so you shouldn't be embarrassed to be seen with me."

"You've no idea how easily I embarrass, Mr. Ezell. The funeral will be at one o'clock at the St. Mary of the Angels church on Finley Avenue. Do you know it?"

"I do. It's known for serving the Hollywood crowd, who aren't always welcome at other churches. Was Matteo a member?" The late cellist juggled so many women, it would be remarkable if he also found time to attend church services.

"No, he wasn't, but he knew Fr. Dodd, and the priest offered to officiate. The entire LA Philharmonic will probably attend. Let's meet in front at twelve-thirty so we won't be forced to sit out front in folding chairs."

Clearly the thought horrified her. "I'll meet you there." He walked her to the door. There was still time to visit Luigi Albano's shop, but first he went looking for CC to borrow a fan.

The Luigi Albano shop's front window held a swirl of gray satin and a beautifully hand-lettered sign stating shoes made to custom order. A single pair of men's black loafers and a pair of women's high heels in a deep purple that appeared navy blue at first glance provided evidence of his talent and skill.

Joe looked down at his own brown oxfords, a serviceable pair he'd brought at Sear's. They were comfortable, and with a frequent polish and new heels when needed they would last several years. He hoped he wasn't shown out of the shop before he could explain the reason for his visit.

Luigi was younger than Joe had expected, tall, good-looking, with prematurely gray hair softly curled over his collar as European men favored. His vivid green eyes were brightened by a deep tan. Rather than a shoe repairman's well-worn leather apron, Luigi wore a white dress shirt, neatly pleated gray wool trousers, and loafers identical to the pair in the window. Clearly he designed the shoes bearing his signature rather than fashion them himself.

Voices came from the workroom behind the well-furnished showroom. Joe could not help but imagine elves from the Shoemaker and the Elves children's story hard at work with needle, thread, and tiny hammers and nails.

Joe spoke before Luigi could greet him, explained his purpose, mentioned Constance Remson, and handed him the photo. "Perhaps you won't be able to identify the stilettos on his woman, but I wonder if you recognize her."

Luigi studied the image. His voice was flavored with a slight accent, "No, I've no idea who she may be. It looks as though the photo caught her in mid-stumble. She can not possibly be wearing my stilettos."

"It must be difficult to walk in such high heels," Joe remarked.

"Not for the women, such as the graceful Miss Remson, who come to me for heels with a perfect fit. We use only the finest Italian leathers, and wearing our shoes is like walking on a cloud.

"Many people don't realize their feet may vary slightly in size," he continued. "They are simply used to having one shoe fit better than the other. Shoe stores measure only length and width, while we take more measurements to insure the ultimate fit. Would you care to try on a pair of men's loafers? We have samples in popular sizes. A custom pair made expressly for you will feel even better."

The shoe designer hadn't looked down and grimaced at Joe's oxfords. It was clever of him not to ridicule a prospective customers' current footwear. "Thank you, but I won't take any more of your time." As he reached the door, he couldn't help himself.

"I understand Matteo da Milano wore Luigi Albano shoes."

Luigi responded with a wide grin. "Indeed, he was a handsome advertisement for us." He bowed his head for an instant. "May he rest in peace. Please come back when you're ready to place an order. You are sure to regret not coming here sooner."

"I'll do that," Joe promised, but he had more worthwhile things to save for at present, and well into the future. He checked his watch, and headed for Bullock's Wilshire.

The luxury department store's Art Deco architecture featured a tower sheathed in copper, now turned a distinctive aqua shade. Joe parked in the rear lot, entered and went first to the ladies' shoe department. A clerk immediately approached him.

"How may I help you, sir? Are you seeking shoes for your wife, or mother?"

Joe explained who he was, and with a brief introduction showed him the photo. "I'm checking everywhere stiletto heels are sold in hopes someone will recognize this woman, perhaps from her shoes."

Alarmed, the clerk's eyebrows shot up. "She may have witnessed a murder?" He'd kept his voice low, and looked around quickly to be certain they hadn't scared off a customer. Fortunately, the other clerk was helping a woman whose attention was focused on the small mountain of shoeboxes surrounding her.

"It's a real possibility." Joe was glad he hadn't frightened him any further by describing her as the chief murder suspect.

"A few women do come in wearing furs, but generally later in the year when they're needed for warmth. As for the shoes, we do have stilettos, but there's no way to be certain hers are from here. I certainly hope not." He shuddered slightly as he returned the photo to Joe.

"We keep sales records to reorders popular styles, but customers names aren't attached. There are records of charge purchases in accounting, but Bullock's certainly wouldn't share them with you."

Joe had expected as much and didn't wait to speak with the second clerk. Instead, he went upstairs to the furs. A clerk wearing a wide smile approached him.

"Furs make the perfect Christmas gift. You're wise to shop early for the best selection. Did you have something in mind?"

Joe hated to disillusion him. "Do you recognize this woman, or her fur coat and hat by any chance?"

"We have similar furs, but I have only been assigned to this department for a few months, and have no idea what we've sold in the past. Perhaps you'll have better luck elsewhere."

Joe knew there was no point in asking to see sales records. The police could get them, if Detective Lynch thought of it, but when the clerk hadn't already seen the photo, it was obvious the police hadn't beaten him there.

He made a quick stop at I. Magnin, another department store catering to women who were unconcerned by the expense of their wares. The clerks were no more helpful than those at Bullock's, however, and Joe thought it a good time to quit for the day.

Friday night, Joe lay stretched out on Mary Margaret's sofa with his head cradled in her lap. After reading about Matteo's death in the *Los Angeles Times*, she'd guessed the cellist had been the central figure in his case with multiple female admirers. He always told her the truth, but he didn't think she would appreciate anything about Constance Remson. Perhaps the less said about her, the better.

"I'm going to Matteo da Milano's funeral tomorrow afternoon at St. Mary's of the Angels," he began.

"Do you expect the murderess to be there?" She ran her fingertips through his hair in a lazy caress.

"She could be. I intend to keep my eyes open, and speak with anyone who'll accept a question or two. Members of the LA Philharmonic might have a different view of Matteo than the women he dated."

"Isn't St. Mary of the Angels the movie stars' church?"

"It's called that, but it doesn't mean any were fans of Matteo."

"Well, if Katherine Hepburn is there, or Cary Grant, will you please ask for an autograph for me?"

He laughed at the thought. "Wouldn't it be in very poor taste to request one at a funeral?"

"Probably, which means you won't be the only one asking!"

He'd escaped having to describe Constance Remson, but simply omitting any mention of her stung his conscience. He sat up. "Let's finish the ice cream in your freezer before I go home."

"What a terrific idea." She leaned close to kiss him. "I can't wait for the time we'll be sharing my cottage."

"Me too." During the war, he'd envied the men who'd showed off photos of their wives and girlfriends waiting for them at home. They had love letters to read, while all he'd had were mystery novels. Mary Margaret had been well worth the wait.

Saturday afternoon, Joe arrived in plenty of time to take note of others attending before meeting Constance. The noted architect Carleton M. Winslow Sr. had designed the St. Mary of the Angels church in the popular Spanish Mission style. The spectacular altarpiece featured glazed terra cotta figures of St. Mary and the archangel Gabriel at the Annunciation with side statues of St. Francis and St. John, all from the renown della Robbia studio in Florence, Italy.

A cello, violin, and flute trio seated at the front of the sanctuary played hauntingly beautiful classical music and set a reverent mood. Undoubtedly members of the LA Philharmonic who'd wanted to pay a musical tribute for a lost friend.

Joe was curious about what members of the orchestra had actually thought of Matteo. Had the cellist playing that afternoon been a close friend, or a fierce rival? There were probably many rivalries among those in the orchestra, and Matteo could have been right in the middle of them.

He waited out front at the appointed time and Constance appeared almost immediately. Dressed in a primly tailored black wool suit and stylish hat, she again made him wonder if she'd presented Matteo with an exciting challenge.

"Are there women playing in the LA Philharmonic?" he asked.

"A few, the harpist is especially fine. Was Matteo involved with one of them, or all, for that matter?"

"Not that I know," Joe replied with an honest shrug. "I need to speak with as many of the orchestra as I possibly can today. Will you introduce me?"

"Of course, I want Matteo's murder solved without delay." She looped her arm through his, and they entered the church and chose a pew toward the rear.

As he watched the church fill, Joe searched for a movie star or two so he could tell Mary Margaret he had seen someone she admired, but he didn't recognize anyone until Fr. Neal Dodd began the service. He was a slim fellow, wore glasses, and had a marvelous resonant voice that easily carried to the back pews.

"Isn't he wonderful?" Constance asked. "He's played the preacher in so many films, *It Happened One Night, The Philadelphia Story*. Too many to count really."

The woman seated in front of them turned with a warning finger to her lips. "Sorry," Constance whispered.

That an Episcopal priest had founded a Hollywood church and gone on to appear in films struck Joe as something that could only happen here. It also reminded him to check when *Arizona Sunrise* would be released. He leaned close to Constance to form the words in a bare whisper.

"I've been in a film myself."

"You don't mean it," she mouthed.

Joe nodded, and turned his attention to the service. Paloma Val Verde was seated across the aisle and two rows ahead of them. Her head bobbed as she wept for the man she'd lost. There were quite a few women weeping, some noisily, and he thought the reception following might degenerate into violence even if he kept Constance out of it. However, if the woman who owned the fur coat and hat was in attendance, she had left them at home in her closet.

He looked over his shoulder and saw Detective Lynch standing in the open arched doorway. Joe nodded and Lynch grimaced, apparently aghast to find him there. Joe loved every little wince he could squeeze out of the straitlaced man.

Latecomers were still filing in and moving into open spaces among those already seated. They were all smartly dressed, and perhaps supporters of the orchestra.

The woman Joe had photographed had appeared tall, but without the stiletto heels, she might merely be of average height. He could cross off any petite types from the suspect list, but that still left plenty of women to investigate.

Lost in thought, he heard little of the eulogy delivered by the concertmaster, the first chair violin, who praised Matteo's extraordinary musicianship, but avoided any mention of his character. The music provided by the trio was superb, and Joe relaxed into the exquisite melodies. He didn't notice the lack of a flower-draped coffin until the service ended.

"He's been cremated," Constance murmured. "Maybe they'll hand out little silk pouches of ashes at the door so each of his women will have something to treasure."

Joe wasn't sure whether or not she'd made an attempt at humor, but he was relieved when there was no such shared distribution of the late man's ashes. Constance stayed with him as they followed everyone from the sanctuary into the adjoining the hall. When Paloma Val Verde rushed up to him, he introduced her to Constance.

"I always admired Matteo for his fascinating selection of friends," Constance responded coolly.

It could have been an insult, or perhaps not. Joe thought it probably was and steered the conversation toward the service. "The eulogy was a fitting tribute."

"He was so much more than merely a superb cellist," Paloma insisted.

"Indeed," Constance added. "Excuse me for a minute, I need to speak with another member of the board."

Paloma watched her walk away. "Was she one of Matteo's women?"

Joe doubted there were many women present who might not be described as such. "Let's concentrate on our memories of him, shall we?"

"I suppose we should." She dabbed at her eyes with a lace-trimmed hanky. She'd worn a simple black dress rather than come in the more colorful peasant apparel she had worn to his office. Her hair curled in soft ringlets over her shoulders, rather than being in an upswept style bedecked with fresh roses.

"Oh, there's someone who bought one of my paintings." She waved. "Wish me luck. I might be able to inspire her to buy another."

"Yes, don't miss the opportunity." As Paloma walked away, Joe noticed the cellist who had played for the service standing alone. He made his way through the crowd to him. "Your music was perfect for the day."

"Thank you, it took a while to cull through Matteo's favorites to make our choices. I'm Sean Dermot." He extended his hand. Slightly-built with dark-hair, rimless glasses showed off his brown eyes. More personable than charismatic as Matteo had been, Joe thought women might find him attractive in a subtle boyish way.

"Joe Ezell." Sean had a firm grip, which was predictable he supposed. "I imagine Matteo must have owned a very fine cello."

"A Stradivarius, while I play one created by a twentieth century master, Gregorio Grisales. It's equally fine. Most people cannot discern any difference when they are played."

"Really? Are they equally expensive?"

Sean laughed, and caught himself when others looked his way. "Of course not. At auction, the opening bid on

Matteo's Stradivarius would be several hundred thousand dollars."

"Who will own it now?"

"Probably his wife."

Shocked, Joe stared in confusion. "I didn't realize he was married." His clients hadn't either.

"Veronica is actually his ex-wife, but they've remained close."

Seeking the distraught widow, Joe glanced over the crowd. "Is she here?"

"No, she lives in New York, and when I called to offer condolences, she was too distraught over Matteo's death to make the trip."

"His tragic loss must be difficult for all who loved him and his music." Joe handed Sean one of his business cards. "I'm a private detective, and I've been asked to look into the case."

Sean frowned as he studied it. "Won't the police be able to catch whomever killed Matteo?"

"There is always that hope."

"How do you go about catching a murderer?" Sean asked. He slipped Joe's card into his jacket pocket.

"It depends on the situation," Joe replied.

"Like all of life. Will you excuse me, I need to cultivate the members of the LA Philharmonic board." He rolled his eyes, as though it were an onerous duty he'd prefer to avoid.

"I understand." Joe watched Sean weave his way through those gathered near the buffet tables and stop at Constance Remson's side. He seemed a much better match for the elegant woman than the more flamboyant Matteo had been. Mary Margaret had fallen in love with him, however, so there was no point in questioning anyone's romantic tastes.

Constance Remson spoke only a few words with Sean before she rejoined Joe. "It seems members of the orchestra are keeping to their groups. Whom would you like to meet first, shall we begin with the woodwinds, brass, percussion, or strings?"

"I've met Sean Dermot, how about the rest of the strings." All were coolly pleasant, rather than forthcoming with revealing opinions of the cellist. By the time the reception drew to a close, he had given business cards to most of those present, and hoped to hear from some of them soon. He'd also gotten Fr. Neal Dodd's autograph on the back of one of his cards for Mary Margaret.

Once home, he changed his clothes, and set out to question the residents of Matteo's second apartment on La Peer Drive. With a sandstone façade and shutter framed windows, it housed six units. The manager lived in number one.

Florence Hayes had a charming English accent. Clad in a flowered dress, sweater, and laced oxfords, she could have easily played the part of the mother in any film shot in the British isles. "Come on in, love. I could use a scotch and soda by this time in the afternoon. How about you?"

Joe always let the person he wished to question set a leisurely pace if they so desired. "I would love one." She showed him into a comfortably furnished living room. He sat on the sofa and glanced through a garden magazine devoted to roses while he waited.

She soon returned with a drink for him in a cut-crystal glass and one for herself.

The club chair to his right was her favorite perch. "I often drink peppermint tea in the afternoons, but when the topic is murder, scotch and soda seem more fitting."

"Indeed it does." He'd set the tone when he had introduced himself at her door. He removed the photo he'd been showing from his pocket. "Does this woman look familiar?"

Florence removed her glasses and polished them on her skirt before taking a close look. "Veronica da Milano has often stayed in her ex-husband's apartment. As I recall, she's worn a pretty fur coat in winter, but this woman could be anyone. Sorry." She handed him the photo.

"Veronica called me yesterday, to say she'd be coming to Los Angeles when she could bear to. She asked me not to allow anyone else to enter Matteo's apartment until she can go through his things. She didn't want anyone taking something she might treasure as a mere souvenir."

"Was she calling from New York?"

"That's where she lives, so I suppose so. Matteo stayed with her when he was there. For a divorced couple, they maintained a very close relationship, but that was their business, not mine." She gave a thoughtful nod and sipped her drink.

"From what I understand, Matteo might have had other friends stay here."

"Now that he's dead, I don't feel obligated to protect his reputation, but those friends were all female, and very beautiful I should add. A time or two he introduced me to a lady friend, but they came and went so often, I didn't make a note of their names. I wish I had as it might be a help to you now."

"I appreciate that you've told me about Veronica. If she arrives for a stay soon, will you give me a call? I'd love to meet her."

"Of course I will. She must want to have Matteo's killer caught more than anyone. If you ever saw them together, it was plain she loved him still. He spread his charm too thinly for my tastes, but she adored him. May he rest in peace."

"Amen," Joe replied. He stayed another few minutes to finish his drink, and Florence offered a tidbit about each of the residents of the building, amusing gossip, but unfortunately not helpful in his investigation.

Rod Cole, a veterinarian, lived in apartment two. A large man with a booming voice, he took Joe's card, but stood wedged in his doorway rather than invite him in as Florence had.

"I barely knew the man," Rod offered. "Florence told me he'd been murdered, or I'd not have known. Thank God he didn't die here. We don't need any howling ghosts disturbing our sleep."

"God forbid," Joe agreed, although he thought it a weird observation. He offered the photo. "Matteo often had female guests stay here. Do you recognize this woman?"

Rod pulled his glasses from his shirt pocket and studied the photograph. "Looks like a dyed ermine coat to me. The weasels' fur turns white in winter, so if you see a woman in a white fur coat, it's undoubtedly ermine. The fur is fine for trimming royal robes, but white is impractical for most use, and the pelts are often dyed."

"Thank you. I'll make a note of that. What about the woman? Is there anything familiar about her?"

"Saturday, my clinic closes at two o'clock. Other days I'm there until after six, come home, and spend the evening in. Matteo could have marched a dozen women past my door, and I'd not have seen them."

Joe slid the photo back into his pocket. "If anything occurs to you later, don't hesitate to call me."

"I will." He stepped back and closed his door.

Florence had described the resident of number three as Suzanne Ritter, a fashion designer, but she wasn't in. Joe took the stairs to the second floor, and knocked at apartment four.

Felix O'Dell came to the door carrying a dictionary, and he turned away to set it aside. "I'm a teacher, but I don't spell nearly as well as my wife, and she isn't home. What can I do for you?"

Joe explained the reason for his visit and showed him the photo. "Do you recognize her?"

He took a quick glance of the photo. "Who could? She's dressed like an Eskimo. That's odd for Los Angeles, don't you think?"

"Others have the same observation. Mr. da Milano often had guests staying here. Did you ever meet any of them?"

"We love classical music, but we're elementary school teachers, and we don't run with the LA Philharmonic crowd."

Matteo would have had expensive tastes, and Joe readily grasped his meaning. "Thank you for your time, if your wife recalls anything about Matteo, please ask her to call me."

"I'll do that."

From Florence's report, Thomas Roach, a car salesman, rented apartment five. He also wasn't home. Matteo had rented number six. Maybe it was only a coincidence that he also had an end unit here too, but he could have preferred not to have neighbors on both sides. Joe doubted he'd learn anything from Susan Ritter, unless she'd dated Matteo, but he'd make the effort to see her soon and hope Thomas Roach would also be in.

Joe took Mary Margaret to the Jumpin' Plate for a couple of the best hamburgers in Los Angeles before they went to the movies. He reminded her who Fr. Neal Dodd was before he handed her the autographed card. "He was the only celebrity I saw, but apparently whenever a script calls for a preacher, he gets the part."

"I know who he is!" she exclaimed. "He played Jimmy Stewart's father in *It's A Wonderful Life*, and when his character dies, Jimmy has to give up his dreams of travel and work in the family's bank." She slipped the card into her purse. "Thank you. I suppose now that you're in the movies, we'll be able to collect quite a few impressive autographs."

"Having a few seconds of dialog in *Arizona Sunrise* isn't really being in the movies. I can't expect much more for the Roy Rogers film that's coming up either."

"It's a start," she assured him. "Maybe I should sign with your agent and play the part of the nurse whenever there's one in the script."

He laughed with her. "It's not nearly as much fun as it looks when you see the finished film, but if you're serious, I'll be happy to introduce you to Archibald Sutton."

"I'm not serious, but thank you for being so supportive. You're going to make such a wonderful husband, Joe," she exclaimed.

"Let's hope so."

"Oh, I do have news. Do you remember the chaplain from Georgia's memorial, Luke Hatcher?"

"Tall thin guy with dark hair?"

"Yes, that's him. He's rented Amy Hudson's cottage and moved in this afternoon."

"Really? He should be quiet, rather than rowdy, shouldn't he?"

"He's a Presbyterian minister, not a monk, but I doubt he'll host wild parties."

"Let's hope not, unless he includes us." He checked his watch, and they finished the last bites of their meal to make it to the theater on time.

When the previews began, *Arizona Sunrise* flashed across the screen. Among the many fast shots of the action, there was a brief focus on Joe and Max at the saloon bar. Joe had wanted to look like a tough cowboy, but his glance was menacingly mean.

"Joe!" Mary Margaret squealed.

"Let's talk about it later," he whispered. They'd come to see *Life With Father*, a comedy starring William Powell as an 1880's stockbroker who seeks to impose the strict efficiency of his Wall Street office on his family. His wife, played by Irene Dunn, ran their home beautifully and managed their four rambunctious sons without his absurd interference, which made for all the fun.

While the rest of the audience laughed as each of the stockbroker's pompous edicts went awry, the shot of Joe in the previews kept repeating in his mind. Leaning on the bar, he'd appeared not merely mean, but cynical and world-weary, as though he'd seen the worst from life. With Mary Margaret's enthusiastic recommendation, her mother and family were sure to see *Arizona Sunrise* and take an instant dislike to him.

After the film, he said so as they shared a banana split at Miss Lucy's Ice Cream Parlor.

"Please don't worry. We barely saw you, Joe, and I thought you looked determined rather than dangerous."

Strawberry ice cream failed to lift his mood as it usually did. "I still hope your mother hates Westerns and doesn't go to see it."

"As a matter of fact, she loves Westerns, and she's been looking forward to seeing you on the big screen."

Dread nearly choked him. "God help us."

"Joe!" she scolded. "You're making a big thing out of nothing. Let's change the subject. How is your murder investigation going?"

"Not much better than my movie career, I'm afraid." He gave her a quick rundown on the people he'd met, including Luigi Albano, who knew a lot about shoes, but had supplied little in the way of useful information.

"Apparently, Matteo kept the second apartment as a place for guests, which included his ex-wife, Veronica, who lives in New York City. She owns a fur coat, but it's unlikely she's the woman I photographed."

"Was she at the funeral?"

"No, although there were plenty of other weeping women."

Mary Margaret swallowed a spoonful of banana before speaking in an excited hush, "Do you suppose she could have flown out from New York, killed Matteo, and caught a return flight home all in the same day?"

"It may be possible, but if they were still so close they visited each other often, it's doubtful she'd harbor such a murderous level of hatred."

"I don't know. Maybe she'd hoped he'd come back to her, and when she realized he never would, she couldn't bear to let any other woman have him."

"Jealousy has been a reason for murder, but there have to be so many local women who'd be jealous, one of them could have gotten to him first."

"True. Do you suppose Detective Lynch has learned anything?"

"If so, he hasn't shared it. Let's change the subject again."

"Fine let's talk about the wedding. I bought a gorgeous gown and will ship it to Seattle in plenty of time for the wedding. It's exactly what I wanted, but I'll not give you a verbal preview so it will be a surprise when I wear it. My mother's feelings will be hurt that I'm not choosing to wear hers, but it's our wedding, after all, and the choice should be mine."

"That's the spirit!" He knew she'd anguished over the issue and was relieved she'd found a way to solve it to her own advantage. "You're going to make a wonderful wife, Mary Margaret."

She laughed with him. "Let's hope so."

CHAPTER 4

Late Saturday night, Joe lay in bed with his head propped on his hands. He didn't discuss all his cases with Mary Margaret, but whenever he did, she frequently saw an angle he'd missed. The possibility of plane travel made Veronica a suspect even if she lived in New York City. He wouldn't be able to get passenger lists, but Jacob Lynch could, if he thought of it.

They hadn't spoken at the funeral, which was a relief, but he still wondered what the detective was up to. None of the people he'd questioned about Matteo had mentioned the police had been there earlier. He supposed Lynch must have a way to tackle a murder investigation, but it remained a mystery.

Sunday, Joe thoroughly enjoyed the lazy morning. He slept in, showered, shaved, and made a fine breakfast with scrambled eggs, bacon, and toast. The big Sunday crossword puzzle in the *LA Times* offered more of a challenge than those printed daily, and he took pride in being able to complete it in less than an hour.

He gave the residents of Matteo's apartment building time to arrive home after church, and then drove to Almont Drive. He climbed the stairs to the third floor, and went to apartment nine. Rita Smith was the name on the mailbox downstairs. A large woman in a flowing blue dressing gown answered his knock. Her gray hair was in tight curls, and her make-up as perfect as a baby doll's. Joe introduced himself.

Rita raised her hands to her rouged cheeks. "I heard Matteo was murdered in his own place! Lord, have mercy! What's become of the world?"

"I ask myself that same question at least once a day, Miss Smith," Joe responded.

"Please call me Rita. Would you like to come in? I've been reviewing the script I'll need for tomorrow and could use a break. I work in radio, commercials mostly, although I occasionally have a small part on a soap opera. Bet you don't listen to those."

Joe followed her into the living room, and found furniture designed for someone of her ample size. "I don't, but a lot of people enjoy the entertainment during the day."

"Well, aren't you the agreeable sort." She picked up the script from the sofa and gestured for him to sit.

Joe chose a roomy wingback chair to face her, and offered the photo for her opinion.

"This looks like Veronica, Matteo's ex-wife. I met her a time or two, and she has a lovely fur coat. I don't wear furs myself, you understand, so I won't be mistaken for a grizzly bear!"

She had a charming giggle, and he laughed with her. "Do you recall the last time you saw Veronica?"

"In the late spring maybe. When did you take this photo?"

"Last Wednesday."

"When Matteo died? This can't be Veronica then. If she'd been here when he died, the whole building would have shook with her screams. She just adored him, and I was embarrassed for her. She'd look up at him with such a worshipful gaze, and he'd respond with a distracted smile. Have you seen couples like that?"

"Indeed I have, although it's often the man who adores a woman who has little time for him. You have my card. Please give me a call if you remember anything about the other women Matteo saw."

"He was one gorgeous man. I thought he ought to be in movies, but he told me music was his life. What a terrible waste." She sprang from the sofa with surprising agility and walked him to the door. "Good luck with your investigation."

He thanked her, and went on to apartment ten, where Bob and Meg Wood were just leaving for the library, each with an armful of books. They took a quick glance at the photo, had no idea who the woman might be and went on their way.

Marc and Rhonda Barker lived in apartment eleven. "We own the cleaners on Burton Way, and Sunday is our only day off," Rhonda disclosed in a whisper. "My husband is taking a nap on the sofa, and I don't want to wake him." She stepped out into the hallway to get a better look at the photo.

"We leave early in the morning and aren't home until late, so we don't see much of our neighbors. I don't recognize her. Is she involved in Matteo's murder?"

"She may have witnessed the crime," Joe replied, not wanting to frighten her.

"I hope you find her then. Wait a minute, let me give you a coupon for free dry cleaning."

"Thank you so much." He'd pass it along to Mary Margaret.

Chuck Meyer came to the door of number twelve carrying the Sunday crossword puzzle, which gave Joe an opening for several minutes of easy conversation. He then broached why he'd come, and showed Chuck the photo.

"Sorry, she doesn't look familiar. I often go to the LA Philharmonic concerts with friends, and we all thought Matteo was a musical genius. He could coax such soulful sounds from his cello, the whole audience would be in tears. We're unlikely to ever hear his equal."

"What about Sean Dermont? He has to be good, or he wouldn't be in the orchestra."

"The second chair cello? I've no idea. Matteo always played the solos."

"I'm sorry I missed hearing him."

"His recordings capture his superb talent. I'd invite you in to hear some of his music, but I have plans for the afternoon."

"That's quite all right. I'll pick up an album." Joe said good-bye, and headed to the apartment house on La Peer Drive.

Suzanne Ritter, the fashion designer, proved to be a beautiful dark-eyed woman, who wore her burgundy hair in a stylish short bob. No one was born with that startling shade, but it looked good on her. In an emerald green striped jacket and slim black skirt, she presented the height of fall fashion, but she was in her stocking feet. He thought such an elegant woman probably wore silk hose rather than nylons.

She leaned against her front door as they talked. When she brushed her thick bangs off her forehead, they fell into place in a wave that dipped over her right eye, Veronica Lake style.

"I knew Matteo, of course, I did. If an attractive woman lived within a mile from here, he knew her. He was a gentleman and never spoke a word about other women, however." She crossed her arms under her ample bosom. "I will tell you something no one else might mention. He loved drinking milkshakes at the close of a romantic evening. I'd never associated milkshakes with making love, but I always will now. I'll miss him."

She held the photo by the corner. "I recognize Matteo's other apartment building, but not the woman. No one dresses like that here, unless she was trying out a Halloween costume."

The coming Friday would be Halloween, so he thought it a reasonable guess. "Do you know Veronica da Milano? She stays in Matteo's apartment here when she's in town."

"I do, poor thing," Rita murmured under her breath. "It's a familiar story. They married very young, and he quickly outgrew her. She didn't understand why he'd left her and never will. She belongs with some decent fellow who'll welcome a houseful of kids. Have I told you too much?"

"No, I appreciate everything you'd care to share." It didn't sound as though she had been jealous of Matteo's casual affairs although she had been one herself. "Do you own a fur coat?"

"No. I've never been fond of dead animal pelts. It's too reminiscent of cavemen for me." She swept him with a slow appreciative glance, and smiled. "Would you care to come in for a drink?"

It was a softly-spoken invitation, not a desperate plea, but he couldn't accept. She had a viper's beauty, and he couldn't help but stare, but he didn't dare get any closer. "Thank you, but I have a wonderful fiancée, and won't stray into an attractive woman's apartment. Tell me one thing more. Why do women wear such uncomfortable shoes they can't wait to take them off, and men expect their shoes to be comfortable all day long?"

She had a deep, throaty laugh. "Women wear high heels because men like the way they make our legs look. Some men adore women's feet, but I've never heard of a woman who loved a man's hairy toes."

"Neither have I." He handed her his card. "Don't hesitate to call me if you think of anything related to Matteo's murder."

"I will," she promised as she closed her door, but she didn't sound sincere.

Joe needed a moment to collect himself before he knocked on Thomas Roach's door. The car salesman wore a sport coat and tie, and appeared ready to leave for work.

He spoke before Joe could. "Tell me you're in the market for a new car, and I'll meet you at Felix Chevrolet. I'm only one car away from my month's quota, and I'll make you a great deal."

"Thank you, but not today." He handed him his business card and the photograph. "Do you recognize this woman?"

"Can't say that I do, but Matteo had women friends with fur coats. I was sorry to learn he'd died. I'd hoped one of his girlfriends would knock on the wrong door and want to know me. Guess I missed my chance."

"Did you know his ex-wife?" Joe asked.

"Didn't even know he had one. We weren't close."

Joe could easily understand why. "If you think of anything more that might be helpful, please give me a call."

Thomas slapped a business card in his hand. "Sure will, and when you're ready for a new car, come and see me."

"I'll do that, Mr. Roach." He hurried down the stairs rather than walk with him, but he'd keep his card on the off chance he could ever afford to buy a new Chevrolet.

On Sundays, Joe liked to spend a quiet afternoon with Mary Margaret visiting someplace new, taking a walk in a park, or staying at the cottage to read and listen to music. When he arrived at Chrysanthemum Court, she drew him in and showed him an album of phonograph records. Johann Sebastian Bach distinctive signature decorated the front along with Matteo da Milano's name.

"I doubted you'd have time to buy any of Matteo's recordings and a friend at the hospital loaned me these."

Joe knew her friends, and thought it odd she didn't offer a name. "Which friend?" When she hesitated to answer, he knew right away. "Gabriel Webb?" The doctor was tall, blond, and handsome, and the thought gave his heart a jealous twinge.

"Yes, now that you mention it, but I didn't want you to worry. He's not my type, and you are." She reached up to kiss him. "From what it says in the album, Bach's six cello suites are a challenge, and Matteo played them beautifully. Let's listen to the first one."

She removed the first record from the album sleeve, placed it on her phonograph turntable, turned it on, and lowered the needle. Joe caught her hand to pull her down beside him on the sofa. He placed a playful kiss in her ear.

"Joe! Let's just concentrate on the music for now."

"How's ten minutes, we don't want to overdo." He closed his eyes to concentrate on the ebb and flow of the superb music. Matteo produced the depth of sound for which he was well known, and when Mary Margaret poked him in the ribs with her elbow, he checked his watch and found half an hour had gone by.

"I'm sorry, but classical music tends to put me to sleep. I can appreciate Matteo's talent from what I did hear though. Let's go out and soak up some sunshine and listen to more later."

"Only if you're good," she teased, and they left for the nearby park for a leisurely stroll.

Monday morning, Joe's first call came from his agent, Archibald Sutton. "You're all anyone is talking about after they see the *Arizona Sunrise* previews. Casting agents are drooling over you!"

"I don't say a word and haven't more than a few seconds in the preview. Are they desperate for talent?"

"Yes, for new talent at least. You're set for the Roy Rogers film at the first of the year, and we might be able to work in another job before then."

"I'm getting married, and can't devote any time to becoming a movie star until after Roy's Western."

"All right, I'll just tell anyone who calls that you're booked until after Roy's next Western wraps. It will make them all the more eager to hire you, so we'll be able to ask for more money."

"Hold that thought." Joe had hired an agent and read for a part only to track a young woman who had died all too soon. He had solved the case, but he'd never thought anyone would want to see him more than once.

His next call was from Hal Marten. "I have another case of possible fraud, do you have time to look into it?"

"Sure do. Does it involve another suspicious theft?"

"No, this case is far more unusual. Our clients, Doug Larsen and his wife, Eleanor, bought a Victorian house. They plan to live on the second floor and run an antique shop on the first. The problem is, everyone they hire gets injured, and he's making repeated claims for their injuries on their California West homeowners insurance. The owner claims the house is haunted, which he considers charming, but enough is enough."

"What sort of injuries are we talking about?"

"The painter fell off his ladder and broke his arm. The plumber slipped on the stairs and threw out his back. The electrician apparently fell over his own equipment and sprained his ankle so badly he won't be able to work for several weeks. I want you to go look at the house. The owner could be making claims and splitting the money with the men he's hired. Tell me what you think of him."

"What if there really is a ghost?"

"Hire a priest to do an exorcism and get rid of it."

"Sure, I'll get right on it." Joe still had his identification card for California West. He'd made a note of the address, drove by the house, and parked across the street. It was a magnificent Queen Ann Victorian covered with fish scale shingles, with a two story circular turret, gingerbread decorative trim along the eaves, tall narrow windows, and a porch that curved around the front. A man stood painting the porch railing's intricate trim white, and he looked up as Joe approached.

"Wonderful house!" Joe called to him. It was a subtle rose hue, not a garish pink, but while the upper story was freshly painted, the scaffolding was still up, and only a few swipes of color had been taken on the ground floor.

"Indeed it is. I'm Doug Larsen, the owner. We'll have an antique store here soon, but we're not open today." Doug was as chubby as Santa Claus, with a fringe of white hair circling his head. He looked to be in his sixties at least, but his fair complexion held only a few lines and wrinkles.

Joe walked up the stairs to the porch, introduced himself, and showed his ID card. "California West wants you and your wife to have a lovely home, but the frequent accidents here are becoming alarming."

"If you're alarmed, imagine how we feel." He laid his brush on the can of paint, and wiped his hands on a rag. "I hate to blame a ghost for the injuries, but apparently Ida doesn't want workers here hammering, clanging on pipes, and doing all manner of noisy jobs, but we can't endanger others to suit her whims."

"Ida is her name?"

"Yes, she lived here more than fifty years, and we bought the house from her heirs, but she just refuses to go."

Joe observed the man closely, he appeared to be stating fact, as though ghosts were a normal part of any conversation. "Have you seen her ghost?"

"Not clearly, she's more of a shadowy mist, as you might expect, but we often smell her perfume even when we don't see her, so we know she's been around."

Joe glanced down the railing to have a moment to think. "You're doing a fine job. Ida doesn't mind if you're out here painting?"

"No, she knows us. You want to come in and see her picture?"

"Thank you, I'd like that." He followed Doug through the wide front door and found the interior already painted a cooling light green. "The painter didn't have any problems until he moved to the exterior?"

"Oh, he had problems aplenty, but they were silly things like his stepladder being moved, or cans of paint hidden in the closets. It wasn't until he put up scaffolding that the troubles began." He crossed to the desk in the parlor and pulled open a little drawer to remove the photo. "You can see she was a beauty in her day."

Joe could appreciate her looks, but her gaze held a serious gleam, as though she saw trouble coming. "Was she married?"

"Yes, but her husband, Walter, was on the Lusitania in 1915 when it was attacked by a German submarine and sunk. He wasn't among the survivors. She never remarried, and may have mourned her husband's loss the remainder of her life."

"You mentioned heirs?"

"Yes, a niece and two nephews, her brother's children. They were happy to sell Ida's home and took our first offer. Not many people want to take on a project this big, but it's perfect for our antiques business, and we had to have it."

"Do you have anything else of Ida's?"

"There was a trunk of clothes in the attic, but they were so old they turned to dust when touched. She had albums of family photographs, but her niece took those. What are you thinking, that there's something here she wants?"

"Frankly, I have no idea what to think." He did understand Doug believed what he said, however. "Have you considered having a priest do an exorcism?"

Doug shrugged. "I think that's just for live people, but I'd hate to chase Ida away. I don't want anyone else hurt, of course. What do you think I ought to do?"

"Have you tried speaking to Ida and suggesting she move on?"

"My wife chats with her. Let me call her." He went to the bottom of the stairs. "Eleanor, will you come down for a moment, please?"

Joe expected a round little woman who could play Mrs. Claus, but Eleanor was taller than her husband, slender, and quite pretty. She had a measuring tape hung around her neck. "The curtains will never be finished if you keep interrupting me. I'm sorry, I didn't realize we had a guest."

"He's from California West, and looking into the multiple injuries here."

"Joe Ezell, how nice to meet you. Your husband tells me you've spoken to Ida."

"Yes, she loves to chat. I believe she's been quite lonely and delighted to have someone here who treats her as a friend."

"What's wonderful for her, but we need to convince her not to harm those who come here to work, or to shop. You'll not be able to sell many antiques if customers fall on the porch stairs, or trip over rugs."

"I'd not thought of that," Eleanor surmised with a slight frown. "How silly you must think me. I could at least ask Ida to move upstairs."

"Would she go?" Joe asked.

"My wife can be very convincing," Doug responded. "Let's give it a try."

"Do that, and I'll call in a couple of days to see if you've been successful. Do you have anyone coming to do any work here this week?"

Doug walked Joe to the door. "No, it's just us for the time being."

Joe said good-bye, but he wasn't satisfied he'd solved the problem of multiple claims. When he picked Mary Margaret up that afternoon after her shift, he told her about the ghost. "Somehow asking her to move upstairs doesn't look all that promising. Do you suppose Reverend Hatcher has any experience removing ghosts?"

"I doubt it, but let's invite him to join us for dinner and ask while we have dessert. I'm baking a chicken, and there will be plenty."

While Joe wasn't happy about having to share his time with her, he accepted her suggestion. The lights were on in cottage five when they reached the Chrysanthemum Court and Mary Margaret knocked on Rev. Hatcher's door to issue the invitation and introduce Joe.

The minister glanced between her and Joe, and broke into a slow smile. "I'd love to come. Should I bring something?"

"No, give me an hour to pull it together before you join us."

"So you're a detective." Luke stepped off the narrow porch to shake Joe's hand. "Do you like reading mysteries? I spend most evenings reading and can never tell who did it until the author reveals him, or her, in the last few pages."

"Why don't you go on home and work on dinner?" Joe suggested, and Mary Margaret left them to see to it.

"I'm fond of Sherlock Holmes," Joe said. "He continually amazes me, or I should say Sir Arthur Conan Doyle does."

"I love Sherlock Homes, too. Would you care to come in for drink?"

"Sure." Joe followed him into the cottage. The solid maple furnishings were what many of the cottages had. He accepted a scotch and soda and took a chair.

Luke was a talkative soul. With black hair, and blue eyes, his gaze was riveting. His angular features couldn't be described as handsome, but he smiled so often Joe doubted anyone noticed. When there was a lull in their conversation, he saw no reason to wait for dessert to mention ghosts. He described the Victorian house and the residents belief it was haunted.

"Have you ever come across a ghost?" Joe asked.

"If you've ever walked through a military cemetery, you can feel a presence there, like a scream just below our level of hearing. Civilian cemeteries are calmer, but most of those buried there didn't die as violent a death as our soldiers did. As for a haunted house, no, I've not run across one."

"Ida may move upstairs as asked, but if she doesn't, is there some ritual you can perform to convince her to move on to heaven?"

Luke couldn't help but laugh. "Not off-hand, but I can probably find one. If you need me to give it a try, let me know, but I won't offer any guarantees."

They talked about Mickey Spillane's mysteries until Mary Margaret called them for dinner. Luke Hatcher wasn't what Joe had expected in a minister, but it had been so long since he'd been to church, other than to attend funerals, he thought he might simply be out of touch.

CHAPTER 5

Joe hadn't been in his office more than ten minutes Tuesday morning, when LAPD Detective Lynch strode through the door accompanied by a uniformed officer. He regarded it as a disastrous way to begin the day. He smiled anyway. "Good morning, Detective."

Lynch ignored the friendly greeting. "You're coming down to the station with us."

Joe stood and circled his desk. "Have you identified Matteo's killer?"

"We'll talk later."

"I've never ridden in a police car. Will you turn on the siren?"

"Shut up," Lynch uttered in a threatening whisper.

Lynch could be counted on to be an ass no matter what the occasion, and Joe slid into the back seat of the unmarked Ford sedan parked out front and kept quiet as they made the short drive. They hadn't handcuffed him, which he took as a good sign. When they arrived at the station, Lynch directed him into his office rather than an impersonal interrogation room. Another plus.

Lynch took the chair behind his desk and motioned for Joe to take one of the two in front. Thick file folders were stacked on the desk, and he opened the top one. It contained the photos Joe had given him. "This case becomes more peculiar by the hour, but you may be the key to solving it."

"Me? How?" Joe asked, sincerely puzzled.

"Didn't it strike you as peculiar that two women would come to see you about Matteo da Milano in a single day?"

"Yes, it was an odd coincidence."

"It may have been more than merely coincidence. Miss Remson and Miss Val Verde could have been working together. Lily Montell may also have been in on the plot."

"You've lost me. What plot is that?"

Lynch laid the photo of the woman in the fur coat on his desk. "They wanted you to photograph this woman, to throw us off the track. Maybe they drew lots, but one of them wore this outlandish get-up, and killed Mr. da Milano, while the other waited in her car at the corner and drove her away."

Dumbfounded, Joe stared at him. Constance Remson struck him as being cold enough to kill, but she was not the type who ever got her hands dirty. Paloma Val Verde probably couldn't even step on a spider, much less murder a man she loved.

"Interesting theory." Joe replied. "Can you prove it?"

"I will, eventually," Lynch assured him. "If you'd like to confess you were part of the conspiracy, I'll call in a stenographer to take your statement."

"This is the first I've heard of it," Joe insisted, shocked Lynch could regard him as an accomplice in such a bizarre undertaking. The detective had a habit of going off in unfortunate tangents, however. "Wait a minute, is this a prank?"

The detective swore under his breath. "I do not do pranks, Mr. Ezell. Most people realize I'm serious whenever I speak."

"It was just a thought," Joe replied. "You may be onto something though. Matteo saw quite a few women, and a couple could have gotten together to kill him, but I doubt it involved Miss Remson, or Miss Val Verde. The woman in the fur coat could have been a witness rather than the murderer, who could have escaped by the apartment building's rear door. I hope you can identify her soon. She's the key to this, not me."

Lynch sat back in this chair. "You've questioned the residents of Matteo's two apartment buildings. Have you no idea how to stay out of our way?"

"Miss Remson hired me to solve the crime. I'm only doing my job."

"You're free to go, but if you do stumble over some helpful information, call me first rather than Miss Remson."

Joe rose. "Sure. I don't suppose you'd like to give me a ride back to my office?"

"Call a taxi."

"See you around." He had no doubt that he would.

After returning to his office, Joe added a card for Suzanne Ritter and placed it on his bulletin board. She appeared to care so little for Matteo's loss, she could have been in on his murder. He rocked back in his chair. He knew only those who had come to him, or who lived in Matteo's buildings. That left the majority of women in Los Angles between the ages of twenty and forty as possible suspects he couldn't name. He didn't want to exclude Veronica da Milano either. He hadn't asked Lynch about her, but maybe he should have to discover what the LAPD knew.

Needing a break, he called Hal Marten to report on the ghost at the Larson's Victorian home. "Mrs. Larson claims to chat with Ida, and promised to convince her to move to the second floor. Most workmen and customers will be on the first floor, so it might work."

"Do you believe there actually is a ghost?" Hal asked.

"I can understand why you're skeptical, and I have a chaplain from the VA hospital willing to help encourage the ghost to go on to heaven."

"This case just gets better and better," Hal replied. "Can you wind it up in under a week?"

"That's my hope."

"Great. *Arizona Sunrise* is opening this weekend, and we ought to go together and make a party of it."

Mary Margaret would love it even if he wouldn't. "This isn't really the type of movie that gets fancy premieres."

"So what? We'll make our own celebration . I'll see you Saturday morning. You want to invite Gilbert to come to the movie with us and bring his girl?"

Joe grimaced at the thought. "Why not? We ought to do our best to fill the theater seats."

He'd just hung up the telephone when Doug Larson called. "The mailman just tripped out on the sidewalk, fell and chipped a tooth. He was in front of the house, not inside it, do you think it counts?"

"Difficult to say. Did your wife talk to Ida?"

"Yes, she did, but Ida might not have been listening. What should we do now?"

Being no expert on ghosts, Joe wasn't sure. "I've found a minister who is willing to come to your house and attempt to send Ida along her way. Let me check with him and see when he's available."

"Swell, just don't make it too far in the future."

"Of course." As he hung up, he wondered if Matteo da Milano's ghost might be hanging out at the apartment where he'd died. He seriously doubted Mr. Perkins, the manager, would let him in to conduct a séance. Constance Remson would laugh at the prospect, but Paloma Val Verde would go for it.

Wednesday was the full moon, and Luke Hatcher suggested it was the best time to visit the Larson's home. "In the reading I've done about ghosts since we last spoke, during the full moon, they are more open to contact. It might be our best shot at encouraging Ida to move on."

"Do we need any special props?"

"Just candles, and I'll bring those and matches. I'll try to be serious, but it will be a challenge."

"Maybe you can conjure up Walter to meet her half way."

"The husband? Yes, that's a wonderful idea."

Mary Margaret went on the ghost mission with them. "What a beautiful house. It's no wonder Ida won't leave," she whispered.

"Concentrate on the glories of heaven to sweep her away," Luke encouraged.

"Singing angels, harp music, lost loved ones?"

"Yes, that's good. We have to look as though we know what we're doing or Ida may see through our efforts and stay put."

Doug and Eleanor Larson were dressed in black and whispered as they welcomed Mary Margaret, Joe, and Reverend Hatcher into their home. "I lit a fire in the fireplace. I hope that's all right," Doug murmured.

"Yes, it sets the mood," Luke responded. "Would you please turn off the other lights? Ghosts prefer the dimness of night."

Doug quickly saw to it. Eleanor helped Luke light the candles. They each took one, and it gave their faces a ghostly glow. Luke motioned for them to move into a circle. There was no furniture in the parlor other than the desk, so they had plenty of room. The smell of fresh paint scented the air.

Luke began with a brief prayer on the joy of this life and the beauty of the next one. His voice held a reverent depth, and sounded totally convincing as he continued, "Ida, we're gathered together this evening to celebrate your life, and to send you on to heaven where you surely belong. Walter has waited for you all these many years, run to him now."

The flames in the fireplace shot up in a rain of sparks, startling them all. Luke raised a hand to keep them silent. "Your sadness will disappear like the dew at dawn. Go now, return to God's love, and you will be joyfully remembered here."

Mary Margaret curled her hand into Joe's, and he squeezed her fingers. She was always eager to join in whatever high-jinx his work entailed. He'd thank her again later for making even chasing a ghost out of a haunted house a pleasure. He held his breath and wished Ida a happy journey. He hadn't felt her presence on his first visit to the Larson home, and felt only the warmth of the fire now.

They waited, five minutes, maybe ten before Luke turned to the Larsons and whispered, "Do you still feel her presence?"

Eleanor closed her eyes and breathed deeply. "No, I believe she is gone."

"Let's leave as quietly as we came," Luke offered. They blew out their candles and Doug shut the front door behind them with quiet care.

Luke didn't speak until they'd climbed into Joe's Chevy. "Lord help us, because I've no idea what to do next if Ida isn't gone."

Mary Margaret turned toward him. "What you said was so beautiful, I'm sure she was as touched as we were."

"Thank you. Let's hope so," he murmured.

Joe started the car and drove to the Chrysanthemum Court. "I'll file a report with California West, and see that you're paid, but I won't tell anyone else if you'd rather I didn't."

"Thank you. Let's see how it goes, before we congratulate ourselves."

"Wise plan," Mary Margaret responded. She invited the reverend to come into her cottage for coffee and cookies, but he thanked her, and entered his own home alone.

Friday was Halloween, and Joe bought several bags of candy in the drug store on the first floor of his building to take to Mary Margaret's. She loved chocolate, and so did he. He bought some Hershey bars for them to share while they gave out suckers to the neighborhood kids.

Mary Margaret wore her nurse's uniform, complete with white stockings and white oxfords. "The kids will think I'm wearing a costume, and it makes the evening more fun. You should have dressed as a cowboy."

"I'm afraid I lack the basic gear, ma'am, but if anyone asks, I'm a private detective."

"That's a good story. Oh, there's the bell." She picked up the bowl of suckers, and he opened the door. A small ballerina and a clown smiled up at her.

"Trick or Treat!"

She dropped suckers into their bags. "Isn't this fun?"

Joe laughed. "Sure is. I loved Halloween when I was a kid. We used to run from house to house to see how much candy we could get before we had to be home." He opened the door and found four children waiting, a pirate, an angel, a cowboy with a cap pistol in a holster on his hip, and a ghost in a flowing sheet.

Each resident of the Chrysanthemum Court handed out their own treats, but on other holidays they planned group parties with everyone attending. Joe knew them all, and was looking forward to a scrumptious feast for Thanksgiving. He and Mary Margaret ate pieces of a Hershey bar between callers.

"Thank you." She gobbled the chocolate, and then apologized.

"It's Halloween, so we can get by without displaying fine manners for a few minutes," Joe said.

Luke Hatcher stood in his doorway passing out candy, and when the last of the kids had come by, Joe walked over to speak with him.

"Wasn't that a lot of cute kids?" Luke asked. "Want some jelly beans?"

"No, thanks. I've not heard a peep from the Larsons, so your ceremony must have worked."

"It's only been two days," Luke cautioned. "Maybe Ida's just taking a nap."

"Do ghosts nap?"

"Maybe."

Mary Margaret walked up behind Joe. "*Arizona Sunrise* opens tomorrow, and Joe has a part in the movie. Would you like to come see it with us?"

"Really? I'd no idea you were a movie star," Luke replied.

"No, I'm not, and have such a small part you'll probably miss me," Joe explained.

"Thanks for the invitation, but I have the late shift at the hospital tomorrow. I sure want to hear about it though."

Embarrassed to the core, Joe muttered a quick good night and walked Mary Margaret back home. He followed her into the kitchen. "That was sweet of you to invite him. Are we going to include him on all of our dates?"

"Please don't be jealous. Half the nurses at the hospital are in love with him, so he can find plenty of dates on his own. I was just bragging about you. That's all." She filled the coffee pot with water.

"Better wait until you see the film. You may want to deny we ever met."

She regarded him a sultry glance. "Never."

Their golf game brought both praise and humor Saturday morning. Gilbert played with a pro's keen eye, and Hal was refining his game with every stroke. Both men inspired Joe to work on his own skills. He needed to spend the occasional free afternoon at the driving range.

As they left the course, Hal invited Gilbert to join them for *Arizona Sunrise*, and the young man blushed deeply. "That sounds like fun, but Marsha invited some friends to her place for dinner tonight, and we'll have to go see the movie on our own."

"Don't wait more than a week," Joe advised. "It might not be in theaters long."

"It will have as good a run as any other Western," Hal argued. "You'll see Joe in the saloon scene."

"Don't blink," Joe advised. "Let's get back to Marsha. It's good that she wants to introduce you to her friends. Are you planning to take something?"

"Like what?" Gilbert asked, clearly perplexed.

"Flowers are good," Hal suggested. "Women always love flowers."

"A box of chocolates is always appreciated too," Joe added.

"Thanks, I'll take both." He walked to his car and turned to wave good-bye.

Hal and Joe stood in the parking lot a moment longer. "We might have to go with him on his honeymoon," Hal whispered.

"We could flip for the honor," Joe responded, and he laughed as a silly image came to mind. "Marsha is probably as naïve as Gilbert, and they should get along fine without a coach."

"Still, maybe we ought to offer," Hal countered, but he was laughing too. "See you tonight at the theater."

"Can't wait." Joe lifted his golf bag into his car's trunk, and sat down in the driver's seat to remove his golf shoes. For the Roy Rogers film, he'd rather have his own boots than limp around in a pair from the costume department. It would be a good errand for the afternoon, and keep his mind off the humiliation he was sure to suffer that night.

Mary Margaret hugged Joe when he came to pick her up. "We've already seen you in the previews, so you shouldn't be mortified about what we'll see tonight."

"Mortified is a good word. I bought a pair of boots this afternoon to wear in my next film. Gene Autry wears real fancy colorful pairs, but all I need is pair that looks like they've been worn on multiple cattle drives."

She looked down at his loafers. "You should have worn them tonight."

"I'd rather not get ahead of myself. January will come soon enough." He took her hand to walk to his car. They parked on the street near the theater and met Hal and

Gladys at the box office. He was surprised to see a line, but there were fans of Western movies who would attend any show with horses.

They bought tickets and glanced over the offerings at the refreshment counter. "Would you like some popcorn?" Joe asked.

"No, I'm so excited I'd probably choke. Some Walnettos would be good though," Mary Margaret replied.

Joe also loved the walnut laced caramels and bought some. The four of them found seats toward the rear of the theater. "This is good," Joe announced. "I won't have far to go if I'm run out of here."

Gladys thought he was joking and brushed his sleeve with a light caress. "Playing a cowboy led to an arrest in an important case. Think of it that way."

"I'll try ma'am." Joe would have touched the brim of his Stetson had he been wearing one. He needed to buy a cowboy hat to go with the new boots. He'd like his own Levis too. A shirt couldn't cost much, and it would be nice to wear his own clothes. That way he'd recognize himself among the riders high-tailing it out of town. The lights went down and the previews came on. Mary Margaret squeezed his hand, and he handed her a Walnetto.

Joe had seen only the saloon scene, and he was surprised when the movie opened with a shootout on the main street of the western town built on the back lot at MGM. Caught up in the action, he forgot his own embarrassment until the hero, the new sheriff in town, strode into the saloon. The camera focused first on the three saloon girls who turned to greet the sheriff with teasing glances and fluttering waves. Then the focus shifted to Joe and Max Reyes leaning against the bar.

They faced the camera as though staring into the mirror behind the bar, and bragged about their horses with a lazy sincerity that hushed the audience. The action soon shifted to an insult laced brawl. Tables and chairs went flying in all directions, and he and Max disappeared for the remainder of the film. Their brief appearance wasn't nearly as embarrassing as he'd feared from the previews, which brought some sense of relief, and he relished another Walnetto.

After the show, the two couples went to a popular bar within walking distance. They settled into a comfortable booth, and Joe waited until they had placed their orders to speak. "You needn't feel obliged to comment on my fleeting part in the film, but-"

"You were the best part!" Gladys exclaimed. "You two looked and sounded like real cowboys, while the star only wore the right clothes."

"It was enough to charm the pretty schoolmarm," Hal argued.

"I loved it," Mary Margaret said. "But your part went by much too fast. You should have been seen again later in the film, walking along the street, or riding in the sheriff's posse."

"I agree," Gladys added. "You added an authenticity that was absent for much of the film."

"I wouldn't analyze it too closely," Joe offered, embarrassed by their compliments. "Now let's change the subject."

"Shall we talk about ghosts?" Hal asked.

"We don't dare, it might conjure them up," Joe insisted.

Gladys mentioned a peculiar legal case that had been in the news, and Joe was grateful the conversation had shifted from him. That he'd agreed to appear in a Roy Roger's film in the coming year stuck him as the height of folly. At least he'd be wearing his own clothes, boots, and hat.

Joe's first call on Monday, came from a woman who spoke in a breathless rush, "Marty Streech says you're the best private detective in Los Angeles. Is it true?"

"I've solved most of my cases," Joe replied, too modest to say anything more. He'd thank the reporter for the compliment the next time he saw him. "First, I'll need your name, and the nature of your problem so we'll know how to proceed."

She signed softly. "This is Thalia Dupré, and someone is trying to kill me."

Joe sat up in his chair. An extra had been killed when a set wall had collapsed on her latest film, but he'd thought Marty had merely been looking for a sensational story when he'd said Thalia might have been the real target. She was a big star, and he couldn't wait to meet her. "Can you come to my office this morning?"

"I'll be there in an hour."

"Fine." Joe gave her the directions and went downstairs to the drug store to study the display of magazines. He flipped through several movie magazines before he found a feature article and photo of Thalia. She was a classic beauty, tall, slender, and blessed with auburn hair and green eyes. Posed against a palm tree, her sarong accented her spectacular figure. He paid fifteen cents for the magazine and took it back to his office to read.

The article focused on the upcoming *Flamingo Lane* film as both romance and adventure, but it had gone to press before the extra had died. The brief bio of Thalia described her as a Southern California girl who's signed her first movie contract right out of high school. There was a list of her recent movies, and he'd taken Mary Margaret to a couple of them. From what he remembered, the camera loved her. She was convincing in her roles, if not a gifted actress.

Thalia arrived on time. Dressed in a navy blue sweater, a blue and green pleated skirt, and low-heeled shoes, she resembled a university coed rather than a movie star. Without the makeup she wore in her movies, she was a very pretty girl, but with it, a sophisticated, stunning beauty.

"Thank you for seeing me so soon," she began. "Ever since Ryan Newnan died on the *Flamingo Lane* set, I've had the eerie feeling I'm being followed. Do you know what I mean?"

"Yes, I've experienced the same sensation. I've spun around hoping to catch them, but no one's there."

She smiled, revealing charming dimples. "Yes, that's exactly what I mean. I've heard whispers that rather than Ryan, I might have been the intended victim. The wall was the background for my opening scene, so it could be true. That's why I need your help before we resume shooting."

Joe took notes on a yellow legal pad. "Is anyone worried one death during filming might lead to others?"

"I am!" she exclaimed. "I've asked for a new title, and changes to the script so it will be a new film, even if it's still set in the South Seas so we won't need new costumes or sets. There was no great expense involved, so I got my way."

"Could an actress who auditioned for your part be mad enough to want you dead or so badly injured you'd have to be replaced?"

She shrugged. "The competition is fierce for leading roles, and there are so many pretty girls auditioning for them. I was lucky to be discovered by a noted talent agent who secured good parts for me from the beginning. Now directors come to me, but I know it won't last. Once a woman turns thirty and can no longer play a dewy-eyed ingenue, the roles are few and far between. I save most of my earnings, rather than splurge on expensive clothes or fancy apartments the way some girls do."

"That's very wise." Joe complimented, impressed by her forethought. "I heard the carpenter who built the wall has disappeared."

"Only for a short while. Ruben Aguirre was found in a Tijuana jail, which is no recommendation for his character, but the police can't prove his shoddy work was a deliberate threat to me, or Ryan. A falling 2x4 struck him on the temple, and he was dead before he reached the hospital. If the board had hit his shoulder, he'd still be with us. His death has left us all uneasy."

"Did you know Ryan well?"

"No, there are too many extras in a film to know them all."

Joe readily understood. He and Max had spent two days on the *Arizona Sunrise* set and had had no chance to mingle with the stars. "Other than a jealous actress, have you stopped seeing a man who might wish you harm?"

"I'm still with my high school sweetheart, but don't tell anyone. He's a pre-med student at UCLA. By the time he's become a doctor and is ready to practice, I might be offered fewer roles. It should help us make our marriage work. I go to Hollywood parties with whomever publicity wants me to be seen with, and vice versa, but I've not been involved in any tempestuous show business romance." She laughed at the thought. "You can't believe everything they write about us."

"Nevertheless, has someone asked you out, and been insulted by your refusal?"

She plucked at a pleat in her skirt. "Men ask me out all the time. I thank them as sweetly as I can, and insist I'm devoting my full attention to my career. No one has been overly upset about it."

"What about an amorous fan? Have you received passionate letters, or seen the same person at multiple appearances?"

"I don't read the letters coming to MGM. I sign photos and publicity mails them out. There's such a crush of fans whenever I appear to promote a film, I'm busy protecting myself rather than scanning faces in the crowd. I'm sorry to be of such little help."

"You needn't apologize. We have several possibilities worth investigating, an actress jealous of your success, a carpenter who may have been paid for shoddy work, a fan who craves attention, or someone who may have reasons we can't yet discern for wishing you harm."

"I'd no idea there were so many reasons to dislike me, but I'm sure someone is following me."

"Then let's begin there. Does he follow you to the studio in the morning?"

"I don't believe so, although I sometime have the uncomfortable sense he's watching me there."

Joe made a star in his notes. "That's a clue right there that he's associated with the studio. Now that there has been a break in the shooting schedule, is someone still following you?"

"Yesterday, the gardener pointed out footprints in the dirt under the front window of my home. When he's coming that close, I felt justified in calling you."

"Definitely a wise move," he responded. "Did you inform the police?"

"It wouldn't be worth the publicity it would create, and if fans learned my home address, they would start coming by my house."

"I understand. I'll follow you for the next few days, very discreetly, of course, and see if we can catch someone trailing you. I'll take photographs of any suspicious persons, and hope you'll recognize them. Give me your schedule, and I'll arrive at wherever you're going first. That way, if anyone is following you, he won't notice me."

He handed her paper and a pencil so she could jot down her plans for the day. "I'm meeting a friend at a dress shop we like," she began. "We'll have lunch at a nearby café. If you were parked across the street, you could see both places." She made a quick map.

"Later, I'll go home to work on the new script, and my boyfriend is coming over for dinner later. Do you think he might be in any danger?"

"If you're being followed by a jealous fan, he might be, but let's not borrow trouble. I'll park in your neighborhood tonight, and if the Peeping Tom reappears, we'll have him. Once filming begins, we'll need to think of a reason for me to be on the set. With luck, we'll catch him before then. I'll call you tonight, and ask for your plans for tomorrow." He gave her the cost of his retainer, and she opened her purse and pulled out a red wallet fat with cash.

"You ought to be careful about how much money you carry," he warned.

"This is mostly small bills, but you're right. Someone might think I carry hundred dollar bills and rob me. Could they be following me with that in mind?"

"It's possible. Let's see what I discover this week." He stood and walked her to the door. She'd been amiable rather than the snooty starlet he'd expected. Mary Margaret would want her autograph, but he'd wait until he'd caught the culprit bothering her before he made such a request. In fact, he'd wait to tell his darling fiancée that he'd met the beautiful star. It wouldn't just be a white lie, but self-preservation.

CHAPTER 6

The Doberman Pinscher slammed against the driver's door of Joe's Chevy with the force of a freight train. Joe jumped so high in fright he hit his head on the roof panel, and the slight padding failed to cushion the blow. The dog had a deep, fierce, growl, and his sharp canines glowed under the streetlight.

The day had passed without incident, but the night sure wasn't going well. He'd parked across the street from Thalia's home to watch for anyone lurking nearby. It was getting late, and he had just reached for the key to start his car when the enraged dog had leaped into view.

It took him a minute to notice a man the size of Paul Bunyon standing in front of the Chevy to block a quick exit from the thunderous hound. Joe wasn't even tempted to roll down his window to speak, but he leaned over the passenger seat and pushed open the small windbreaker window.

"Call off your dog!" he yelled. "I'm a detective working for one of your neighbors." He hoped the man lived in the neighborhood rather than being someone who roamed the streets looking for human dog toys.

The man stared at him through the windshield, but after a long wait, jerked on the dog's leash. "Come, Achilles, sit."

Expecting the worse, Joe held his breath until the Doberman ceased barking, and ran to the man's side. He again called through the small window, "I'm being paid to watch for strangers. Do you live around here?"

The man moved to the passenger side of the car and leaned down to look in. "You're the only stranger I've seen today."

"Thanks. I'll be on my way."

"Wait! Just who are you working for?"

"I'm not at liberty to say, but there have been reports of a Peeping Tom."

"There's only one person worth peeping on around here. Are you working for Thalia?"

Joe was deliberately vague. "I promised not to reveal any names."

"I'll take that as an affirmative. I walk Achilles every night, and I've not seen a man lurking around her house. Wouldn't you be better off watching from the inside of her home rather than out here?"

"If I were seen going in, I'd be recognized the next day. It would hinder the surveillance."

"Yeah, I see. What you need is a big dog to help you catch the creep. Achilles' mate had puppies a month ago, you want to see them?"

Joe imagined of a basket of black and tan pups, all teeth and snarl, and wasn't remotely tempted. "My landlord doesn't allow pets."

"Rather than a pet, he'd be a working watch dog. Your landlord might like to have one himself."

After a quick glance at Thalia's house to make certain he wasn't missing what he'd come to see, he made the effort to leave. "Can't speak for the landlord." He handed his card through the small window. "You might need a detective someday."

The man laughed. "Not with Achilles here, no one messes with me."

"Good night." Joe started his car and eased it away from the curb. He'd gotten away without being bitten, so he'd call it a productive night.

Tuesday, Thalia planned to stay home and study her script. "The new title is *Orchid Lane*, and it's much easier to find colorful orchids than trained flamingoes, if any exist."

The tall, gawky birds had beautiful pink plumage, but Joe doubted they'd had much of a part in the *Flamingo Lane* script. "Keep your doors locked, and don't open your front door unless it's someone you know. Even then, be careful."

"Will do. Talk to you later."

Paloma Val Verde called a half an hour later. "I'm scared, Joe. Detective Lynch came by my studio yesterday afternoon. I'm proud of my paintings, but he eyed them with a dismissive glance, and warned not all prisons offer art programs. He said I'd receive the best deal from the DA if I were the first to confess to my part in Matteo's death. How could he think such an awful thing?"

Joe was disgusted, but not surprised. "He may say it to every woman who knew Matteo in the hope he'll eventually receive a tearful confession. Please don't worry that he's singled you out."

"How do I not worry? I cried for hours, and I'm too depressed to paint today. Do you think I should hire an attorney?"

Lynch had had the wrong person indicted in the past, but Joe offered what reassurance he could. "Not yet. Do you have a solid alibi for the afternoon Matteo was killed?"

"Yes, I was in the gallery where my work is shown, but Lynch said I didn't have to be at the murder scene to be involved." She burst into heartbroken sobs. "This is the worst thing that's ever happened to me."

Joe had her address, and it wasn't far from his office. "Why don't I come by and take you to lunch?"

"Thank you, but I couldn't eat."

"You could have a cup of tea while I eat," he suggested.

She sniffed loudly. "All right, I suppose I could. Give me half an hour to dress."

"See you then." Other than Mary Margaret, Joe had never dated his clients, and this certainly wasn't a date. It was more of a rescue.

Before he could leave, a brisk knock sounded on the door. "Come in," he called.

A buxom woman peeked in the door, and took a quick look at Joe's office before entering. She tossed one of his cards on his desk. "Did my husband hire you to follow me?"

She had the muscular physique of a lady wrestler, and he chose his words with care. "I've no idea who your husband is, madam. Would you care to take a seat while we talk?"

"I don't plan to stay long." She sat, pulled the hem of her gray dress over her knobby knees, and clutched her handbag in her lap. "Russell is a big man. If you'd met him, you'd remember him."

A sudden sinking feeling filled his chest. "Does he raise Doberman Pinschers?"

Her smile resembled a Halloween pumpkin's scary grimace. "Yes, that's Russell. Did he hire you to follow me?"

Joe wondered why Russell would want him to, but it was an uncharitable thought he promptly suppressed. "No, we talked briefly when he was out walking Achilles last night. I pass out business cards to everyone I meet. He didn't ask me for one."

"Then why did he hide it in his sock drawer?"

"I've no idea. If you two are having issues, perhaps you should speak to your minister."

Her laugh ended in a rude snort, and she pushed her frizzy brown hair out of her eyes. "You'll never see Russell in church. All he worships are his precious dogs, while I'm left to clean up after them. He couldn't raise them without my help, but I still have to remind him each year when my birthday comes around. I always bake him a nice cake, and buy him a present. Don't get much back in return though."

Joe checked his watch. "I'm so sorry, Mrs.?"

"I'm Helga Sauter. I should have introduced myself when I came in."

"Nice to meet you, Mrs. Sauter. I have a lunch meeting with a client, and mustn't be late." He stood and waited while she rose. "I hope I've relieved your mind about your husband."

Another snort. "You're not the only detective in town, are you?"

He couldn't argue with that, and waited for her to reach the bottom of the stairs before he locked up. Even then, he waited another minute to make certain he wouldn't meet her again on the sidewalk.

Paloma had turned the front room of her home into her studio. At first glance, it appeared to be a colorful mess. With further study, however, Joe found the tall bookcases were filled with the wooden birdhouses she built to serve as models for her paintings. Tubes of paint were organized by color into small bins on a table near her easel. Brushes were gathered in jars. A tarp splattered with paint protected the hardwood floor, and finished paintings were stacked in a row along the far wall. The scent of turpentine hung in the air.

Paloma followed his gaze, and she uncovered the painting on her easel. The two by three foot canvas held a neat sketch of a tall, thin birdhouse she's just begun to fill in with several shades of red and pink paint.

"I use various combinations of yellow, orange, red, and pink, or greens and blues with a touch of lavender. That way, I can produce multiple paintings from a single birdhouse. They can also be turned slightly to show different angles. Do you like it?"

She'd dressed in the long, embroidered turquoise dress she's worn to his studio. Her eyes were puffy from crying, but her expression was so hopeful Joe couldn't disappoint her.

"I like it very much," he replied. "Your work has a fanciful charm, as though the little houses were designed to be homes for magical birds."

"Yes! Thank you. Some people see that right away, others want me to add a robin or blue bird."

"What do you say to them?"

"If they're buying the painting, I add a canary, or whatever they'd like. At this point in my career, I need to sell more than I need to insist on the purity of my vision. Does that sound silly?"

"Not at all. I admire such a practical view. Is there someplace special you'd like to go for lunch?"

"There's a café I walk to when I need to clear my head. They have good sandwiches. Would you mind walking there?"

"Not at all. I often go for walks after lunch."

Archie's was more deli than café, but they had a few tables. Paloma chose one near the front window. "Now that I'm here, I think maybe I'll have a tuna sandwich."

Joe ordered it and a corned beef sandwich for himself. Pausing occasionally for a bite, Paloma talked through much of the meal, and all he had to do was nod to show he was listening. She knew everything about the Los Angeles art scene, and he knew nothing whatsoever, so it was both informative and entertaining. Once she'd finished her sandwich and eaten her last potato chip, she grew solemn on the walk home.

"Is Detective Lynch as awful a person as he seems?" she asked.

"I'm prejudiced, you understand, but indeed he is. His only asset is a handsome wardrobe. It's best to simply ignore him. Are you feeling well enough to paint this afternoon?"

"Yes, thank you, I do. I'm alone too much, dwell on Matteo's death, and become so depressed, I end up a weepy mess. I should get out and see people every day, even if it's only a trip to the market. Unfortunately, I need to stay in and paint as well."

"Can you strike a balance, paint for most of the day, and go out in the afternoon?"

"You give such good advice. Do you mind if I call you sometime just to talk?"

They were standing on the sidewalk in front of her house, and he hated to depress her again by saying no, but he sure couldn't say yes. "I always try to be helpful, but I must reserve my telephone for conversations with new clients. I'm sure we'll speak again before Matteo's case is closed though."

She smiled and turned toward her home. "I just hope I won't have to call you from jail."

When he became a detective, he'd expected to provide answers and solve crimes, but when advice was desperately needed, he gave it. Usually questions involved romance, and what Paloma needed was an attentive boyfriend. He hadn't said so, because she would have asked him to find her one. He knew better than to start down that slippery incline.

Later that afternoon, Sean Dermot called Joe and asked if he could come by his office. Joe hoped the cellist had some useful insights, but Sean had thought the same of him.

"I really miss Matteo," he began. "We were comfortable sitting side by side. He was a brilliant musician, and his like won't come again. Have the police said anything about a diary or calendar that might show whom Matteo expected to see the afternoon he died?"

"Not that I've heard, but with so many girlfriends, he must have had a way to keep them from bumping into one another."

"You'd think so." Sean sipped the coffee Joe had poured for him. "He was a genius in many respects, maybe he kept it all in his head."

"The real question is why."

Sean couldn't help but chuckle. "Because he could. All that really mattered to him was being the foremost cellist in the world. Women were merely a hobby, the way some men play golf. He toyed with women's hearts and never looked back. Apparently it finally caught up to him."

"Did he date any of the orchestra members' wives?"

"Other than casual comments about having a date later, he didn't confide details so I don't really know. We all have the same rehearsal and performance schedule, so the husbands would have been free whenever Matteo was. It would have provided an unnecessary complication when he charmed women so easily."

Joe stood to refill their cups with hot coffee. "His reputation as a lady's man didn't make women leery of becoming involved with him?"

"Do moths realize the danger to a flame? But he wasn't actually involved with any of them. Maybe he allotted each woman a limited number of dates and moved on before they expected more of him than what must have been a spectacular afternoon or night."

"I wish he'd left the rest of us some notes," Joe added.

"Me too. He could have sold a million copies." Sean looked up at the clock. "I didn't mean to take so much of your time." He finished his coffee and set the empty cup on Joe's desk. "I need to go home and practice."

"Do you have new music to learn?"

"No, but everything I do know won't sound nearly as good if I don't put in several hours of independent practice each day. It's not a life everyone would enjoy, but I love it."

After he had gone, Joe regretted not asking him if he were taking Matteo's place and moving up to first chair. It had to be a challenge to take the place of the most celebrated cellist in the world. He added Sean's name to his bulletin board, off to the side with those who knew Matteo, but weren't suspects.

If all the orchestra members practiced their instruments at home as devotedly as Sean, their wives could say they needed to do some shopping, or meet a friend for lunch to get away. A conspiracy might have emerged after some of them compared notes. He made a card for orchestra wives, and pinned it to his board.

Constance Remson was a great contact, and he called her. "How well are you acquainted with the wives of the philharmonic members?"

"Not well at all," she replied. "They're not included when we're doing a party for sponsors, or publicity for a concert. Do you think one of them might have killed Matteo?"

"Possibly, and they shouldn't be overlooked as suspects."

"I could host a tea to thank them for their support of the orchestra. That would get them together without tipping our hand."

"How much time do you need to arrange it?"

"A simple tea? I can plan one in my sleep. Are you free this Thursday afternoon? No one does anything on a Thursday, so they should all be free. Not every musician has a wife, by the way, so it won't be as large a group as you might think. I can start calling them now to issue the invitations."

Joe's calendar was disappointingly empty. "I do have Thursday free."

"Good, once we have them all together, I'll mention Matteo, and you'll be able to see how they respond."

"That's the plan." Joe hadn't expected Constance to take up the effort so enthusiastically. He said good-bye and penciled in the tea on his calendar. He wondered if he should dress as a waiter to see what he could overhear.

When Joe picked up Mary Margaret at the end of her shift, she wore such a miserable expression he knew something dreadful must have happened. He wrapped her in a warm hug. "Did you lose a favorite patient?"

"No, it's worst than that, but let's wait until we get home to talk about it."

Joe saw her comfortably seated in his car, and as they drove to the Chrysanthemum Court, he made no effort at cheerful conversation. She was usually such an upbeat, positive person, he hoped whatever her problem might be, he could help to resolve it.

When they reached her home, she dropped her purse on the small table by the front door, and took his hand. "Come sit with me." She pulled him down beside her on the sofa, and kept hold of his arm.

"My mother called this morning just as I was leaving for work. She went to see *Arizona Sunrise,* and found your brief appearance so frightening she wants me to break our engagement and come straight home."

Joe had hoped her mother wouldn't see the film, but her response was even worse than anything he'd imagined. He drew in a deep breath and released it slowly. "What did you tell her?"

The threat of tears brightened her pretty green eyes. "I told her I couldn't be late for work, and that I'd call her this evening. What are we going to do, Joe?"

He was relieved she still thought of them as a couple. "Tell her it was a movie role, and not who I really am?"

"I said so this morning, but it didn't lessen her fears." She bit her lip. "She also thought you were too old for me."

He couldn't deny he was eight years her elder, but it had never been a problem, until now. The war had made them all older than their years, but that wouldn't impress her mother.

"Is she hoping you'll meet a cheerful looking guy who just graduated from high school?"

She pulled her hand from his. "This isn't funny, Joe."

"I'm not trying to be funny." He dropped his arm around her shoulders to pull her close.

He wouldn't make her choose between making a quick trip to Seattle to allay her mother's fears a month or so before they'd return for the wedding, and having a honeymoon. It was the actual choice, however. "What do you suppose your sisters and brothers think about me?"

"None have called, but I don't need a committee decision. I'm marrying you regardless of anything they might say."

That she loved him was a constant thrill. "Thank you, but this is your family, love. Maybe you should speak with everyone."

"I think I'm going to be sick." She made a dash for the bathroom, and he handed her a glass of water when she came out. "I'm sorry. You're right, I should speak to all of them before my mother convinces them I've lost my mind."

"Do you want to talk to them in person? We could catch the Coast Starlight train tomorrow."

She placed the glass on the counter with deliberate care rather than hurl it against the cabinets. "I've arranged for time off in December for the wedding, and I can't ask for additional time now. I'll begin with my sister, Sharon, we've always been close."

Before she could look up the number in her address book, a knock came at the door. "Would you see who that is, Joe? I don't feel like entertaining company."

Luke Hatcher stood on the stoop with a measuring cup in his hand. "Hi, Joe. I'm sorry to bother you and Mary Margaret, but I'm making macaroni and cheese and ran out of milk. Could I borrow a cup?"

"Let me check." He left the door partially ajar. "Can you spare a cup of milk for Luke?"

"Yes, but only if he'll come in and offer advice."

That very day Joe had advised Helga Sauter to consult a minister, so he couldn't say no. Joe welcomed him. "Please come in and sit down for a minute."

The minister laughed. "That sounds as though you're going out back to milk a cow."

Mary Margaret gave him a shaky smile. She told him how badly her mother had reacted to Joe's performance in *Arizona Sunrise*. "I'm marrying Joe regardless of what she says, but there would be no point in traveling to Seattle if my family will boycott the wedding."

Luke nodded and pursed his lips as he considered the problem. "I'm sorry I wasn't able to see the movie over the weekend. That's not the issue, of course, but people often have trouble separating actors from their roles. It might be a good idea to give your mother a few days to cool off before you broach the subject with her."

Joe and Mary Margaret stared at him. "'Broach the subject,'" she repeated. "That's all you've got?"

"Not worth a cup of milk?" he asked.

She shook her head. "Perhaps I understated my mother's reaction, but she was in a furious rage when she called this morning."

Joe tried not to laugh, but Luke appeared to be totally flummoxed by their situation. "You must have an occasional family disagreement with the VA's treatment of a patient."

"It happens," Luke agreed. "For my trouble, I got punched in the jaw in August, and now I avoid those situations unless I'm actually asked to help. We begin in the chapel with a prayer. I can make it so long and tedious tempers have time to cool and people forget why they're there. I'm sorry, but I've not had my own congregation, and haven't had any experience with adults dealing with difficult parents."

"You've not been married either," Joe reminded him.

"Yes, that might be a factor as well," Luke agreed.

Mary Margaret took his measuring cup and carried it into the kitchen. She quickly returned with the requested milk. "You don't want your macaroni to get cold while you're making the cheese sauce."

Luke stood to take the cup. "Thank you. I'm teaching myself to cook, and the dish seemed easy."

Joe walked him to the front door and whispered, "Thanks for trying to help. It's appreciated."

The minister nodded and left. Joe turned back to Mary Margaret. "Is Sharon your married sister?"

"No, that's Rose, and we've never been close. Sharon is more like me." She ran a finger down the numbers in her address book.

"Should I go out for a walk?"

"No, please stay." Her expression brightened. "Maybe you can talk to her after I explain why I'm calling."

Joe figured as long as he didn't mention any murder cases, he might do all right. When Sharon's voice sounded so much like Mary Margaret's, he liked her right away. "I appear to be a much better actor than I thought, but I don't scare children on the street."

"That's good to hear. Why don't you have some photos taken with Mary Margaret and send them to our mom. If you look real sweet, hold some flowers or a kitten if you must, but do your best to look pleasant and friendly. That ought to prompt her to reconsider her initial poor impression of you."

"Did you see *Arizona Sunrise*?" he asked.

"No, but I'm going to a matinee tomorrow, and I'll take Rose with me. Tell Mary Margaret not to worry about the boys. They don't care whom we marry."

Joe thanked her and handed the telephone back to his fiancée to say good-bye. "I'll talk to Pete about having photographs taken of us tomorrow after work. If he has time to develop them quickly, they can be in the mail this week. Do you want me to stay while you talk to your mom?"

"Yes, please, I won't have the courage to call her without your being here." They returned to the sofa for a warm snuggle before she dialed her mother's number. The telephone rang and rang, but no one answered. Mary Margaret hung up and redialed the number, but again, there was no answer.

"That's odd, my mother is usually at home in the evening. Maybe she took several friends to see *Arizona Sunrise*, and isn't home yet. I'll try later. I don't feel like making anything more involved than a grilled cheese sandwich for dinner. Will that be enough for you?"

"Yes, you make a terrific grilled cheese."

"Oh, Joe, you say that about everything I make."

"It's true." He slid his arms around her waist and gave her a fond squeeze.

She reached up to kiss him. "Having photos taken was a swell idea. It's sure to impress my mother. I've always thought you were very handsome, and she will too."

Joe thought love must be clouding her vision, but he'd not argue.

When Joe met Mary Margaret the next afternoon, she looked much happier than she had yesterday. "I didn't reach my mother until this morning, and I didn't give her a chance to speak. I told her we were having photos taken we'd send soon so she could see what a truly nice guy you are. I said good-bye before she could insist it would be an unnecessary expense. You gave me a wonderful photo of you in your Coast Guard uniform. I think we should include it."

"Whatever you like." He'd worn a sports coat and slacks, and hoped he looked sufficiently respectable to please her mother. She had changed into one of her favorite dresses after work and looked especially pretty.

The owner of Pete's Cameras had set up a portrait studio in the back of his shop, and he welcomed Joe and Mary Margaret. Joe had told Pete the situation was dire when he'd made the appointment.

"You want to appear sincere," Pete commented. "A pleasant smile rather than a wide grin should work best. Let's have you sit on the stool, Mary Margaret, and you stand beside her, Joe."

It was a high bar stool, and Joe picked her up to place her on it rather than watch her struggle to climb on it herself. "You're always a gentleman," she exclaimed. "I'll tell mother that."

"I do my best." He kissed her cheek. They got the giggles when Pete worked on their pose, and the photographer had to wait for them to regain their composure. Joe did his best for Mary Margaret's sake, but he feared Pete didn't have much to work with when it came to him. With his features, it was a lot easier to look menacing than friendly but it had always worked to his advantage in the past.

"Your relaxed pose is perfect." Pete took several shots, and then changed their angle to the camera for a few more. "These should be exactly what you want."

"I'm sure they will be," Mary Margaret replied. As they left the shop, she took Joe's hand. "Let's go to the Jumpin' Plate for dinner. I was too worried to eat much yesterday, and I could do with a juicy hamburger tonight."

"Whatever you like, my love." Joe never turned down a good hamburger and an order of fries, and with Mary Margaret's company, it would be the perfect meal.

CHAPTER 7

Joe had just closed his copy of *The Complete Works of Sir Arthur Conan Doyle* to get ready for bed when Thalia Dupré called. "Slow down, I didn't get any of that."

She took a deep breath, and spoke slowly. "My neighbor saw someone peering in my front window, and his dog bit the man's leg, but he still got away."

"Are you talking about Russell Sauter and Achilles?"

"Yes! How do you know them?"

"Met them on the street. Did Russell see the man's car?"

"No, he was busy calling off Achilles, and the man leaped a couple of hedges and got away around the corner. What do you think I ought to do if I'm not safe in my own home?"

"I've met Achilles, and the man won't return tonight." There were Doberman puppies that needed good homes, but she traveled often and couldn't provide for one. Maybe Russell could loan her a trained watchdog when she was home. "Are you going to the studio tomorrow?"

"Yes, will you come with me?"

"I will, and we can both watch for anyone limping, and you'll know if someone who should be there hasn't come to work." *Arizona Sunrise* had been shot on the MGM lot, and he looked forward to again visiting the sprawling studio.

Autumn is a glorious season in Southern California. The days are clear and bright, and the temperatures hover in the high seventies. It's perfect weather to shoot a picture on one of MGM's outdoor sets. *Orchid Lane* was complete with sand dunes, palm trees, and a pier that extended into what would appear to be a peaceful lagoon when the movie arrived in theaters.

Thalia's character lived in a typical island colonial home with a wide veranda and louvered windows. A profusion of silk orchids appeared to grow over the end of the veranda. Real orchids would take their place for close-ups.

"They have changed the story," Thalia explained. "Initially, the plot centered on a sea captain who meets a girl on an exotic isle. A mysterious character, who may have been good or evil, is murdered, and the girl's father believes the captain did it."

"And she works to prove him innocent?" Joe asked.

"Of course," she laughed. "Now the captain arrives after a terrible storm. While the crew works to repair his ship, he falls for me. The boy I've hoped to marry has never left the island, and he makes a brave attempt to compete with the captain's tales of adventure on the high seas."

"Which man does she choose?" he asked.

"The writers are still working on the ending, but I'm pulling for the boy who has loved her all his life."

"The safe choice?"

"True, but the captain may not be what he seems, so there's an aspect of danger surrounding him. My costumes are all sarongs. Thank God the seductive drape is sewn into them, so I won't have to worry about them fluttering free on their own."

A large trailer held racks of costumes, lots of white shirts, and khaki pants for the men, and a colorful array of sarongs for Thalia. She slipped behind a curtain to dress in a pretty green one, and then wearing sandals, led him to the makeup trailer.

A smiling gray haired woman in a lavender smock greeted them. "Dennis is home sick today, so I'll be doing your makeup."

"Thanks, Hazel. This is Joe Ezell, who's working for me today. Joe, Hazel is the best there is."

Hazel swept Joe with a discerning glance. "You've got a great face for movies. Do you act?"

"Only when I have to," he replied.

The spacious trailer held everything needed to turn anyone into a great beauty or hideous villain, and half a dozen makeup artists were working on the other leads in the cast. Thalia sat down in front of a mirror, and Joe stood back out of their way.

"Did Dennis say what the problem was?" he asked.

Hazel picked up a slip of paper and handed it to him. "He called in, so all I got was this note, which doesn't give any details. Between you and me, I'd prefer not to have a list of complaints. Some people will go on and on about their every ache and pain. I choose not to bore anyone with my health concerns."

"I'm with you, Hazel." He met Thalia's eyes in the mirror. "Is Dennis ill often?"

Thalia sat up straight so Hazel could drape a cape around her shoulders. "He's worked on most of my films, and never missed a day. Do you suppose he could have met with a misadventure?"

"My thoughts exactly." And yet, Joe didn't trust answers that came so easily.

"Hazel, do you know where he lives?" Thalia asked. "I'd like to stop by when we're finished today, and take him some chicken soup."

"I'll get it for you. He lives near here in Culver City," Hazel replied. "Dennis adores you, and he'd leave his deathbed if you rang his doorbell."

Joe met Thalia's glance in the mirror. "I'll keep a watch for anyone else who might prove of interest."

"We've nothing but people of interest here." Hazel laughed. "Movie studios are filled with them."

"Yes, that's why I'm here." Joe considered asking Hazel for the name of anyone who had suddenly begun to limp, but thought better of it. She was the chatty sort who might share his concern with every actor who sat in her chair, and unintentionally warn the culprit before he could be identified.

He turned and went to the door of the makeup trailer to look out. Everyone rushing by walked with a steady gait. When Thalia tapped his shoulder, he turned to find her movie makeup had again turned her into a remarkably beautiful young woman.

"Thank God I don't have to go around made up like a goddess everyday. I'm due on the set. If you stand behind the cameras, you won't be in anyone's way."

They walked over to the outdoor set. "Did they rebuild the wall?"

"No, now the movie opens with me strolling the beach. I'll catch sight of a magnificent sailing ship, and wait for it to dock at our private pier. It won't actually be there, but will be edited in later. Movies are made in little bits and pieces, but they're edited together beautifully before they reach neighborhood theaters."

Joe had learned that on his brief appearance in *Arizona Sunrise*. "Do you walk out on the pier to welcome the captain?"

"No, I make the him come to me."

"Smart girl." Joe found a place out of the way to watch, but kept his attention on the crew. They shifted positions with a lively agility and none showed any hint of a leg injury. He'd seen Achilles' teeth, and if he'd bit any of these men, they wouldn't have been doing their jobs with such confident strides.

The lights creating a warm island sky were hot, and he moved into the shadows. Thalia stood behind a palm tree, watching the captain as he approached. She'd starred in other films with the actor, but regarded him with an apprehensive glance as though he truly were a stranger.

They reshot the scene half a dozen times before running through the opening dialog. Joe thought they'd done it perfectly the first time, but again the director called for new angles and retakes. Joe could appreciate how diligently Thalia and her co-star worked to please the man, but something was always off.

Thalia had given him a pass to be at the studio, and with his notebook and pen in his hand, he looked as though he belonged and was on his way somewhere important. Thalia sensed she was being watched, and that meant the man had to be close enough to observe her without calling attention to himself. Actors thrived on attention, so he probably wasn't a member of the cast. He could be a member of the crew, however, who had also called in sick. While there was a break in the shooting, he walked over to men handling the lights.

"Good morning, I'm doing a quick check for the accounting office. Are any of the crew missing today?"

The lightening engineers looked around. "We just started this shoot, so it's too soon to say. We're going to be paid on time, aren't we?"

"Of course," Joe assured them. He'd seen a trailer with a red cross painted on the side, and wondered if the injured man could have sought treatment there. The door was open, and a nurse sat at the desk placed just inside the door.

"Good morning, I'm from accounting, and just checking on a strange report of someone being bitten by a dog. Have you treated anyone for a bite today?"

"A dog bite, goodness no. If anyone came in with such an injury, we'd send them to the hospital to they could begin shots to ward off rabies."

"Thank you." Joe left before she could ask why someone from accounting would be investigating dog bites.

He couldn't get to a pay telephone until that afternoon when they stopped for chicken soup on the way to Dennis Nesbit's house. He seldom if ever called Mary Margaret at work, but he knew the number on her ward. When she came to the phone, he made a quick request.

"I'm sorry to bother you, but I'm on a case that involves a dog bite and wonder if you could check to see if a man came into emergency last night with such a complaint. He might have gotten a rabies shot."

"I can do that," she offered. "If no one came here, would you like me to call other hospitals nearby?"

"Do you have time?"

"I'll do it on my break. There is a series of shots to prevent rabies, and unfortunately, they do make some people sick."

"How sick?"

"Symptoms similar to the flu, nausea, headache, and fever."

He drew in a deep breath. "Thank you, you've been a big help. See you later."

He told Thalia what he'd learned as they drove to Dennis's home. "He could actually be ill, or it may be a reaction to a rabies shot. Let's just be attentive, and see what we can learn."

"Should I mention the Peeping Tom?"

"Let's see how it goes before we do."

Dennis Nesbit's house was painted a bright yellow, with green shutters, a red front door, and neatly trimmed hedges lining the walk. It was so cute it could have been featured in a children's book. Joe rang the bell, and then stepped back to allow Thalia to greet Dennis first.

Dennis opened the door only a crack to peer out, and then dissolved in a coughing fit when he found Thalia on his porch. She waited for him to catch his breath before she offered the container of soup.

"This is my friend Joe Ezell. I was worried about you, and he volunteered to drive me here on the way home. You've never missed a day on any of my movies, and I missed you. Hazel does a beautiful job as well, but she isn't nearly as entertaining."

After wiping his nose, Dennis reached out to take the soup. He was a tall, thin fellow whose dark hair was spiked from sleep. He blinked his teary eyes. "I'm so sorry I can't invite you to come in, but I don't want you to catch this awful bug."

"How long have you been sick?" she asked.

"What is today? I've lost track of time."

"It's Wednesday."

Dennis needed a moment to think. "I woke up feeling sick early Saturday morning. Spoiled my whole weekend, but I'd hoped I'd be well enough to work today."

"Don't come to the studio until you feel truly well. With such a tight shooting schedule, we can't have anyone else falling ill."

"I hope you weren't bitten by a rabid dog," Joe offered. "Once you develop the symptoms of rabies, it's too late to seek treatment."

Dennis stared at him. "A rabid dog? What an odd thing to say. I do like dogs well enough, but don't have one. Have there been reports of rabid dogs roaming Los Angeles?"

"No, of course not," Thalia assured him. "Joe is simply trying to be helpful. If you haven't seen your doctor, maybe you should give him a call." She turned to leave and Joe followed.

"Thank you for coming by and bringing the soup," Dennis called and closed his door.

"He's not our man," Joe announced as he started his Chevy's engine. "He wasn't favoring a leg as he talked with us, and thought a question about a dog bite was absurd. Which it is. If the man Achilles bit went to an emergency room last night, I'll find him."

"Thank you. Can you come with me to MGM tomorrow?"

"I'll pick you up, but I'll have to leave at noon to attend a tea party. Don't ask, it's for another job."

"Sounds fun. I can get a ride home. Talk to you tomorrow night."

Before walking her to her front door, Joe checked the dirt beneath the front window for footprints. They were there, although the Peeping Tom had taken off to escape Achilles with a speed that had smeared them so there was no point in buying plaster of Paris to copy the impressions the way the police did. He made a mental note to buy a small bag to use the next time he encountered telltale footprints.

Mary Margaret waved as she came down the hospital steps. "A man did come in late last night for treatment of a dog bite. The physician who saw him gave him the first rabies shot and convinced him to check-in for a couple of days to be certain no infection sets in."

"He's still here?"

"Yes, he is. Want to see him?"

"I sure do." He took out his notebook and pen. "Just show me to his ward, and I'll do the rest. What's his name?"

"Ralph Snyder."

She walked him to the ward, and waited outside. Joe took a moment to get into the professional mood he needed to project, rather than gleefully force Mr. Snyder to admit how he'd been bitten. The injured man was in the second bed in the ward, with his right leg propped up on pillows. A sandy-haired fellow with eyes of a doll's innocent blue, he looked up as Joe approached his bed.

"Mr. Synder?" Joe extended his hand. "You entered the hospital complaining of a dog bite. Is that correct?"

"Sure is. I went out for a walk and this monster of a dog attacked me, for no reason at all."

Joe opened his notebook. "Can you tell me exactly where this occurred?"

"I was lost in thought, as they say, so I can't pinpoint the exact spot, and wham, the dog bit me. Thank God the owner caught him, or he might have gone for my throat and killed me."

"Horrible possibility. Could you identify the breed of dog?"

"Not really, but he was big and black with a mouthful of sharp teeth."

"Is the place you work sympathetic, or will they dock your pay for the days you miss?"

"I'm a carpenter at MGM, and if I'm not there with my hammer in my hand, I'm not paid. I've saved a little money, so it's not a disaster, but I don't want anyone hired to take my place."

"Of course not. Isn't MGM where Thalia Depré makes her films?"

Ralph's grin extended nearly ear to ear. "It is, and I've worked on several of them. She's gorgeous, isn't she? Her real name is Susan Ann Smith, by the way. She's real friendly, not stuck up as many of the stars are."

"Have you ever asked her out?"

He laughed. "No, she wouldn't go out with me, so there's no point in embarrassing us both by asking. I've heard she has a boyfriend, probably some rich guy who can take her everywhere she wants to go in some big convertible."

"It sounds as though you have a crush on her."

"Who wouldn't?"

Joe turned the page in his notebook. "As a carpenter, what do you know about the wall that collapsed on her latest film?"

"*Flamingo Lane*? Now it's *Orchid Lane*, as if changing a title would ward off evil spirits, if they exist. Ruben Aguirre worked on the wall, and he drinks more than anyone suspects, so his work is often shoddy. It caught up with him this time. I built the house where Thalia's character lives in the South Seas. When I build something, it will withstand a hurricane. You can count on it."

"You obviously take pride in your work."

"Of course, don't you?"

"Yes, I do." Joe handed him his business card, and produced the fiercest expression he could muster. "I'm working for Miss Dupré, and know exactly what you were doing last night before you were bitten." He watched the healthy tan drain from Ralph's face. "Do you make a habit of peeking in windows?"

"No, sir, I don't."

"I'm tempted to call the police and report you, or you can give me your word you won't ever go near her house again, or follow her, or bother her in any possible way. Is that clear?"

Ralph bobbed his head. "She's just so pretty...."

"Your word, Mr. Snyder."

"Yes, I won't go near her home, or follow her ever again. She's way out of my league, I know that."

"Just drool at her movies. Is that clear?"

"Yes, sir."

"What branch did you serve in?"

"The Navy, in the Pacific."

"Be grateful you survived the war, and find yourself a nice girl to date, and never compare her to Thalia."

Joe walked out and found Mary Margaret standing outside the ward with both hands over her mouth to stifle her laughter.

Thursday morning, Joe picked up Thalia with plenty of time to drive to MGM. "I found the Peeping Tom at the VA hospital recovering from a dog bite. He's Ralph Snyder, a carpenter who's worked on several of your films. Do you know him?"

"I don't recognize the name, but maybe I would if I saw him. There are so many men on the set, and...."

"You needn't apologize. I made him swear he'd never bother you ever again, or I'd report him to the police for peeking into your windows. He told me Ruben Aguirre has a drinking problem, and did a crummy job on the wall that collapsed. It wasn't part of a plot to hurt you."

"That's a relief." She hesitated a long moment. "Do you suppose the studio should provide a body guard to make certain I'm always safe?"

"If it would make you feel better, go ahead and ask. You also need to have the publicity department save any letters addressed to you that are in any way threatening. They need to keep the envelopes with them, so I can pay a call on anyone who needs a personal warning to stay away."

"You'd do that?"

"If they're local, sure, it's part of my service."

He hadn't been asked to trace dangerous fans for anyone else, but he was game to try. "I would like an autographed photo for my fiancée. Her name is Mary Margaret."

"It will be in the mail for you today."

Joe picked up the photos from Pete's Cameras, took them to his office, and laid them on his desk.

When CC came by, he invited him to offer an opinion. "Look at these, will you? I'm trying to impress Mary Margaret's mother. I need to look wholesome rather than dangerous."

"Wholesome?" CC mused thoughtfully. "Mary Margaret looks real pretty, doesn't she?"

Joe noted CC had dodged his request. "She sure is. With any luck, she's all her mother will see."

"I like this one," CC offered. "It's a more relaxed pose, and you're leaning into each other. That's real sweet."

"Thank you. Sweet is exactly what I need."

CC picked up the wastebasket to empty. "I took my wife to see *Arizona Sunrise* last night."

Joe held his breath. "What did you think?"

"You're the best part of the movie. You looked like a real cowboy, and we both wished you'd had a bigger part."

"That was all I could handle," Joe confessed, "but thank you anyway, I appreciate your support."

"Any time, Mr. Ezell." He emptied the wastebasket into the trash container he rolled down the hall, and left Joe to ponder the photographs on his own.

When the phone rang, Joe counted to three before answering. "Discreet Investigations."

"Yes, thank you. The man I've been seeing might be married. A friend said I needed a detective to find the truth. Do you do that kind of thing?"

"I most certainly do, Miss...."

"I'm Grace Adams. Do you have time to see me today? I want to get this over with quickly before I lose my courage."

"Can you be here in the next half hour?"

"Perfect. I have the address."

Joe told her good-bye, took out a new manila folder, and reached for a legal pad to take notes. This was the type of follow and photograph case he did most often, and wouldn't be nearly as exciting as being on the MGM lot yesterday.

Grace Adams proved to be older than Joe had expected, easily in her sixties. She wore her silver hair in an attractive bob, sat with a proud straight posture, and was remarkably pretty.

"I met Louis Dowell at the Beverly Hills Library six months ago. We were both browsing the mystery section and struck up a conversation about favorite authors. We each checked out a book the other had recommended, and met for coffee later in the week to discuss them. I liked him right away because he's intelligent, and fun. I've invited him to dinner in my home several times, but he's never free to come."

She laid an index card on the desk. "Here's his address, and telephone number. He sent me a card for my birthday last month, and the address in the telephone book matches the return address. I'm not going to ring the bell at his home when his wife might answer."

"It always pays to be cautious," Joe agreed. "Other than not accepting your dinner invitations, is there anything else that troubles you about Louis?"

"No, not really. He says he's a retired corporate attorney. He never mentions being married. I'm a widow and won't bore any man with sweet memories of my late husband, but I always make it clear I've been married."

"Did you ever ask him if he'd been married?"

"I should have, shouldn't I? After knowing him for six months, it's too late now, isn't it?"

"Not necessarily, but if you'd like me to discover how Louis spends his evenings, I'll be glad to do so. If he lives with his wife, it will be impossible to hide. When will you see him again?"

"We meet at noon on Fridays." She gave him the library address, and paid his retainer.

"I'll be there, but if you happen to see me, ignore me as though we'd ever met."

"I understand, Mr. Ezell. It will be our secret."

"Exactly." Now, he had to get ready for a tea party.

CHAPTER 8

Constance Remson's white columned home resembled Scarlett O'Hara's Tara, in *Gone With The Wind*. It was larger than the frat houses at USC; it was just plain huge. With tall hedges masking the long curved driveway, it wasn't visible from the street. The front gate was open to the sidewalk, and a bouquet of bronze and gold chrysanthemums streaming orange ribbons added a welcoming touch.

Joe had come early, but the front door was already open, and Constance answered his knock. In a beautiful print dress in vivid fall colors, she looked to be part of the festive decorations.

"It's such a beautiful day, I thought we'd be happier on the terrace by the pool than indoors."

He followed her down a long wall outside to the terrace, where seven circular tables with pale gold tablecloths and centerpieces of chrysanthemums matching the bouquet on the gate added a colorful touch. A wide stretch of deep green lawn framed the fenced pool. It appeared close to Olympic in size, and past it, there were tennis courts.

"Lovely place you have here," he complimented sincerely.

"My father's family struck oil in Texas, and my parents have thoroughly enjoyed their success. They're at the Balboa Island house today, and will miss all the fun. The tiny sandwiches, scones, and sweets are ready to be served, and we'll pour plenty of champagne as well as tea. I'm hoping for a relaxed afternoon, where conversation will flow easily, and you might find answers to any questions you ask."

She glanced at her watch. "We have a few minutes before the first guests arrive. Please feel free to tour the house while I make a last check on our kitchen staff."

He wasn't sure where to begin, but retraced their path to the front door and turned into the living room. The walls were a vivid blue, with tasteful furnishings in shades of blue and gold. The art on the walls had to be originals. He wondered if Constance ever played the baby grand piano.

A door opened into a study, with bookcases lining the walls, with popular fiction among the leather-bound volumes of the classics. He sat at the desk, removed his notebook from his sport coat pocket, and made a few notes. He wouldn't naively ask if any of the ladies had enjoyed a close friendship with Matteo. He'd simply mention the cellist's name, and welcome whatever the response might be.

Constance returned to the front door to welcome her guests as they arrived. Dressed for an afternoon tea, they wore attractive suits, or full-skirted dresses with narrow belts to emphasize a trim waist. Their hats were small and cute, and all had worn dainty white gloves.

Two maids in black dresses with snowy white aprons showed them to the tables on the terrace and poured champagne into the delicate crystal flutes at each place. When the first table had six women giggling over the champagne, Joe joined them.

"Good afternoon, ladies. I'm Joe Ezell, a private detective, and I'm working with Miss Remson on Matteo da Milano's untimely death. This is such a lovely party, isn't it? I swear my whole family could live here and not run into each other in a week."

As he'd expected, the comment on the palatial estate drew smiles and put them at ease. "Do you all know each other?" he asked.

The ladies gave their names, along with their husband's instrument. "This is such a wonderful idea," a woman named Geraldine enthused. "The board does so much for the Philharmonic, and it's so nice Miss Remson wanted to do something for us."

Joe offered a word here and there between bites of the small cucumber sandwiches. He thought teas were the only place they were served. He'd never heard anyone say they were looking forward to eating the cucumber sandwiches they'd brought in their bag lunch from home.

The woman next to Joe leaned close. "Do you have any idea who might have killed Matteo?"

"I'm still gathering information. Do you have any thoughts?"

The other conversations at the table abruptly ceased. "My worry is that other members of the orchestra might also be in danger," a young woman named Karen exclaimed.

The woman by her side scoffed. "No music lover would have killed Matteo. It had to have been one of his many women who took offense at his behavior. I heard tomcats are choosier."

Laura, the prettiest woman at the table concentrated on a scone. "I'm sure that's not true, and we shouldn't gossip about the dead."

"On the contrary," Joe interjected. "A casual remark might reveal an important clue." When no one offered anything he hadn't known, he passed out his business cards, excused himself, and moved on to the next table to introduce himself.

Constance Remson waited until all her guests had arrived to extend a warm welcome. "Thank you for responding to my invitation. I'd hoped to provide an opportunity for all of us to become better acquainted away from the concert hall."

She complimented them on their devotion to their talented husbands, as well as their enthusiasm for the symphony.

The woman who'd introduced herself as Eunice to Joe's left leaned close to whisper, "Do you suppose there are any of Matteo's girlfriends among us?"

"Maybe, what have you heard?" he replied.

She checked to make certain the others at the table where listening to Constance. "Only that he was fishing off a dock too close to home, if you know what I mean."

"I do. There are many beautiful woman here today."

"There are, but from what I heard, he liked them young."

Joe glanced over his shoulder at Karen, who'd worried other members of the orchestra might be in danger. Had she wanted to focus the attention on the musicians rather than risk speculation on Matteo's pretty conquests?

The women at each table he joined were curious as to what he had learned, but none offered any significant new information. They all had his cards, however, and he hoped to might hear from one of them soon.

He stood with Constance as she bid her guests goodbye. True to her usual mood, she closed the front door with a deep sigh, as though being pleasant all afternoon had been unbearably taxing. "This was a really nice party, and no one appeared to suspect they were here solely to talk about Matteo. Let's finish the last of the champagne."

Once seated on the terrace, she took a tiny bite of a sugar cookie topped with chopped pecans. "They did have fun, didn't they? I might make this a yearly event. Did you learn anything useful?"

"I did hear a whisper or two that Matteo might have been seeing one of the young women here, and there were some beauties among them. Sean Dermot came to see me, and from what he said about the orchestra's rehearsal, and performance schedules, it would have been difficult to arrange the logistics of avoiding the husbands to date one of the wives."

"Matteo was free when the husbands were also, is that what he meant?"

"Yes, but perhaps he enjoyed the risk in seducing other musicians' wives."

Constance shook her head. "It's a shame you never met Matteo. He was a veritable wizard with a magical charm. If he smiled at a woman, she would give herself to him willingly, so not much in the way of seduction was required. That's why I came to you in the first place. I couldn't believe his lavish declarations of love were real."

Joe could have argued Matteo might have wanted to have a life with her, but she was far too cynical to believe such a remote impossibility could exist. "Each of your guests left with one of my business cards, and one might call me with information she wouldn't disclose in front of others."

"Let's hope. Would you like to take the rest of the scones with you? Otherwise, I'll just reduce them to crumbs and feed them to the birds."

"Sure, I'd love to take the scones. Were they baked here?"

"Everything came from our kitchen. The cook's food is sublime. I'll get you a bag. Before you go, I have a check for you. Will you give me your home telephone number in case something occurs to me after your office hours?"

"Sure." He didn't usually give it out, but she wasn't the typical client by any means, and he wrote it on the back of his card. He'd deposit her check first thing in the morning. Now, he'd call the Larsons and hope Ida was gone for good.

He called them from his office. "It's Joe Ezell, how are things going for you there."

"No one has even tripped over a loose shoe lace, so I'd say they are going well," Doug Larson exclaimed. "We don't even mention the name of the person we wished gone for fear of conjuring her up again, but Eleanor doesn't feel her presence as she used to. I'd say Reverend Hatcher did the trick. Please thank him for us."

"I will. Let me know when you open your antique store, and I'll come by."

"Sure will. It will be such fun to decorate for the holidays, we're hoping to be open before Christmas."

Joe wondered if Doug ever dressed like Santa, but was too polite to ask.

He made his next call to Hal Marten at California West Insurance. "The ceremony the reverend conducted for the Larsons appears to have banished their ghost. Could you bring my check when we meet for golf on Saturday? I want to split the money with Rev. Hatcher."

"I will, it will save you a trip downtown. How are you doing with the cellist's murder?"

"Slow but sure, I'm afraid. See you on Saturday."

Mary Margaret found the scones absolutely delicious. "These are wonderful, Joe, so light and flavorful, but I can't picture you at a tea party."

"The wives of the Philharmonic were quite welcoming, and each left with my business card. One of them might know something she'd not confide in front of others."

She licked a crumb from her lips. "Matteo appears to have been tireless in his pursuit of women. It's surprising he had time to even tune his cello, let alone play."

"I've thought the same thing." She was such a sensible girl, he doubted she would have fallen for Matteo's well-practiced charms. It was also a relief she'd never met him.

Friday afternoon, Joe drove to the Beverly Hills Library to see what Louis Dowell looked like to avoid a waste of time in following the wrong man. Walking among the stacks, he appeared to be earnestly searching for a title without success. Grace and Louis were seated in a nook by an arched window and enveloped in the rosy glow of the afternoon sunshine.

Joe remained where he could watch them without being noticed. Louis laughed at something Grace had said, and reached out to touch her arm. His gray hair was clipped short, his dress shirt sparkling white, and his tan slacks looked freshly pressed. His brown loafers shone from a recent polishing. When they stood, Joe followed. After they'd checked out their books at the counter, Louis walked Grace to her car, and then got into a black Ford sedan.

After quickly making a note of the license plate, Joe hurried to his Chevy to follow Louis. He had the man's home address, but while Louis headed in that direction, he angled off to the east. After a ten-minute drive, he pulled into the parking lot of the bougainvillea-draped Fair Oaks Convalescent Home. A two story structure with a red tile roof, the white exterior sparkled in the sun. Louis entered carrying a book.

Joe parked across the street and waited. Louis' mother, sister, or dear aunt could still be alive. Or, perhaps Louis's wife could be a resident. He'd passed a florist on the corner, and needing a way to get more information, he'd buy a bouquet.

The shop had a humid warmth, and held the mixed scent of a dozen flowers. The owner looked up from the workbench where he was counting roses.

"If people want a dozen roses, they get twelve. Years ago, I sent out a vase with thirteen roses, and the recipient feared it was a curse of some sort." He laughed at the memory. "I told her not to worry, and to put the extra rose in a bud vase. What can I do for you?"

"My aunt moved into the Fair Oaks Convalescent Home last week, and I want to take her some flowers when I visit."

"Very thoughtful, but elderly women can be sensitive to scents and don't enjoy bouquets as much as you'd think they would. I'd advise a small philodendron in a pretty pot. See if there's one you like on the shelf near the front."

"Thank you. I have a philodendron in my office, and it thrives on minimum attention."

"That's what makes them the perfect gift."

One lush plant grew in a pretty blue pot, and it wasn't more than he wished to add to his expenses. He took one of the small free cards by the cash register, and wrote only Dowell, Fair Oaks Convalescent Home. He walked down the street and entered the home's glass front doors.

A cheerful woman in a ruffled green dress seated at the desk greeted him warmly. "What a lovely plant. Is it for one of our guests?"

Joe looked at the card as though he hadn't written it himself. "All I have here is Dowell. Does that match one of your residents?"

"Yes, Patricia Dowell has been with us for two years. Poor dear had a disabling stroke and is unable to speak, or care for herself. Her husband comes by every day to visit and read to her. He often stays to help with her dinner. Just leave the plant with me, and I'll see it goes to Mrs. Dowell's room. Only close friends and family are allowed to visit our guests."

Joe placed the plant on her desk. "I understand. All we had at the floral shop was the last name, and it's an anonymous gift."

"How wonderful Patricia still has such devoted friends."

"Yes, it's a blessing."

Joe returned to his car, and took a couple of photos of the convalescent home. After waiting an hour, he saw no point in staying any longer when he now knew how Louis Dowell spent his evenings. He wondered whether Grace Adams would be sympathetic, or insulted Louis hadn't told her about his wife. It would be a good question to bring up with Mary Margaret that night.

She listened attentively as Joe described what he'd found. "He just met your client at the library?"

"Yes, and sometimes they went for coffee at a place nearby, but he didn't respond to her dinner invitations. That's what brought her to me."

"Discussing books certainly doesn't betray his wife, but it's odd he didn't mention her. Perhaps he's tired of receiving sympathy for her sad situation. If I'm ever disabled to such an extent I couldn't care for myself, please feel free to find attentive female company elsewhere. Couples really should discuss such an eventuality before they marry."

"I'd not abandon you," Joe exclaimed. He gave her hand a fond squeeze.

"Of course not, but if you dropped by on Sunday afternoons, it wouldn't bother me at all if you'd spent your Saturday nights elsewhere."

Their conversation had turned more personal than he'd anticipated. "How do you know how you'll feel twenty or thirty years from now? Maybe you won't be so generous then."

"That's precisely why we should discuss this now. I'd not abandon you either, but I doubt you'd want me knitting by your bedside if I'd rather be seeing friends."

"How close are these friends?"

"Joe!" She couldn't help but laugh. "Maybe I'll make up something scandalous just to keep you entertained."

He grabbed her in a bear hug. "Don't you dare!"

She pulled away. "I'm serious. If one of us dies, the other should feel free to look for love with someone new rather than grieve themselves into an early grave."

"You're the only woman I've ever loved, Mary Margaret, and your place in my heart couldn't be filled with anyone else."

"How sweet you are." She leaned close to kiss him. "I feel so sorry for my neighbor, Patrick Wood. He's been alone for years longing for his late wife. I can't believe there haven't been nice women who've come into his shop with a watch needing repair. You and I met when I needed a detective. If I were gone, please don't miss a chance for love when another terrific woman consults you."

"There are no women as terrific as you. We've strayed off my original question. Let's talk in more general terms. If a man has an invalid wife, when should he mention her to a woman he's just met?"

She gave it serious thought. "Well, if he were just chatting with a woman at the library, and didn't expect to see her again, he'd have no reason to refer to his wife. But after they'd met again, and enjoyed discussing books, he should have explained he was married. When your client asked him to dinner, he should definitely have spoken up about his wife. Maybe he was afraid she wouldn't see him again, but he should have taken that chance and told her the truth."

"I agree, but I'll let my client decide on her own. Now let's have the ice cream I brought for dessert, and talk about something else."

"That's fine with me, but difficult questions can't be ignored." She left the sofa for the kitchen.

He followed. "I don't even know what the difficult questions are. Will you give me a list, and we can discuss them when we're walking in the park, or eating ice cream, or doing anything that won't leave me deeply depressed."

She gave him a quick kiss. "I'll work on it, but you already know about my mother's concerns, and I wouldn't have hidden them from you. That would have increased the problem tenfold. Do you want one scoop or two?"

"That's my kind of question. I'd like two please." He'd mailed their photos to her mother, and could only hope for the best while they awaited her response. He'd not waste a minute of their evening together worrying over it now.

Saturday morning, Hal and Gilbert met Joe at the golf course. Gilbert stared at him wide-eyed. "I took Marsha to see *Arizona Sunrise* last night. You might have had a small part, but you looked like you'd been driving cattle and hanging out in saloons your whole life. Marsha was really impressed that I play golf with you."

"She must impress easily, but I appreciate your taking her to see the movie."

"We love movies, and it was fun to see someone I know. I realize you're not a star yet, but it sure looked like you have the talent to become one."

"That's an overstatement for sure, but thank you. Now we're here to play golf, let's go."

Hal wore an amused grin Joe didn't appreciate, but he wouldn't say another word about his brief movie career. Inspired to focus on his game, he came close to meeting Gilbert's score, and that was something new.

As they walked to their cars, Gilbert turned shy. "I wouldn't ask this, but Marsha was wondering if you had photographs. She'd love for you to autograph one for her."

Joe drew in a deep breath, and reminded himself how innocent an individual Gilbert was. "I'm sorry, but I don't have publicity photos for fans as yet. Maybe after I do the Roy Rogers' film next year, I'll have some made. I'll be sure to save one for Marsha."

"Great." Gilbert nearly jumped up and down with excitement. "See you next week."

Joe walked with Hal to his car to pick up the California West check. "Thank you again for being so generous. Rev. Hatcher deserves most of this, and if you have any other cases involving ghosts, I'll call on him again."

"This was the first account of a ghost I've seen," Hal responded. "So they must be rare, but I'll keep you two in mind. Say, when you have photos, save one for Gladys, will you?"

Hal was laughing and Joe didn't care. "Sure. I'll give you two so you'll have one to carry in your wallet."

"Can't wait."

As Joe drove to his office, he counted Saturday golf games as a great way to spend a morning. As for the afternoon, he called Grace Adams, and asked her to come to his office for his report. She was there in half an hour. With Mary Margaret's encouragement, he stuck to the facts, and gave an account of what he'd learned at the Fair Oaks Convalescent Home.

When she stared at him wide-eyed, as though he'd referred to a difficult algebra problem, he tried again. "Louis is devoted to Patricia, who'll be an invalid for the rest of her life. Clearly he enjoys discussing books with you, but that may be all he can manage at present."

Grace's eyes filled with tears. "He should have told me he has a wife, even if she is bedridden. It isn't as though he led me on. He made no promises at all, but he still should have told me he's married."

"I agree. Now knowing what you do, you can choose how to proceed."

She removed an embroidered hankie from her purse and dabbed her eyes. "You mean that I can tell him I've learned he has a wife, or just be quiet about it and not expect more than a library friend?"

Joe leaned back in his chair. "There's another option, Mrs. Adams. Speak only about yourself. Tell Louis how much you enjoy his company, and wonder aloud if your friendship can become anything deeper."

"He'll have to tell me he's married then, wouldn't he?" She rolled her hankie into a damp ball. "I suppose the humiliation of asking would be worth it."

"If he doesn't mention his wife, you'll know all he wants is someone who loves to read. In that case, you'd be better off spending your time with another man who can meet your expectations."

She sighed sadly. "Maybe I'm too old to expect more than a buddy who loves visiting in the library."

"Nonsense," he responded. "I'll bet there are widowers at your church who'd love to keep you company."

"Maybe. I'll have to think on it."

The retainer she'd paid covered his time and expenses. He stood and moved to open the door for her. "I've enjoyed meeting you, Mrs. Adams. Please don't hesitate to consult me if you ever have the need."

"I'm grateful for your help, but I hope I'll have no further reason for your services."

After she'd left, he wondered how things would turn out for her and Louis, but he wasn't sufficiently tempted to sneak around the Beverly Hills library to find out.

With that job finished, he turned his attention to furriers. Constance would know where to begin, and he made a quick call and found her home.

"I'm thinking a furrier might recognize the mystery woman from the photo. Where would you buy a fur, if you were so inclined?"

"I'm not, but my mother likes William H. George LTD on Wilshire Blvd., they might care more about protecting their clients' privacy than being helpful, but I suppose it's worth a try."

"Thanks, I'll let you know if I find anything useful."

"Please do."

The popular furrier's building was another example of Los Angeles' exquisite Art Deco buildings. Scrolled leaf designs above the door and windows were frosting on an already perfect cake. The stark interior gleamed, and models waited to show off whatever the customer might desire to see in furs.

A smartly dressed salesman met Joe as he came through the door, and he quickly described the purpose of his visit before he could be shown out. "I realize it may be difficult to recognize the woman in the photo, but do you have any idea who she might be?"

The man reacted as badly as Joe had feared. His nose even twitched as though he had caught a whiff of something utterly revolting.

"No, sir, I do not. If you're not interested in selecting luxury furs, may I suggest you shop where they sell wool coats with detachable red fox collars."

Joe laughed in spite of himself. "For all you know, I could be an eccentric millionaire, who might wish to order a dozen mink coats for Christmas gifts."

"I seriously doubt that, sir." He pushed open the front door, and Joe walked out.

He had no more luck at any of the other furriers he'd found listed in the telephone book. Although he did learn mink stoles were becoming popular and costing between $200 and $300, they were more affordable than a full-length coat. Unfortunately, it didn't add to his store of practical knowledge. He'd record the hours spent when he returned to his office, but it wasn't nearly enough when he'd met another dead end.

CHAPTER 9

Saturday night, Joe and Mary Margaret drove downtown to Clifton's Cafeteria on Broadway. It was a popular place with a forest décor that included a waterfall and stream. It was as close as Joe cared to go to camping out. They were both in the mood for macaroni and cheese, and savored every gooey bite.

"I can't tell you how much I look forward to spending weekends with you," she exclaimed. "Often we're so busy with our patients, we don't have more than a few minutes to gulp down lunch. I should eat more for breakfast."

"Bacon and eggs are among the few things I know how to prepare. Or, I can pour cereal into a bowl with the best of them."

She paused for a bite of lime Jello. "We're going to have so much fun together, Joe, it could be difficult to remember to go to work."

They might swiftly starve to death if she quit her job, but he was too happy to be marrying her to risk discussing money, or the lack thereof. It was probably one of the difficult subjects couples needed to discuss, but later.

After dinner, they were going to Thalia Dupré's latest movie, *Lavender Lace,* a Cinderella story where the pretty seamstress designing dresses for the ball lacks the time to create her own. He was confident a spectacular gown would be found in the nick of time, and the prince would surely fall in love with her. Mary Margaret would love the romantic story, but he was looking forward to *Orchid Lane*, a film with a sea captain and schooner he could relate to. He would save the autographed photo Thalia Dupré had sent him until a time he really needed to impress Mary Margaret.

Monday morning, he was busy sharpening pencils when the telephone rang. "Discreet Investigations."

"Mr. Ezell?"

"Yes, how may I help you?"

"We met last week at Constance Remson's tea. My name's Karen. I doubt you remember me."

"Of course I remember you. You were worried other members of the Philharmonic might be in danger."

"Yes, and I still do. Can you meet me in Plummer Park at ten o'clock this morning? I take my son there whenever I can."

"I'll be there." He found her by the swings with soft bucket seats for babies. Her chubby one-year-old son was giggling with every push. "What a handsome boy!" he called to her.

"Thank you. Kevin is so good-natured I can take him anywhere, and we'll both have a good time."

There were other mothers with small children gathered around the sandbox. But they were the only ones at the swings. He checked over his shoulder, but no one was close enough to overhear their conversation.

"I expect you had a good reason to call."

"I thought I did, but now I'm not so sure." She was a slender young woman with curly dark hair and brown eyes. She'd bundled up her son, and worn a sweater over her cotton dress to ward off the slight chill in the morning air.

"Let me decide. Did you know Matteo well?"

"No, but he'd brush by me whenever we happened to be in the same room. He had the most incredible smile, an inviting grin. Do you know what I mean?"

"Yes, I do."

"The last time I saw him, maybe a month ago, he slipped his business card into my hand, and winked at me. It was all very sly and teasing, but I knew exactly what he wanted. I wasn't even tempted and threw away his card, but that doesn't mean there weren't other wives who'd welcomed his attentions. Symphony musicians can be so focused on their instrument and performances, they devote little time to their family."

"It's a common mistake across many careers, I'm afraid. Do you have any idea who any of these lonely women might be?"

"Any of the young, pretty ones, but I won't mention names when I'm not sure. Matteo appreciated women in general, and maybe it was a hunger he had to satisfy. A woman who'd wanted him all to herself might have killed him in a jealous rage."

For a woman who'd not seen the bloody murder scene, she'd described it well. "He appears to have given many women a motive."

She pulled her son out of the swing seat and gave him a loving hug. "Even if I can't name any suspects, I wanted you to know he wasn't above poaching other symphony members' wives."

"Thank you. If anything more occurs to you, please let me know."

"I will." Kevin waved as she carried him away, and Joe waved to him. Kevin was a cute kid, as all babies were, but he was in no hurry to become a father.

When Joe returned to his office, he called Henry Hilburn, a retired LAPD detective who had access to information a private detective couldn't get. "I'm working on Matteo da Milano's murder. Have you heard anything interesting about the case?"

"I might have heard a word or two. Want to come over?"

"Sure, I'll be there soon and bring the beer."

Henry lived in a modest home in the San Fernando Valley. A tall, thin, bald man, he resembled an inverted exclamation point. He ushered Joe out to the back patio, pulled two chairs away from the table, and invited him to sit. They sipped their beers in companionable silence until Henry was at last inspired to speak.

"You have to be an excellent private eye, Joe, because you know how to listen. It appears to be a lesson many find difficult to learn. As for Matteo da Milano, Detective Lynch is interviewing every woman he can find who's dated him. He began with some society dame, and followed what she knew about Matteo to the next woman, and then she points him to the next, like links in a chain. Of course, he's overlooking all the women who aren't known to have had affairs with the cellist, or won't own up to it."

"Married women you think?"

"Sure. Apparently Matteo was as fine a virtuoso of women as he was of the cello. I have to admire his stamina, if not his lack of morals. He reminds me of gamblers who won't quit until they've lost their last dime. Apparently, Matteo never ran out of charm."

"Clearly it wore thin with the woman who killed him."

"True. She must have been the exception."

Joe liked that thought. What made her different from the women Matteo had loved and left, probably without sending a last bouquet of roses? He sat up in his chair. "I'll bet he sent flowers, and Lynch won't think to check with florists, will he?"

Henry tipped his bottle in a salute. "Matteo must have sent a ton of flowers, and a florist would have a record of where they went. I won't keep you here, when there's time left in the day to pursue such a good lead."

"Thanks again, Henry."

* * *

Joe called Constance Remson when he reached his office. "It's Joe Ezell. I had no luck with furriers, but now I have another question. Did Matteo ever send you flowers?"

"Yes, a beautiful bouquet of red roses when we first began seeing each other. Why?"

"It's a way to track the women he dated. Do you remember which florist delivered them?"

"I saved the card in the little envelope. They were from a place called the Wonder of Roses on Wilshire Boulevard in Beverly Hills. It's near the Beverly Wilshire Hotel."

If she had been there, Joe would have kissed her. "Thank you! I may not be able to find out all I need to know today, but I'll call you next week."

"I'll meet you there," she offered. "My name will mean something to them, and I'm betting yours won't."

"Good point."

The Wonder of Roses had a corner spot on Wilshire Boulevard. The shop's windows were filled with gift items and beautiful rose bouquets. Joe had waited outside only a few minutes when Constance arrived.

Joe greeted her with his plan. "Let's tell the manager we're hosting a memorial for Matteo, and don't want to forget anyone who was important to him. Monday has to be a slow day for the shop, which should work to our advantage. If they have a file for Matteo, we can copy the names and addresses and be on our way."

"I know the owner. Let me speak to him first."

"Give it your best shot." He crossed his fingers and pulled open the front door for her, and the unmistakable perfume of roses rolled over them in the humid air. Glass refrigerator cases lined one wall of the shop with a colorful array of roses in tall ceramic vases. Arranged bouquets in the last case showed off the florist's talents. Two women and a young man were working at a long workbench along the opposite wall creating matching bouquets.

When a gray-haired man wearing a white shirt, khaki slacks, and a green apron approached them, Constance stepped in front of Joe. "I want to tell you again how beautiful the centerpieces were for my tea last week. They were absolute perfection. Charlie Bloom, this is Joe Ezell."

Charlie shook Joe's hand. "For special clients, I do work with chrysanthemums, but you mustn't tell anyone I admitted it. What would you like today, Miss Remson?"

She returned his warm smile. "We're hosting a gathering to remember Matteo da Milano. We don't want to miss anyone who might have been important to him. Do you keep files of customers' orders we might see?"

He pursed his lips. "Usually, we'd not violate a client's privacy, but Matteo certainly can't complain, can he? Come to my office, and I'll show you what I have."

The door at the back of the shop led into another workroom, with more refrigerator cases with centerpieces waiting to be delivered for a formal dinner that night. Charlie's glass-walled office held his desk, chairs, a telephone, and file cabinets so full some drawers couldn't be fully closed.

"He has to be under the Ms, doesn't he? They're in this cabinet. We have a clerk who handles filing as well as shifts at the register. Unfortunately, she can't do much when the files are bursting with receipts. I need to buy another cabinet."

"Do you need to keep track of sales that are several years old?" Joe asked. He hadn't handled enough cases for even a single drawer of his file cabinet to be filled, let alone crowded, but he could see how to solve Charley's problem easily enough.

"Of course not, there's no reason to save the receipt from every sale I've ever made." He laid Matteo's file on his desk. "Take as long as you like."

"Thank you so much, Charlie," Constance nearly purred as he left them.

Joe had brought a yellow legal pad inside a manila file folder. He removed his pen from his pocket. "Why don't you read the names and addresses to me, and I'll write the list. Let's keep track of the dates as well." He sat down behind the desk, and she took a chair in front.

She glanced through the orders. "I'll bet the dates are closer than any real gentleman would need."

"If this is too difficult for you, I can do it alone," Joe offered.

"No, I never trusted Matteo, so I can easily manage without weeping. There are ten orders. Shall we skip the one that's more than a year old?"

"I'd like to keep track of them all," he replied. He wrote the Wonder of Roses across the top of the page and looked up at her.

"All right. The first is a FTD order for December 1945, a dozen red roses to be sent to Veronica in New York with a card reading Happy Birthday. His continued devotion to his ex-wife is endearing, isn't it?"

"Down right inspiring. Who's next?"

"March, 1946, Charlotte Eaton. Her father is on the symphony board. I went to her wedding that summer, so it's doubtful she would be a suspect now."

"Agreed."

"In May, Linda Skye, apartment seven in Matteo's Almont building. Did you meet her?"

"No. Her friend Tanya Olson is living there while Linda is working in London. She might not have known Linda dated him. At least she didn't mention it. Tanya called the police when I found Matteo. She was wearing a pink dressing gown when I knocked on her door, and it occurred to me later than she could have gotten out of her bloody clothes after she'd killed him. She's sweet and rather dim, so she didn't strike me as the type to murder anyone."

"Maybe she's neither sweet, nor dim. Better put a star by her name."

"Will do. Who's next?"

"August, Suzanne Ritter, who lives on La Peer. Could it be in Matteo's building?"

He glanced up to read the address. "That's it. I spoke with her, and she didn't appear to be distraught over

Matteo's death, but maybe she's a good actress. She's a fashion designer, who could have assembled the fur outfit on the woman I photographed."

"If she dated him more than a year ago, you'd think she would have attacked him much sooner."

"The same could be said for Linda Skye. Who's next?"

"December 1946, there was another FTD order for roses for Veronica in New York. Has she come to Los Angeles?"

"I would have heard if she has. How did Matteo do this year?"

"February, 1947, Andrea Donovan. She lives on Mildred Avenue in Venice Beach. Looks like he widened his geographical search there. I'm next in May, a Paloma Val Verde received roses at the end of July. I was still seeing Matteo when I came to you in October, so clearly there was some overlap there."

"Looks like it, I've been to Paloma's house. She does paintings of whimsical birdhouses."

"I know someone who has one." Her eyebrows twitched at the thought. "They're almost too cute."

He couldn't imagine her hanging such a sweet, colorful painting in her spectacular home. "So is she."

"In September, he picked up a dozen roses, so we don't know where they went. Did you learn anything useful?"

Matteo was then also seeing Lily Montell, maybe he hand-carried the roses to her. "Yes, I think so. Will Charlie sell me a single rose? I can't afford to buy a dozen for my fiancée."

"To repay his thoughtfulness today, I'll buy a dozen roses to take home and give you one. How's that?"

"Perfect." He carried the gold box holding red-orange long-stemmed roses to her car. A cream-colored Mercury convertible, the top was up, but he could easily imagine her hair flying as she drove along the beach with the top down.

Constance rested the box on the hood of her car, and removed the lid. "Do you want to pick a rose, or shall I?"

The roses were snuggled in green tissue paper. "Aren't they all the same?"

"Of course not. They're as individual as people and each has its own personality."

Joe sincerely doubted it. "Give me the one on the top, please, it looks real pretty and cheerful."

"Good choice." Constance pulled a sheet of tissue from the box to wrap it. "There you are. Let me know what you find out about the Venice Beach woman."

"I'll contact her tomorrow."

Joe handed Mary Margaret the gorgeous rose when he picked her up at the hospital. "Happened by a flower shop today, and thought of you."

"Oh, Joe, it's so pretty and smells absolutely divine. Thank you. Were you there working on a case?"

He explained how thoughts of Matteo had led him there. "It was just a sudden inspiration, which makes me think I might have missed a dozen likely clues in other cases."

"They were all solved satisfactorily, weren't they?"

"Yes, but maybe I could have solved them sooner. I cashed the California West check to pay Luke. I hope he won't object to being paid, after all, he did banish the ghost."

"I believe ministers are paid when they perform a wedding or a funeral," she responded. "I'll have to ask my mother how much we should pay Reverend Barker to do our wedding."

It was another expense he'd not expected. "I love your optimism, but we haven't heard from your mother as yet."

"How long do you suppose it takes mail to reach Seattle?"

"Not long." Maybe her mother had already received the photos he'd sent and was too appalled to respond. Mary Margaret might be awash in happy thoughts, but he felt a dismal black cloud hanging above his head.

Joe had put Luke's money in a business envelope and after describing how it had been earned, he handed it to him.

Luke peeked in the envelope. "I appreciate the thought, but this is way too much."

"It's what California West believes is fair pay for ghost removal. I'm not prepared to argue with such a big firm. Spend it however you wish."

Luke nodded. "Fine, there are patients who could use a little cash when they check out. I'll save it for them."

"While we're talking about money, how much does a minister expect to receive when he performs a wedding?"

"It depends on the size of the church. Many have a list of set fees. Are you wondering about the cost of your wedding?"

Joe would still prefer a quick exchange of vows at city hall. "I learn of some new expense every day, Luke. I'm barely able to keep up with what's required."

"That's the bride's job, and you have the much easier part. You'll host the rehearsal dinner, and show up for the wedding on time. That's it."

"Now I'm even further behind than I thought. I didn't even know there was a rehearsal dinner."

Luke laughed. "Maybe you ought to check out a book on weddings from the library and go over it with Mary Margaret."

"And let her know what a fool I am? I don't dare do that, but thanks again for the suggestion."

"Any time, and I appreciate the ghost money. I'll put it to good use."

Joe wished him a good night, and went back to Mary Margaret's cottage. "Whatever you're making smells wonderful!"

"Pork chops, one of your favorites. The enticing aroma is from sautéing the onions and bell peppers with garlic before I fold them into the dressing."

"As always, your food is extra delicious, for which I'm very thankful. Speaking of talents, the florist I met today was named Charlie Bloom. Flowers must have been his destiny."

"Maybe, or it might be a name he uses for business, the way an actor has a stage name."

"Of course, things are not always what they seem. I should have that saying engraved on a plaque and hang it in my office." Rather than drool over her shoulder, he went into the living room to read the paper while she finished preparing dinner.

Tuesday morning, Joe received a call before he could telephone Andrea Donovan. "Discreet Investigations."

"This is Carla Morrisett. I've been betrayed by my best friend, and I need you to straighten out the mess she's made."

Joe leaned back in his chair. "Tell me more about the problem, so I'll know if I can be of any help."

"My friend's dachshund had four pups. She promised me the pick of the litter, but she's given me the runt!"

He'd hoped for a real case, but no, this was another goofy inquiry that would lead absolutely nowhere. "Small dogs are awfully cute, need less space to play, and eat less dog food. Are you sure your friend hasn't actually done you a favor?"

"Dachshunds are already small, a tiny one isn't what I wanted."

"Give it back to your friend and tell her to sell it to someone else."

She gasped. "Oh, you're brilliant, you summarized the problem right there. She gave me the little puppy after she'd sold the rest of the litter, and no one else wanted her."

"Thank you. I'm glad to be of help. Remember it's not the puppy's fault, and she could be the best dog you ever had. Perhaps rather than another puppy, what you really need is a better friend."

"That's undoubtedly true. You give wonderful advice, how much do I owe you?"

"We solved your problem so quickly, there's no charge, Miss Morrisett. Just remember my firm whenever you need a detective."

"I sure will."

He supposed he should have charged at least fifty cents, but he doubted he could have collected it. He dialed Andrea Donovan's number, and she answered on the seventh's ring.

"Miss Donovan? This is Joe Ezell, I'm a detective with Discreet Investigations. I'm working on a memorial for Matteo da Milano, and wonder if I might come by your home this morning to discuss it."

"How did you get my name?"

Her voice had a brassy defensiveness, and he spoke softly rather than annoy her any further. "I'm a detective, and it's what I do. It won't take more than a few minutes of your time."

She sighed unhappily. "It's not like my day is so full I can't work you in. I suppose you already have my address."

"Are you still on Mildred Avenue?"

"Yes. It's the blue duplex. You can't miss it."

"Thank you. See you soon." Joe wondered what Matteo had seen in Andrea, but when she opened her front door, she proved to be a remarkably pretty young woman, even with the dark roots showing in her blonde hair. It was the black-haired, brown-eyed baby boy on her hip that startled him. He couldn't help but wonder if he could be Matteo's son.

Andrea stood aside to let him in. "I'm babysitting for my sister while she's at work at the Bank of America. As soon as she finds another responsible person to look after David, I'll apply there too. I'm a high school graduate, and can count dollar bills with the best of them."

She gestured toward an overstuffed chair, took a place on the threadbare sofa, and put David on a toy-filled baby quilt at her feet. Not quite able to crawl, the little boy wiggled over to a teddy bear and sucked on its paw.

"Handsome little guy," Joe offered.

"He's a real cutie, isn't he? Now what is it you wanted from me?" She brushed cracker crumbs from her sweater, and then dusted off the knees of her slacks. "If you're expecting me to pay for part of the memorial, you're out of luck."

"The cost is already covered. A little information is all I need, nothing more. How did you meet Matteo?"

She leaned back and crossed her arms over her chest. "I was selling programs at the Hollywood Bowl, and he stopped by the stand to get one. It's not every day a good-looking man wearing a tuxedo gives me his card, and I called him the very next day. We went out a few times. It wasn't anything serious, just fun. He sent me roses. Do you believe that? That was a first. I saved a few petals in a book."

She was awfully cute, but younger than the women Matteo usually dated, and not nearly as sophisticated. "You hadn't dated any other men from the LA Philharmonic?"

"Are you kidding? Most are married, or too old, but Matteo, he was just right. We didn't have a great love affair, but I cried when he died. I saved the newspaper photo with the rose petals. When is the memorial?"

"We don't have a firm date as yet, but I'll make certain you're invited. Don't get up, I can see my way out."

"I've got more manners than that." She showed him to the door, and closed it quietly behind him.

CC entered Joe's office in the afternoon and found him studying the cards on his bulletin board. "How is your investigation going? Looks like you've got quite a few suspects."

"All I actually have are people who knew the murdered man. None of them appears to have had any hostile intentions, but they could be lying through their teeth."

The custodian carried the wastebasket into the hallway to empty into a rolling cart. "I doubt the murderer would ever tell the truth."

"Probably not. I just need to catch them in a lie. Are you having a good day, CC?"

"Yes, sir, I am. Good luck with your case."

"Thanks, I certainly need it."

Mary Margaret hadn't called, so maybe she hadn't heard from her mother. When he picked her up after work, her smile wavered, and he feared he'd been wrong. "What did your mother say?"

"She hasn't called yet, and I'm going to call her when I get home. Take the bull by the horns, so to speak."

"That's a brave approach."

"I'm so tired of worrying about her opinions. She thought I ought to become a librarian rather than a nurse so I wouldn't have nightmares about blood. She didn't hide her disappointment when I came to Los Angeles to work for the VA. She's simply a fearful person, and probably won't ever change. Is that disloyal of me to say?"

"Not when it gives me a better understanding of her. Was your father much older than your mother?"

"No, she was the elder by two years, and age was never an issue between them. My father was a wonderful man. I don't believe he and my mother ever exchanged a cross word. When he had a heart attack and died, it was a terrible shock to us all, but especially my mother. He left her well cared for, so money hasn't been a problem, but she misses him terribly."

The telephone rang as they entered Mary Margaret's cottage. She sent Joe an anxious glance and answered. She covered the telephone to speak to him. "It's Sharon, and she thinks you're very handsome in your uniform."

"Thank God. Tell her I love her already."

Mary Margaret did, and listened attentively as Sharon related their mother's response. "Thank you for the warning, I'll call her now. Love you."

She turned to Joe. "Apparently Mother has decided your appearance isn't as much of a problem as your age. She's afraid I'll be widowed with small children to raise."

"God forbid, but if it happened, you'd go home to live in Seattle, wouldn't you?"

"Probably, but I'll not have her hoping you'll drop dead so she'll see her grandchildren more often."

"I'll wait outside this time, and you can give me a summary latter." He gave her a quick kiss and stepped outside. Luke Hatcher waved to him as he came up the walk.

"How are things going, Joe?"

Joe walked over to meet him. He spoke softly, "Not well. Mary Margaret's on the telephone with her mother. You know Mrs. McBride thought I was too frightening in *Arizona Sunrise*, and now she's decided I'm too old."

Luke paused by his doorstep. "I've been giving your situation a lot of thought. From what I've read, sometimes the current issue isn't really the problem at all, but just an excuse. Mary Margaret's mother might even have a list. When you convince her you're barely out of your teens, she'll switch to the uncertainty of your income and your ability to provide for her daughter. Anyone with his own business can't guarantee their yearly income."

"That's true. She could also complain I have no family here to support us with any problems that might arise."

"Yes, that's a frequent complaint. 'Well, who are his people?' type of reasoning. You might want to prepare answers to stay ahead of her. You must believe Mary Margaret is worth whatever aggravation her mother causes."

"I most certainly do. Thank you, even if that wasn't a pep talk."

"My pleasure." Luke unlocked his front door. "Don't forget to add religion to the mix. It's caused more problems than all the others combined."

"Right." Joe walked out to the street and up and down the sidewalk to keep moving rather than stand and fret in place. He'd felt at ease with Mary Margaret from the moment she'd come into his office. She was so pretty she almost glowed, and he was delighted to report that whenever her sailor fiancé wasn't with her, he lavished his attentions on a string of other women.

She hadn't shed a single tear over the sad news, but straightened her shoulders and thanked him for finding the truth she'd suspected. He had suggested they go to lunch rather than have her brood over the tragic facts alone. She'd smiled, as though she already knew how much he liked her, and they'd been together ever since.

If there was a time to discuss important issues, they must have missed it before falling in love. He certainly didn't want a battle with his future mother-in-law, but he wasn't about to lose his darling Mary Margaret no matter what it took.

CHAPTER 10

Joe pulled his notebook from his jacket pocket as he walked back to Mary Margaret's cottage. Maybe he couldn't accurately project his income for the year, but it had grown steadily since he opened Discreet Investigations, and he was also working for California West as well. That was a big plus. As for his family, his parents were born in Oklahoma and had moved to Los Angeles in the 1930s. His father had worked for the Post Office, and his mother had been an elementary school secretary. They were wonderful parents, and he wished they could have met Mary Margaret.

"Joe?" Mary Margaret called from the doorway. "Mother wants to talk to you. Do you feel up to it?"

Luke had left him better prepared to tackle the challenge, and he smiled as he stepped over the threshold. "I'm looking forward to it."

He picked up the telephone and lowered his voice to a warmly convincing depth, "Mrs. McBride, how wonderful to have a chance to speak with you. We should have done this months ago."

"Yes, we should have, Mr. Ezell. I'm sure Mary Margaret must have mentioned my misgivings about your engagement."

Misgivings scarcely described her hostility toward him, but he refused to argue over her choice words when she'd made it plain she didn't consider him good enough for her daughter. "Yes, she has, and I'm glad to have the opportunity to assure you that I'll strive everyday to make her happy."

"When she works in a hospital filled with professional men, I can't understand why she'd be interested in a private detective who calls himself an actor."

She had been horrified by his brief appearance in *Arizona Sunrise,* so he should have anticipated it. "I think of myself as a detective, Mrs. McBride. My small film role came from a case I was investigating. It did lead to the arrest of a murderer, so it was a worthwhile enterprise."

"Do you routinely solve murders?"

"No murder can be described as routine, but I'm proud my investigations have led to arrests."

"That's too dangerous an occupation for a married man."

Upon occasion, he had suffered some physical abuse, but he'd survived. "Most of my cases are unrelated to any acts of violence, or crime."

"So you say. Do you have considerable savings set aside to give Mary Margaret the life she deserves?"

She had him there. Thanks to assignments from Hal Marten, he had been able to add to his savings account, but he'd yet to reach four figures. "In addition to my own firm, I'm handling cases for California West Insurance, and I make regular deposits," he assured her.

"So the answer is no. Do you attend church on Sundays?"

Luke had warned him she might bring up religion. "Not lately, I'm afraid, but I grew up attending the Presbyterian Church in Azusa. They had a wonderful youth group and all my friends went there. I mixed the Kool-Aid and passed out graham crackers for vacation Bible school."

"We're Episcopalian," she informed him proudly. "Do you plan to attend church with Mary Margaret?"

"Yes, I will."

Mary Margaret reached to take the telephone from him, and he didn't protest. "Mother, let's make this the first of many conversations. Please save some questions for the next time you speak with Joe. I'll call you later in the week. Love you. Good-bye." She hung up before her mother could edge in a cross word otherwise.

"I'm sorry, but she's my mother after all and naturally concerned with my choice of husband."

"Of course, she is." Joe drew his beloved into a warm hug. "I had answers for all her questions, even if they weren't the ones she wanted."

"I'm the one marrying you, so it's my opinion that matters. I'm making fried chicken for dinner, and it always lifts our spirits."

"Wonderful excuse for fried chicken, although we don't really need one." Every hour he spent with her was a joy, and he forgot all about her mother's doubts with the first bite of a delicious crispy fried wing.

Wednesday morning, Joe's first call came from a woman who wanted proof her husband cheated on her whenever he went home to visit his mother in Peoria, Illinois.

"I'm so sorry, but my detective's license is valid only here in California, so I'll have to pass on the job. Why don't you call information in Peoria and ask for the numbers of private detectives working there? Good-bye."

The telephone rang again before he'd had time to take a breath. He waited three rings. "Discreet Investigations."

"Mr. Ezell, this is Florence Hayes, the manager at Matteo da Milano's La Peer apartment building."

"Good morning, Mrs. Hayes. How are you today?" Hoping for good news, he sat up in his chair.

"I'm fine, thank you. You wanted to know when Veronica da Milano arrived in Los Angeles. She flew in last night, and came straight to Matteo's apartment. She still had her key, so I didn't ask for a copy of his will to see if she had that right."

"I'm sure it's fine, and thank you so much, Mrs. Hayes. I appreciate your remembering me. I'll come by to speak with her this morning. Talk to you then." He leaped from his chair, and would have danced around his desk if he'd had any music. The purchase of a radio could be justified to follow local news, and for music to dance to when the occasion warranted it. He'd buy one soon.

Reining in his enthusiasm, he sat down to make some notes. If Veronica had a key for the La Peer apartment, did she also have one for the Almont place? Could she have flown into Los Angeles, and killed Matteo when he came home? She could have had a taxi waiting at the corner, gone straight to the airport, and flown home to New York before anyone knew she'd paid a quick visit to Los Angeles.

Time-wise, it could have worked, but why would she have killed her ex-husband with a stiletto heel when it seemed like such an impromptu weapon? And why would a woman from New York come to town in the furs that would give away her identity? That didn't make any sense either, but murderers didn't always make logical plans. He'd have to wait until he'd spoken with Veronica to judge how her mind might work.

Veronica da Milano was tall and thin, with long golden-brown hair, and her bangs brushed her eyelashes. Her big hazel eyes were red from crying, and her nose a bright pink, but she was still pretty. Her black sweater and slacks fit her mood.

Joe introduced himself, gave her his card, and the reason for his visit. "May I come in to speak with you? I promise not to take more than a few minutes of your time."

She moved aside to welcome him in. "If it will help catch the rat who killed my husband, you may stay all day. I'm sorting the few things he kept here, but when this is so difficult, it will take weeks to pack his belongings at the Almont Avenue apartment. Even then, I'll not know what to do with them."

Unlike Matteo's stark, modern home, traditional décor had been chosen here. The walls were painted in a pale apple green, and the furnishings were in a matching green and joyful yellow. The charming apartment could easily have been a sunny hotel suite rather than a place anyone called home.

"I need some coffee. Would you like a cup?" she asked.

"Yes, thank you, I could use one." He followed her into the kitchen, which was again green and yellow. "This is a real cheerful place," he mused aloud.

"It is, isn't it? It's fully furnished for guests, and I suppose I'll have Mrs. Hayes ask the next renters if they'd like to keep any of the furnishings. I don't need more furniture, and I'm certainly not attached to the coffeepot, or pots and pans."

"I understand. I met Mr. Perkins, the manager on Almont, and I hope he will be more helpful for you than he was for me. Did Matteo give you a key?"

"No, I only have a key for here. I've spoken with Mr. Perkins a time or two, and he was polite enough. Maybe you caught him on a bad day."

"That's probably it."

They sat at the dining table to drink their coffee. He took his black, but she added sugar and cream, took a sip, and added more cream. "How long do you plan to stay in Los Angeles?" he asked.

"I'm too overwhelmed to make any plans beyond today. Matteo left everything he owned to me, but his cello is too precious a keepsake to ever sell. His attorney told me the will is straightforward, and there are no other heirs to contest it. Nothing is ever as simple as it sounds though. Matteo's agent will handle the record contracts he negotiated. I certainly couldn't do it. When we were married, Matteo taught me how to use our money wisely, so there's no danger I'll run through it all in a year. That's a comfort."

"Yes, indeed. Have you taken off time from work?"

She shook her head. "I met Matteo at Julliard. I'd planned to become a concert pianist, but there were so many more talented students there, I gave up the dream. I'm qualified to teach music, but I've never applied to any schools. I suppose I should, just to keep myself busy so I won't keep missing Matteo so badly." She pulled a handkerchief from her pocket to dry her eyes.

With her heartbreak so raw, he couldn't believe she'd had anything to do with her ex-husband's murder. She'd loved him too much to wish him dead. "I'm so sorry for your loss."

"Thank you. What was it you wished to ask?"

He took his notebook from his pocket, and turned to a fresh page. "You two remained close. Did Matteo ever mention anyone had threatened him, or caused him any sense of danger, or alarm?"

"No, he always sounded happy when we spoke. We talked about his upcoming concerts, travel, when he'd next be in New York, that type of thing. If he'd been worried about an over-zealous fan, or anyone else, he'd not have mentioned it to me."

He showed her the photo of the fur-wrapped suspect. "This woman may be an important witness, do you recognize her?"

She picked up the photo by the corner and studied it closely. "I used to have a similar fur coat and hat, but I don't anymore. I've no idea who this might be."

The doorbell rang, and she appeared to be too tired to answer. "Let me get that," Joe offered. Expecting Florence Hayes, he swung open the door and found Sean Dermot holding a giant bouquet of yellow roses.

"Mr. Ezell?" Surprised, Sean frowned, then forced a smile. "Continuing your investigations?"

"Yes, I am."

"Is that Sean?" Veronica called. "Show him in, please."

Joe was annoyed their conversation had been interrupted, but perhaps it would work to his advantage. "Would you like coffee? Veronica just made a pot."

Sean leaned down to kiss her cheek before placing the tissue wrapped roses in her hands. "Thanks, I would." He sat by her side.

"These are gorgeous, Sean, and will be so pretty here."

"That's what I thought. Do you have a vase for them?"

"There should be a couple under the sink."

"I'll look," Joe called. He found two vases perfect for long-stemmed roses and filled one with water. He carried it into the dining table. "Here you are."

She stood to arrange the roses in the vase, and set it at the other end of the table. "I love yellow roses. Thank you again, Sean." She gave his shoulder an affectionate squeeze before returning to her chair.

Joe brought Sean's coffee, and he drank it black as he had in the detective's office. "We were discussing possible threats to Matteo's life. Did he mention any such worries to you?"

"No, we talked about music, the talents of guest conductors, upcoming engagements, and not much else." Sean turned to Veronica. "I don't have to ask how you're doing when you look so miserable. What can I do to help?"

Joe could have excused himself and left then, but he was too intrigued to go. He sat back, and watched how effortlessly his companions conversed. Despite Veronica's current despair, a smoldering grudge over the divorce could have prompted her to kill her ex-husband. If she no longer owned a fur coat and hat, had she thrown them away rather than take the bloody garments to a cleaners in New York? Lost in thought, it took him a moment to notice Veronica and Sean were staring at him. He stood to go.

"Thank you for your time, Veronica. I'll take my cup into the kitchen on my way out." Once out of their view, he made a quick note on how well they appeared to be acquainted. They could have known each other for years, but with Matteo's death, everything between them might change.

Rather than go straight back to the office, he knocked on Mrs. Hayes' door. She answered carrying her knitting and welcomed him in.

"I can't wait to hear how your investigation is going."

Joe followed her into the living room and waited for her to turn down the radio and be seated before he took the chair opposite her. "I'm tracing multiple leads, and hope to have answers shortly. Sean Dermont came to see Veronica as I was leaving. Does he visit often when Veronica stays here?"

"The name is familiar. Slim, dark-haired fellow with glasses?"

"That sounds like him."

"I've seen Veronica leaving with him a time or two on her visits here, but he could have come and gone other times while I'm at the market, or running errands. There are apartment managers who keep close track of the residents, but I'm not one of them. People pay their rent on time, and they are justified in expecting privacy."

Sean had known to bring yellow roses to go with the décor, so Joe bet he'd been there more than twice in the last couple of years. "Thank you, Mrs. Hayes. I'll let you get back to your radio program. I'll see myself out."

"Let me know when there's an arrest so I won't have to wait to read about it in the *Los Angeles Times*."

"Will do." He closed her front door quietly, and glanced out at the walk. Sean could have walked across the grass to enter the front door and reach the elevator without being seen from Mrs. Hayes's window. While Sean hadn't admitted it, Joe wondered if Sean and Matteo could have compared notes on Veronica.

When Joe returned to his office, he called Henry Hilburn, the retired LAPD detective. "Veronica da Milano is in town, and I wondered if Detective Lynch ever checked on her whereabouts the day of Matteo's murder."

"Talked to my friend who knows about the case only yesterday. Let me get my notes."

"Go right ahead." Joe waited not all that patiently until Henry returned to the phone.

"Lynch surprises me sometime, and apparently he is smart enough to check on ex-wives when a man is murdered. Veronica can prove she was in New York City. She kept her usual appointment at a beauty salon, and went to lunch with two friends on the day Matteo died. Lynch even followed through and spoke with the owner of the beauty salon, and the friends she'd given for an alibi. If you were thinking she might have been in on the murder, you'll have to think again. Unless, she orchestrated it from there."

"She's a weepy mess, so I don't think so. Thank you for staying on top of the case."

"Sure, keeps me out of mischief."

Joe appreciated a little mischief now and then. The phone rang a few seconds after he'd told Henry goodbye. "Discreet Investigations."

A man asked, "May I please speak to the owner?"

"This is he. How may I help you?" Joe leaned back in his chair, and hoped for a case that would be both complicated and good for his savings account.

"My name is Nathan Skidmore, and I won't discuss the issue over the telephone. If you're free now, I'll come to your office."

The man knew the address and arrived twenty minutes later. He was an imposing fellow, tall and broad, with thinning gray hair. His well-tailored suit was clearly expensive, and Joe provided an appropriately serious welcome.

The man spoke before Joe could ask any questions. "I'm an engineer, with my own company. My father founded the firm and invested wisely, so the family should have no financial worries even if I dropped dead tomorrow."

Alarmed, Joe leaned forward. "Do you feel your life is in jeopardy?"

Mr. Skidmore waved the question aside. "No, but I'm worried about my daughter Jocelyn's boyfriend. He's a fine engineer and a credit to the company, but I doubt his affections for her are genuine."

"What makes you suspect they aren't?"

"Well, he overdoes everything. He sends her flowers nearly every week, and takes her to concerts and nice restaurants, but unless they're on some fancy date, they don't see each other. You'd think they'd go to the movies occasionally, but they don't."

"How old is Jocelyn?"

"She's twenty-three, and graduated from UCLA with a degree in art history. I don't expect her to ever have to work, but she ought to be doing something with her time other than primping for dates with Stephen. His last name is Hartfield, and he's thirty-one. He's too old for her, but she won't listen to anything I say about him."

Mary Margaret's mother insisted Joe was too old for her, but he had to give Nathan Skidmore a reasonable response. "Yes, he might be ready to marry and have a family, while Jocelyn could want to travel and see the world before she'd be ready to settle down."

"That's exactly what I told her."

"Whose side is your wife taking?"

"Jocelyn's mother passed away several years ago, and I've remarried. Jocelyn has never cared much for Kate, her stepmother, so my wife has stayed out of it."

Joe readily understood why his daughter might be anxious to leave home. "Does Jocelyn have close friends?"

"Sure, but they've scattered since they left UCLA. Her best friend from college married last summer. Jocelyn was a bridesmaid, and was all caught up in the wedding planning, but now her friend has no time for her."

"That's a shame." He could imagine Jocelyn as a lonely young woman who was enormously flattered by an older man's lavish attentions. "What is it you want me to do?"

Nathan leaned forward. "I'd like you to follow Stephen Hartfield and see what he does with his time when he's not with my daughter. I doubt he's just washing and ironing his shirts. He's a tall, good-looking man, fair-haired and blue-eyed." He produced a 3x5 card from his pocket. "I have the license plate number for his Chevy, and his home address. Will you need anything more?"

"No, that's fine. Please remember your daughter is of age, and doesn't need your approval to date whomever she chooses. Let's say I find Mr. Hartfield is seeing multiple young women. I'll provide photos. What do you plan to do?"

"You needn't worry, I won't tell Jocelyn and crush her spirit. I'll deal with Stephen, give him a reference, and suggest he seek a job out of state." He pulled out his wallet. "Now what do you need to get started?"

The case had disturbing elements of his own situation, and Joe hesitated to take it. "I may find Stephen spends his time reading in the library, or playing golf with friends. If there are no other women, will you stay out of your daughter's life and let her romance follow its natural course?"

Nathan drew in a breath and puffed his cheeks while he pondered the question. "I suppose I'll have to, but I sure won't like it."

"Your daughter is a grown woman, and it might be time to trust her to make her own decisions."

Nathan responded with a disparaging grunt, but he agreed to Joe's retainer and usual fees and paid with cash. "Don't plan to spend more than a week on this, Mr. Ezell. If Stephen is straying, you'll discover it soon enough."

"Yes, I expect so too." He opened the door for his client, and tried to be grateful for the job. He supposed no father ever thought any young man was good enough for his daughter, but he still had a very bad feeling about the case.

CC came by moments later. "New client, Mr. Ezell?"

"Yes, but I'm not certain I should have taken the case. Did you ever have a bad feeling about something, and find out later you were right?"

"Yes, I have, sir, but I didn't realize it soon enough with my first wife."

Joe had also discovered a lot about women the hard way, and laughed with him. "You're happy with wife number three, and my fiancée is a peach, so we shouldn't have to face another unfortunate situation with the ladies."

"Amen to that. Have a good afternoon now."

Joe parked across the street from the Nathan Skidmore's building and waited for the office to close for the day. Several nice looking young men exited, and one drove away in Stephen's car. Joe followed him to a market, where he bought a bag of groceries, and trailed him home to his apartment building.

If Stephen were seeing someone, he would probably leave by eight o'clock. Of course, he could be seeing a woman who lived in his building. Joe left his car and went to study the names on the apartment's mailboxes. There were only four units, two upstairs and two down. A couple rented number one. Stephen had number two, a Mr. Jackson lived in number three. The woman in apartment number four, Hazel Morgenstern had written her name with a flowery cursive that reminded him of his mother's beautiful handwriting. He bet Hazel was old enough to be Stephen's mother rather than his love interest.

With nothing to see, he went home and called Mary Margaret. "I hope you had a good day," he began. Fortunately, she had. They'd had a birthday party for a patient that included the whole ward, and it had done wonders for everyone's morale.

"His mother brought cake and ice cream, and we sang songs everyone knew and could join in on. We need to have more parties here. Not all our patients have relatives living nearby, but it won't cost us much if we provide an occasional cake or two. We agreed we ought to celebrate more and create a joyful mood. Luke Hatcher agreed. He has a wonderful tenor singing voice and added a lot to the party."

Joe bit his lip rather than make some stupid, jealous remark. "I'm glad you had some fun to make up for the days you don't." He glossed over his day, and wished her good night. He went into his kitchen to find something for dinner, and realized he should have gone into the grocery store while Stephen Hartfield shopped.

Joe had not asked Lilly Montell about receiving roses from Matteo da Milano, and Thursday morning, he gave her a call before leaving his office to follow Stephen Hartfield during his lunch hour.

"Hi, Lily, I wondered if you ever received a bouquet of roses from Matteo."

"No, was that his usual routine? Not that I'd be insulted to be neglected, mind you."

"He did send bouquets from the Wonder of Roses on Wilshire to several women. I'm curious as to whether he patronized any other florist. How are you getting along?"

"Truthfully, I'm growing dreadfully tired of performing at Sherry's. Do you suppose it's too late to consider going to college?"

"Not at all. What are you thinking of studying?"

"I haven't gotten that far." She laughed. "I suppose teaching is out, because no one would want their child taught by a former stripper."

"Use your own name, Bernice, and they'll never discover you've been an exotic dancer."

"With my luck, the father of one of my students would be a regular at Sherry's and recognize me at Back to School Night. I'm thinking business might be the best option. After all, a lot of businessmen lack a sterling reputation."

"That's certainly true. I need to go out on a job, Lily, but let's keep in touch."

"Sure, Joe. Good luck with your case."

Joe arrived at Nathan Skidmore's engineering firm at eleven-thirty, and parked where he'd have a good view of the front door. Thirty minutes later, Stephen Hartfield came out with two other men. The trio walked down the sidewalk, laughing about something they all found funny.

Joe left his car and followed them to a nearby café. They went in and were shown to a table right away.

It was doubtful Stephen could work in a romantic rendezvous after lunch with co-workers. With no reason to stay, Joe drove to Sears and bought a small radio for his office. He plugged it in, but left it on the floor rather than add it to the philodendron and coffee pot atop the file cabinet. It struck him as unprofessional to place it on his desk next to the typewriter.

When CC came by, he noted the new radio. "What you need is a table. There's one in the storage closet downstairs that you might like. Want to see it?"

"Sure." Joe followed the custodian to the first floor and stood back as he opened a door at the end of the hallway.

CC leaned in to turn on the light. "I've got a box of light bulbs on it, but it's a good little oak table that will match your desk."

"Whose is it?" Joe asked.

"It's been here for years, and no one has claimed it. Want me to bring it upstairs so you can give it a try?" He moved the box of light bulbs, and dusted off the table.

It was a small sturdy table, just what Joe would have bought if he'd gone shopping. "If it's not too much trouble."

"I work here to keep the tenants happy. Let's go."

They placed the table against the wall beside the bulletin board. Joe could easily turn the new radio on and off while seated at his desk. "Thanks CC. Now I have everything I need."

The telephone rang, and CC left before Joe answered. "Discreet Investigations."

"I have what will probably be an unusual request," the woman began.

There was little he hadn't heard or seen since becoming a detective, so he doubted it. "Why don't you tell me what the problem is, and then I'll decide."

"All right, I suppose that will work. I'm a secretary in an insurance office, but the boss comes by my desk several times a day to chat, and he prevents me from getting my work done. Several times, he's asked me out to dinner, but I've told him I have a jealous boyfriend and don't date anyone else.

"The problem is, I don't actually have a boyfriend, and I wondered if you could play the part this evening. You could just come in and say you'll wait out front for me to get off work. I'll introduce you to my boss, and it should prompt him to turn his affections elsewhere."

Joe glanced toward his painting and wished he were standing in the tranquil desert setting. He couldn't claim he wasn't an actor now that he'd appeared in a movie, but he doubted it would be wise to accept the job. "That's not the type of case I generally take."

"Would you make an exception just this once? It will only take you a few minutes, and I'll be happy to pay whatever your hourly fee is. Please? My only other choice is to quit and find a job elsewhere, but I like working with everyone else here. Please?"

It was the last frantic *please* that got him. "All right. Give me your name and the address of your office. I'll come and go within minutes. How will I recognize you?"

"My name is Bobbie Beasley." She quickly provided the office address. "I'm wearing a dark green dress, and have curly black hair. My desk is to the right of the office manager, Miss Newton's, so I'll see you when you come in. How will I recognize you, Mr. Ezell?"

"I'm six feet tall, and I'll wear a trench coat and gray fedora. I'll give Miss Newton your name."

"Can you be here a few minutes before five today?"

Nathan Skidmore's engineering firm closed at six. It would be tight, but he thought he could do both jobs if there weren't a problem. That was his first mistake.

The insurance firm where Bobbie Beasley worked was located near Joe's office. He walked in with a confident stride, and asked for Miss Beasley. Miss Newton, a prim, gray-haired woman, swept him with a critical glance.

Clearly she did not condone boyfriends visiting during business hours. After a brief frown, she appeared puzzled.

"Weren't you in *Arizona Sunrise*?"

Bobbie approached on his left. She was wearing green, but she'd not confided with her ample figure, she'd resemble a Christmas tree in motion. He turned to smile at her before answering, "My part was so small, I'm surprised you recognized me."

"Why didn't you tell us you were dating a movie star, Bobbie?" Miss Newton handed Joe a piece of company stationery and a pen. "Would you please give me your autograph? I collect as many as I can, but you're the first star to come through our front door. Do you need any insurance?"

"No, I'm fine, thank you." Joe wrote his name with an impressive flourish, and handed the stationery and pen to Miss Newton. Drawn by the receptionist's comments, several secretaries left their desks to see who'd come in. They expected to find someone famous, and appeared confused when they didn't recognize Joe. He just nodded and smiled. "I came in to let Bobbie know I'm here to take her home. I'll wait out front."

"Oh, wait," Bobbie asked. "I want Mr. Wilson to meet you. Will you call him, Miss Newton?"

"Certainly. It's not every day a movie star comes through our door." She reached for the intercom.

Mr. Wilson proved to be a round little fellow with slicked back hair. Joe couldn't even imagine him romancing Bobbie Beasley when he'd have to leap into the air to gain sufficient height to kiss her. He extended his hand. "Good afternoon, Mr. Wilson. I didn't mean to interrupt your work day, I just stopped by to take Bobbie home."

Wilson gave his hand an enthusiastic shake. "Happy to meet you. Weren't you in *Arizona Sunrise*?"

"For a few seconds only," he replied. It had not even occurred to him that he might be recognized. Bobbie Beasley stepped closer, peering up to get a better look at him. Apparently she hadn't seen the film, yet. "I'll wait for you," he promised, and left before he could get himself into further trouble.

It was only a few minutes to five o'clock, and Bobbie soon followed. She took his arm. "Where's your car?"

"It's the Chevy sedan parked at the curb just ahead. How do you usually get home?"

"I ride the bus, but I live only a few blocks away. It won't take you a minute to drop me off. How much do I owe you?"

Joe hadn't considered the distance she might live from her office, another error. "This didn't go the way I expected, so there's no charge, but I won't play your boyfriend again. Just don't make up any wild tales about a boyfriend from now on, until you meet a nice man."

"Okay, but why didn't you tell me you'd been in the movies?"

He hadn't even thought of it. "It was related to a case, and I didn't realize it would be pertinent." He followed her directions and walked her up to the door of her apartment.

"I really appreciate what you did," she said. "Do you want to come in for a drink?" she asked.

He checked his watch, and was grateful he had a ready excuse. "I've another job scheduled, so I'll tell you good-bye here." He walked out to his car, and made what he regarded as a quick get-away.

After work, Stephen Hartfield stopped by a drycleaner to pick up a suit, and several dress shirts on hangers, before driving home. Joe parked and waited until eight o'clock. With no sign of Stephen, he left, and stopped by Mary Margaret's cottage on the way home.

She drew him in and kissed him soundly. "I ate leftovers for dinner and don't have a thing to fix for you unless you'd like a sandwich."

"I didn't come by looking for supper, but I wouldn't turn down a sandwich now that you've mentioned it."

He tossed his coat and hat on the sofa, and followed her into the kitchen. "I took an absolutely silly job this afternoon that isn't worth describing, but people recognized me from *Arizona Sunrise.* I didn't expect it, and it didn't interfere with the job, but I have to be as close to invisible as I can be when I work, not some two-bit celebrity."

"No one would refer to you as a 'two-bit' anything, but I understand being recognized is a problem."

He stood by the stove as she made him a grilled cheese sandwich. "Maybe I should grow a mustache."

Her glance turned decidedly skeptical. "I doubt it would be becoming, but why don't you get one from a costume shop? You could just slap it on as a disguise when you needed it."

"Great idea, maybe I'll pick up an eye patch too. I can keep them in my glove compartment with my flashlight."

"I'm being serious, Joe."

"So am I," he swore, but he wasn't really.

"You could get a pair of glasses with clear lenses like Clark Kent," she added. She flipped the sandwich over, and waited a minute before placing it on a plate.

She sat with him at the dining table, and sipped coffee. "Maybe you ought to wear a big bushy mustache when you make the Roy Rogers film. Use a disguise for it, and go out on jobs clean shaven as you always have."

"Another great idea. Dare I ask if your mother has called?"

"No, but I promised to call her again, and I'll wait until the weekend. Do you have any ideas on anything new I could say?"

"No, but it's important for parents to step back and let their adult children make their own decisions. Most of the time, they'll make the right choices."

"That's what I love about you, Joe. You're always so optimistic. It's a joy being with you."

"That's what you ought to tell your mother," he replied between bites.

Mary Margaret left him to make a note of his comment before she forgot. He hoped that wasn't a bad sign.

CHAPTER 11

Friday at noon, Stephen Hartfield waved to the men he'd had lunch with yesterday, and crossed the street to his car. Joe followed him to the nearby Mountain View Motel. Stephen parked in front of bungalow six, and a pretty blonde opened the door and welcomed him in with an enthusiastic kiss. Joe barely had time to raise his camera, but he caught the photo he needed.

The blonde couldn't have been the dewy-eyed Jocelyn, but a woman in her thirties who knew precisely what she wanted and Stephen Hartfield was the special of the day. He'd wait to see if they parted with the same lavish affection, and their lingering farewell kiss provided plenty of time for more photos. The woman drove away in a gray Packard, and Joe took a photo of the license plate, but he wasn't being paid to follow her, and didn't.

Before returning to his office, he stopped by Pete's Cameras. "If you could have this film developed by Monday morning, I'd be enormously grateful."

"You got it," Pete replied. "Happy to help you wrap up a case."

Joe leaned against the counter. "Let's hope this one doesn't end in chaos."

"Is that a possibility?"

"The man paying for the investigation swears it isn't, but I'm not sure he can be trusted."

"Can you ever be sure of a client's intentions?"

Joe straightened up. "Unfortunately, no, but thanks for your help." He was still worried as he unlocked his office door. Maybe he'd delay calling Nathan Skidmore an extra day or two next week. Putting off the meeting probably wouldn't change how Skidmore reacted, but it would give him time to craft a report that confirmed his client's worst suspicions without enraging him.

Saturday, Joe played golf with Hal and Gilbert, and that night took Mary Margaret to see *Song of the Thin Man*, staring William Powell and Myrna Loy. The comedy-laced crime film opened on board the gambling ship, *Fortune,* where a charity benefit is taking place. When the bandleader is shot, Nick and Nora Charles investigate the murder. With the series' usual convoluted plot, it ends with Nick gathering all the suspects together to solve the crime.

"Maybe that's what you ought to do, Joe. Invite the suspects in Matteo da Milano's death to an informal memorial, and shake the truth out of them."

"Nick Charles is a movie character, love. He's read the script and knows who the murderer is."

"That's true, but it doesn't mean it won't work. Promise me you'll think about it."

"I will definitely give the idea the thought it deserves. How is that?"

"Oh, Joe. Let's go to Aunt Lucy's for ice cream and argue there."

"We never argue, my dearest. We merely pose differing views." He intended to keep it that way. She looked skeptical, but responded to his ready grin with the kiss he'd always prefer to a silly argument neither would be able to recall the following day.

Monday morning, Joe picked up the photos from Pete's Cameras. He laid them on his desk, and was pleased they were as clear as he'd hoped. He certainly wasn't a gifted photographer by any stretch, but when he pointed his camera at someone he'd followed, the results were uniformly good. He hoped the thought wouldn't jinx his next case, and slipped the photos into a folder for Nathan Skidmore.

Deciding it was cowardly to postpone calling him, he dialed Skidmore Engineering. "Good morning, Mr. Skidmore, I have photos for you. Would you like to pick them up today?"

"May I assume you've found the evidence I was seeking?"

"You may."

"I'll be right there."

Joe hung up and stood to stretch. He made the first pot of coffee for the day, and hadn't finished a cup when Nathan Skidmore arrived. Once his client was seated, Joe spoke in his most serious tone, "While I can never be certain how a case will end, I do hope you'll stick to your original plan, and send Stephen Hartfield on his way with a reference."

"Why wouldn't I?" Nathan responded. "Let's have the photos." He opened the folder Joe slid across the desk, and gasped sharply. "Is this some kind of a joke?"

"You've lost me. Do you recognize the woman?"

"Of course, I do. She's my wife." His face reddened, and he glared at Joe. "I don't know which is worse, that Stephen would betray Jocelyn so cruelly, or that Kate would betray both me and my daughter." He rose, pulled a hundred dollar bill from his wallet and tossed it on Joe's desk. "I'll not thank you for these photos when it's my own damn fault you took them." He grabbed them, and left in the same hurry he'd arrived.

"Good Lord." Joe couldn't have stopped Skidmore, but he could at least warn Stephen Hartfield before Nathan smeared him all over the company office. He dialed Skidmore Engineering for the second time that morning and asked for Stephan.

"Mr. Hartfield, this is Joe Ezell, a private detective. Nathan Skidmore hired me to confirm his suspicions on your commitment to his daughter. I just handed him photos of you and his wife, and you need to grab your coat and get out of the office before he comes back."

"Who is this?"

"My name doesn't matter. Weren't you at the Mountain View Motel with Kate Skidmore last Friday?"

After a long pause, Stephen reluctantly admitted it. "Yes, but…"

"If you value your life, get out now. Tell me the Skidmores' home address, and I'll cut him off there." Or at least he'd try too. He hurriedly wrote the address, locked his office and ran down the stairs.

With any luck, Skidmore would have gone to his office to deal with Stephen first. The Skidmore home in Beverly Hills proved to be a sprawling one-story modern structure facing the street with more glass than solid walls. Only the verdant landscaping made it look like a home. The bright red front door stood open. Joe could hear hoarse shouts as he ran up the walk.

He'd had no speech ready to give Kate Skidmore other than to warn her get out, but clearly something more forceful was urgently needed. He followed Nathan's angry voice into the living room, and slid to an abrupt halt. Nathan was waving the incriminating photos in one hand, and brandishing a Luger someone must have brought home from the war in the other.

"Mr. Skidmore!" Joe ordered. "Put down the gun and let's behave as civilized adults."

Up close, Kate was even prettier than she'd looked in Joe's photos. Terrified, her blue eyes were open wide, and while her mouth moved up and down, only a tiny squeak came out. Her bright blush reached clear to her fingertips, and she gripped the wing-backed chair she'd taken refuge behind with a frantic clutch.

Joe took another step into the room. He pitched his voice low with a comforting edge. "Anyone would be furious,

Mr. Skidmore, but no one will be better off if you're charged with murder."

"You think I care?" Nathan yelled.

"Yes, this isn't the man you'd want your daughter to see."

As if on cue, Jocelyn came through the front door dressed in tennis whites and carrying her racquet. Horrified by the unfolding scene, she halted and called to her father, "Should I call the police?"

"Go!" Joe shouted, but growing unsure of what she'd interrupted Jocelyn hesitated.

"Here!" Nathan hurled the shocking photos toward her.

Joe caught one, but the others landed at Jocelyn's feet, and she gathered them before he could. She shuffled them quickly, and looked up at her stepmother. "Kate, what were you doing with Stephen?"

"That's obvious, isn't it?" her father shouted. "They were sleeping together and laughing at both of us."

Devastated, Jocelyn crumpled like a rag doll, sat down hard, and cried in loud, gulping sobs.

"Put down the gun." Joe moved closer. "Your daughter is heartbroken and needs your loving attention."

When Nathan turned toward his sobbing child, Kate made a dash for the door. Nathan swung back and fired, and missing her, the shot splintered the wood on the bookcase. Greatly alarmed, Joe crossed the final distance between them and grabbed for the larger man's arm.

"Get off me!" Nathan broke away, but Joe caught another hold on his sleeve and held on.

"Drop the gun!" Joe shouted. Intent upon shaking free, Nathan spun in a circle. It was all Joe could do to hang on and remain on his feet.

Stephen Hartfield strode in and caught sight of his boss's Luger. He knelt beside Jocelyn. "We need to get you out of here." He slid his arms around her waist, but she remained limp, too miserable to respond.

The sight of Stephen hugging Jocelyn pushed Nathan beyond all reason. He caught Joe in the eye with a fierce elbow jab and fired. He'd meant to put a prompt end to his daughter's loathsome fiancé, but with an unsteady aim, he hit her instead.

Stunned, Nathan allowed Joe to take the gun from his hand. Joe pocketed it quickly, and rushed to Jocelyn's side. Stephen's white shirt was already covered in blood. Nathan followed. "Is she dead? Have I killed my baby?"

"You bastard," Stephen yelled.

"Hush," Joe ordered. He covered the wound with his handkerchief and pressed down. "The shot grazed her scalp, and head wounds bleed. Go get some towels from the bathroom." Stephen ran to do so. Sirens wailed in the distance, and Joe hoped Kate had called the police. Stephen returned and dropped a handful of snow-white towels.

Joe grabbed a bath towel. "Thanks. Call for an ambulance. All she needs is a few stitches, and she'll be fine."

No one in the room was going to be fine for a good long while, but Joe took care of Jocelyn, and left the others to fend for themselves.

Beverly Hills has its own police force, and the officers arriving promptly arrested Nathan. Joe handed them the Luger. "He meant to shoot his wife." He pointed out the bullet lodged in the bookcase. "I tried to take the gun away from him before he could fire twice, but I couldn't hold him. His second shot grazed his daughter."

The ambulance attendants were seeing to Jocelyn, while Stephen Hartfield hung back to stay out of their way. "He meant to kill me," he volunteered.

"You deserved it!" Nathan yelled as an officer marched him out to a black and white car.

Once Jocelyn had been taken to the awaiting ambulance, the sergeant in charge, a man named Simmons, drew out a notebook. "This has to be a good story. Who wants to tell it?"

Kate peered into the room to be certain she'd be safe before joining them. "My husband came home with photos of me with another man."

"His daughter's fiancé," Joe added.

"That's me," Stephen murmured.

"I doubt you're still engaged," Simmons observed.

"Probably not." Stephen reached for Kate's hand, but she recoiled, and moved closer to the sergeant.

"It was my fault," she insisted. "I should have left my husband before I began seeing Stephen. I meant to, but just hadn't gotten all my ducks in a row."

Joe bet those ducks wore dollar signs. "Mr. Skidmore doubted Stephen Hartfield's intentions where his daughter was concerned, and he hired me to follow him and take photos." He handed the officer one of his business cards.

"You're a private detective?" Simmons asked.

"Does that surprise you for some reason?"

"I suppose not." He picked up a blood-splattered photograph near his foot. "This is you, ma'am?"

Kate stepped close to see. "Yes, I'll not deny it. Stephen and I were lovers. I just never expected Nathan to find out."

"Were there others before him?" Simmons asked.

"That really isn't the issue, is it?" she answered.

Joe took that for a yes. Kate had an exquisite face and figure, but she was real short on morals. He bet Nathan Skidmore had married her for her looks and youth, without once considering her character. He almost felt sorry for him.

"May I leave?" Stephen asked. "I'd rather not stay here in this bloody shirt."

"First I'll need your full name and address."

Joe added a last thought. "Once you have fresh clothes, you might want to stop by your firm and clean-out your desk."

Stephen glared at Joe. "I've already thought of it, and then I'm going to the hospital to see Jocelyn. She didn't deserve to be hurt like this."

"Your concern for her is a tad late, Mr. Hartfield. You may go." Simmons turned to Kate. "Has your husband been violent toward you before today?"

She shrugged slightly. "He was wonderfully sweet when we met, but once we were married, he began to criticize nearly everything I wore and did. We've only been married a little over two years, but our marriage is over now. I'll call a divorce attorney this afternoon."

Simmons nodded to Joe. "You're going to have a black eye for sure. Do you want assault added to the charges against Mr. Skidmore?"

Skidmore wasn't the first client to punch Joe. It was an unfortunate hazard of his profession. "No, he's in enough trouble as is."

After photos had been taken of the splintered bookcase, a policeman pried out the bullet, and retrieved the second bullet from the front door jamb. Simmons closed his notebook. "You need to take care, Mrs. Skidmore, and get as far away as you can before the afternoon is over."

"Yes, I will." Kate waited for Simmons to leave before she reached for Joe's sleeve. "You need some ice for your eye. Come into the kitchen."

The whole side of his face ached, and he followed her. The kitchen was filled with bright, shiny appliances, and he doubted Kate had ever used a single one. She wrapped ice cubes in a dishtowel and handed them to him.

"Thanks." He pulled up a stool and sat down. "Give me a minute, and I'll be out of here."

"There's no rush," she responded, her voice honey sweet.

He couldn't help but wonder if Stephen Hartfield was the only man she was currently seeing. "How do you usually spend your time?" he asked.

She leaned against the counter. "I have friends, and we go shopping, and to the movies. Sometimes, we try new restaurants for lunch. Nathan didn't want more children, and I didn't argue with him. I should have walked out when he went from adoring to critical. This was my first marriage though, and I wanted it to be a success. Kind of stupid of me, wasn't it?"

She focused on her brightly polished nails. She'd not bothered to mention the time she spent with her hairdresser and manicurist, but Joe bet it was considerable. "We all make mistakes," he offered.

"Well, marrying Nathan was a gigantic one, and it's not a mistake I'll repeat. Can you show yourself out? I need to decide where I'm going and get there before Nathan makes bail."

"Good plan. Where's the household help this morning?"

"The cook and I plan the menus, and she does the shopping Monday mornings. She should be here soon. The housekeeper was here, but when Nathan began shouting at me, I heard the backdoor slam, so she's gone."

Joe laid the wet towel in the sink to let the ice melt. His face felt marginally better, and he'd had a chance to study Kate. She had the most innocent expressions, and a heart-melting smile. He doubted she'd be alone for long. He couldn't help himself and handed her one of his cards.

"Keep this. You might need a detective yourself someday."

She studied the card. "Thanks, I'll do that."

Joe sat in his Chevy to collect himself before driving away. He'd known the job would go sideways when Nathan Skidmore had hired him, and he should have refused it right there. Still, he'd arrived in time to save Kate's life, and Stephen's as well. That was a fine day's work in his view. Jocelyn's life was now a sorry mess, however, and unable to cope with anything more, he called it a day and drove home.

Joe called Mary Margaret that night rather than pick her up at the hospital where she would have squealed when she saw his black eye. He ought to make a chart for his bulletin board to tally which eye gathered the most hideous bruises in a year. He listened as she described her day, and relaxed when she failed to mention Luke Hatcher.

"What about you?" she asked. "Anything eventful?"

"I'll say, but I'll wait to tell you in person."

"That bad, huh?"

He could imagine her curled up on her sofa with the telephone cord laced through her fingers. Once they were married, he wouldn't be able to hide the occasional battering he received on the job. She'd always been sympathetic, and had never asked him to look for less dangerous work. She might though. Maybe he could work the counter at Pete's Cameras. He covered the phone to muffle his laughter.

CHAPTER 12

Tuesday afternoon, Joe waited for Mary Margaret to end her shift. He knew how bad he looked, but raised his hands before she could fuss over him. "Ran into a flying elbow, and it's not as bad as it looks."

"Really? Because it looks awful. How about stopping at the market to get everything for spaghetti? It's wonderfully restorative."

"I agree." He would have agreed to liver and onions if she'd liked. He waited until they'd finished their dinner before he told her about Nathan Skidmore and what a disaster the job had proven to be.

"Wait a minute, Joe. Let me get a piece of paper so I can take notes." She was back at the table in an instant. "Don't you realize what you have?"

"Other than a black-eye, no."

"Well, you've got the makings for the a terrific noir film! There's the suspicious husband who hires a detective, the sweet daughter who doesn't question her wandering fiancé's affections, the beautiful stepmother who is definitely a femme fatale, and the young engineer who falls for the stepmother when he has to know he shouldn't. Mixed all together, it's a story literally dying to be a film."

Joe gave it some thought. "A femme fatale who betrays her husband isn't anything new."

"So what? With different actors playing the parts, no one will care. We ought to take notes on all your cases."

"I've kept records of them, but no one would come to me if they realized I was gathering ideas for movies, or novels."

"Novels! That's even better. Besides if you worked with a novelist or screenwriter, no one would know the detective involved is you."

"Don't forget my movie career, it has already cut into my detective work. Now what about you? Stories featuring doctors and nurses are popular. Have you considered writing a novel about your patients?"

"That wouldn't be ethical, Joe. They depend on me when they're at their worst. It just wouldn't be right."

"But my clients are easy game?"

She sat back in her chair. "I can see the difference even if you can't. You could mix up the details from one case with another, and no one would admit that they had inspired it. Just think about it, Joe. Maybe someday you'll want to write a novel, and you'll have plenty of material in your files."

"Did your mother call?"

"That's a swift change of subject, but yes she did. She's been talking to my sister, and Sharon is on our side, but Mom still has misgivings. If I sent her a photograph of the way you look tonight, she'd never agree to our wedding."

"I'm not having more photos taken, so there's no risk to that. Of course, we'll have to hope I don't run into any elbows before we catch the train for Seattle."

Her shoulders slumped. "Oh Joe, I hadn't thought of that. Can you be careful with the jobs you take in December?"

"I shall have to be. What I need to learn is how to refuse jobs that don't feel right. It might cut into my income, but it will be worth it in the long run."

She reached for his hand and gave his fingers a squeeze. "You could say you're up for a movie role, and that wouldn't insult the prospective client. After the Roy Rogers film, your agent said there's lots of work for you."

"He did, but I never intended to be an actor."

"That's why you look so natural," she exclaimed. "We should go see *Arizona Sunrise* again."

Somehow, the thought didn't appeal to him, but he kissed her anyway.

Once home, Joe turned in, but couldn't sleep. He got up, carried a pen and paper into the kitchen and sat down at the table. The police had made no progress on the Matteo da Milano murder, or Henry Hilburn would have called to let him know. Thwarted love, or jealousy was a powerful motive for murder, as Nathan Skidmore's rampage had shown so clearly. With Matteo sleeping with women from all over town, there had to be plenty of jealous women who'd wanted him dead. Their boyfriends or husbands could also have wanted him gone.

Money was also a potent motive. As Matteo's sole heir, Veronica profited from his death. Sean Dermot's career received a boost as he replaced Matteo as the first chair cello at the Philharmonic. Was he talented enough to actually capitalize on the opportunity? The director would know, and he ought to speak to him. Believing Constance Remson's connections to the orchestra would be helpful, he ended his notes with a promise to call her in the morning.

Constance listened to Joe's questions about the Philharmonic director. "There's a guest conductor here now, Gunnar Ingvild from Norway. He'd certainly be the person to comment on Sean Dermot's talent, or lack thereof. Do you want me to see if he's free for lunch today?"

That was more than Joe had hoped. "Yes, but I'll be happy to buy him a drink after rehearsal if that's better for him."

"Let's shoot for lunch. I'll call you in a minute."

"Great." Joe was continually amazed by how easily Constance arranged whatever she desired. Would she have killed Matteo herself, or hired a hit woman, if there were such a person, to handle it? He couldn't imagine her stepping through the cellist's blood, so she'd have hired out the job for sure.

He was making notes when the custodian came by. "Oh no, Mr. Ezell, another black eye? Maybe you should be wearing a helmet when you go out on a job."

"It's not a bad idea, CC. Do you recall the job that worried me? Well, I may have saved a couple of lives, so that's a big plus, but next time I'll trust my instincts and not accept a job that doesn't feel right. Say, have you ever heard of a woman who worked as a hit man?"

"In mystery books you mean?"

"Wherever you might have come across such a person. The guilty party isn't caught for many of the murders in Los Angeles, but women aren't usually the suspects."

"No, they're better at driving a man to drink." He laughed at his own humor. "I can see you're busy. Have a nice day."

"Thanks, I intend to." He called Henry Hilburn to ask about women working as hit men.

"Doing contract killings you mean? I've never heard of one, but if one exists, she might be too good to be caught. Do you want me to check with my sources?"

"If it's not too much trouble."

Joe added the possible hit woman card to his bulletin board, but it was difficult to believe if a woman had been hired to kill Matteo, she would have arrived armed only with stiletto heels. He studied the photo of the fur-clad woman. It would have been a great disguise in New York, but she stood out in Los Angeles. It was mistake a professional wouldn't have made.

Constance called at 11:00 o'clock. "Gunnar wants to meet us at Philippe's at noon. He loves the French Dip sandwiches and while I generally avoid places with sawdust on the floor, I like the food too. Do you want to meet us there?"

"Thanks, I sure do." Joe got hungry just thinking about Philippe's sandwiches. He preferred the pork, with the French roll dipped in the roasting pan's drippings. It would be crowded at noon, but he needed to speak with Mr. Ingvild, and a passion for Philippe's sandwiches should put the man at ease.

Gunnar Ingvild stood six feet four inches tall. His pale blond hair was nearly white, and his eyes were a vivid blue. With his muscular build and dark tan, he could easily have been mistaken for a lumberjack. His deep laugh carried over Philippe's noisy luncheon crowd, and Joe liked him instantly.

The women at the counter not only took orders, but made the sandwiches as well, and collected the money. The lines were long, but moved quickly, and they found good seats at one of the long tables near the front windows. Joe waited until Gunnar had finished his meal to speak.

"I'm investigating Matteo da Milano's murder, and would appreciate your thoughts. Did it appear to you that Matteo was well-liked?"

The Norwegian's accent lent a musical lilt to his words. "He charmed men as easily as women, but I don't know if he had any close friends in the orchestra. He was such a talented musician, and he was admired, or envied, by most. His death is a great loss to all lovers of classical music."

"Is Sean Dermot equally capable?" Joe asked.

Constance took a sip of her lemonade and leaned closer. "Sean has taken Matteo's place, hasn't he?"

"For the time being, yes, but there is an enormous difference between technical proficiency and true artistry. Matteo's talent was a rare gift."

"So Sean can play the right notes, but that isn't enough?" Joe guessed.

"Sadly, no, but it isn't my opinion that truly matters here, but his," Gunnar mused. "If Sean believed he was Matteo's equal, he would have had a powerful motive for murder."

Struck by the Norwegian's insight, Joe glanced toward Constance. "Let's say professional advancement was the motive. There would have been no point in killing Matteo if Sean doubted his talents and thought he would soon be bumped aside by a more accomplished cellist."

"No, he has to believe getting rid of Matteo would allow him to finally come into his own," she posed. "But who was the woman in the fur coat? I've never seen him with a date at any of the after concert parties. She'd have to be far more than a casual date to commit murder for him."

"You doubt he could inspire such a murderous devotion?" Joe asked. He couldn't imagine the mild-manned man even coming close. Matteo could have easily, however, with his magnetic charm.

"Sean is sweet, but no, I can't believe it of him," she answered.

Gunnar glanced over his shoulder, but no one could overhear them above the nearby conversations and laughter. "Do the police regard Sean as a suspect?"

"They don't share their thinking," Joe answered. "Please don't tell anyone what we've discussed today. I'm just considering possible motives, and don't want anyone to believe I'm accusing Sean of being an accessory to murder."

"I understand," Gunnar responded. "Would it be rude to ask if your black eye is related to your work?"

The deep purple shade had faded slightly and taken on a green tinge. "Not at all. I objected when a client took a shot at his wife."

Constance gasped. "Did he kill her?"

"No, but he took a nasty nick out of the bookcase."

Thursday morning, Joe got a call from Henry Hilburn. "You were right, Joe, the LAPD detectives have had reports of women contract killers. They've largely dismissed the *lady killer* possibility as absurd, however, which works to the women's advantage. If no one believes women are capable of violence, they won't become suspects in unsolved crimes."

"Thanks, Henry. I don't suppose you know how anyone could get in touch with such a woman."

"I'm not looking, Joe, and I'd advise you not to search for one either. It would be far too easy to insult a woman packing a gun in her purse, and the results could be horrific."

"Thanks, Henry. I see your point."

As soon as he'd hung up, he dialed the number for King's Bail Bonds. Paul King's sister, Jade, answered. "Good morning. This is Joe Ezell. Does Paul have a minute to answer a question or two?"

"I'm sorry, Joe, he's not in. Could I be of some help?"

She was such a lovely young woman, he hated to take advantage, but with murder as a motivation, he did. "I'm researching the idea of a female contract killer. Not that they'd show up at King's Bail Bonds, but do you recall ever hearing a mention of one?"

A brief silence followed as she gathered her thoughts. "Contract killing requires a degree of professionalism we don't see in the women coming here. Besides, a good one, man or woman, would never be caught."

"I'll take that for a no," Joe replied.

"I'll tell Paul you called. Maybe he's heard of one."

"Thank you, Jade. I'm just wondering if such a creature exists, I don't need a name."

"You needn't worry, he wouldn't give you one," she dismissed the thought with a coolly voiced good-bye.

Joe made a fresh pot of coffee, and rocked back in his chair. No one had suggested Black Dahlia's murder might have been the work of a contract killer. It had been a grisly murder if there had ever been one. A man who'd kill, and then chop his victim in half to drain her blood had to be among the very worse of humanity. He'd probably killed more than once, and would continue to kill pretty young women until he was stopped. Joe hoped that would be soon.

Banishing thoughts of the heinous crime, he turned to his bulletin board thinking he probably had the murderer's name on an index card. It was a chilling thought. He turned the bulletin board to the wall, and left for a long walk to clear his head. He liked the sandwiches at the place he'd found on another extended stroll, and ate his lunch slowly to savor the freshly baked bread, and thick slices of ham and cheese. He took his time getting back to his office, and was surprised to find the door unlocked.

He questioned CC. "I locked my door when I went out for lunch, but found it unlocked now. Did you stop by my office while I was out?"

"No, sir. After my lunch break, I've been cleaning bathrooms. Is something missing?"

"Maybe, I haven't looked yet."

"Well, let's check." When they reached Joe's office door, CC crouched down to study the lock. "Nothing looks wrong, but if someone picked the lock, they would have been careful not to leave any telltale scratches."

"I don't keep money in my desk, so if someone broke in, they must have been badly disappointed."

CC stood and followed Joe into the office. "The painting looks good, and so does the plant. Your new radio is on its table, and the coffee pot is where you leave it. It doesn't look as though anyone came in. Are you sure you locked your door, sir?"

He'd been thinking about suspects when he'd left, but he hadn't been so distracted he'd forget to lock the door on his way out. "Yeah, I'm sure. Thanks, CC. I didn't mean to interrupt your work."

"Don't you worry, Mr. Ezell, my work always waits patiently for me. I'll ask if any of the other tenants has found their office door unlocked."

"Let me know if they have." Joe went over to the window and watched the cars driving by. He might not keep money in his office, but he did have files on all his clients, and someone might have wanted that information.

He opened the file cabinet drawer, and fingered his way through the file tabs. He kept a list of his cases in the first folder, and there were no missing files. Maybe he had left his door unlocked after all. After turning the radio on low, he sat behind his desk and reached for his bulletin board. He'd arranged the 3x5 cards so carefully, but every single one was gone, and the thumbtacks lay scattered on the floor. A tingling chill shot up his spine, as though someone had stepped on his grave.

He'd had names of people involved on the fringes of Matteo da Milano's life, as well as those who'd been close and possessed a motive to kill. Whoever had snuck into his office had no doubt found their own name on the bulletin board, unless it had been one of the Philharmonic wives. No one else would have broken in and taken the cards as a prank.

So what did it mean? Even as a subtle warning, it showed someone must be worried about what he knew, and what he could prove. It was inspiring to be so well thought of, but he didn't want to be popular with the woman who had hammered Matteo to death with a fiercely wielded shoe.

He stood, walked around his desk, and leaned back against the front. Someone he had questioned had begun investigating him. He had nothing to hide, so no one could blackmail him to force him to keep quiet about Matteo's death. A few stolen index cards could be easily replaced, and he'd do that this afternoon. He'd also place a note on the bulletin board every time he left his office to warn whomever had broken in that he'd catch them, and soon.

Paul King called while Joe was printing names on new cards for his bulletin board. "I hope Jade didn't think my question was absurd, but I'm just curious."

"You know what curiosity did to the cat. Can you meet me at the Golden Bear Lounge at 6 o'clock?"

"I'll be there." Joe hung up thinking whatever Paul knew, it was too dangerous to discuss over the telephone. What had he stepped into now?

The Golden Bear Lounge was among Paul King's favorites. The dark mahogany paneling and deep green leather booths provided a touch of class. Mitch, the mustachioed bartender, claimed his mother owned the place, but no one had ever met her. Joe was seated at the bar when Paul walked in. He slid onto the barstool beside him, and ordered a scotch and soda.

"Get that black eye working on a case?" he asked.

"I'll not deny it. I should get a make-up kit like the ones they use in the movies to cover the occasional black eye. I could also use one to create disguises."

"Definitely a business expense for a man in your line of work." He raised his glass in a silent salute. "What is it you really want to know?" Paul asked.

The bail bondsman always looked as though he belonged in a display window at an expensive menswear store. Joe admired his classy tastes, but he couldn't afford them. "A woman murdered Matteo da Milano." He showed Paul the photo. Apparently whoever had broken into his office hadn't found it mixed among the other photos in the top drawer of his desk.

"This has to be a goofy disguise for a California woman, but it worked, and she's impossible to identify. It crossed my mind that she might have been hired to do the killing. Several of the possible suspects could afford such a person."

Paul laid the photo on the bar. "There are female contract killers, but I doubt they'd knock on a man's door. From what I've heard, they are more likely to follow a man and strike when he's alone at night. An attractive woman walking a man's way wouldn't alarm him as an approaching man would. He'd be dead before he drew his next breath. Besides, wasn't Matteo bludgeoned? A hit woman wouldn't take a chance the man could over-power her. She'd shoot to kill and walk away."

"So, it's possible to hire a woman contract killer, but she wouldn't have attacked Matteo with a stiletto heel?"

"She killed him with a shoe?" Paul shook his head. "Too many things could have gone wrong, so it looks as though a contract killing is out."

Joe ordered another round for them both. "Have you actually met such a woman?"

Paul responded with a slow smile. "I once dated one. She was a lovely girl from New Orleans with a seductive southern accent. She'd call me when a job brought her to Los Angeles. I intend to marry a Chinese woman, so there was never anything serious between us. I was younger then and enjoyed the risk, but I wouldn't date her today."

It wasn't only the handsomely tailored bespoke suits that set Paul apart. There was a dangerous edge to the slender man, and the bail bondsman had just confirmed it. "I know what you mean. I'm a lot smarter now than I used to be. Thank you. You've been a great help, and I'll cross a contract killer off my list."

"I'm happy to help. LA has so many male contract killers there might be one seated at the end of bar." He laughed when Joe leaned over to look. "I'm joking." He offered his hand and Joe shook it. "Good luck with your case."

Joe certainly needed it. He pocketed the photo and left for home. He'd call Mary Margaret, but not admit he'd gone off on a wild goose chase looking for a contract killer, or that someone had entered his office while he was out. She had enough on her mind planning their wedding, and didn't need him to add to her worries.

Friday morning, a woman called to demand an immediate appointment. Joe counted to ten. "Yes, that can be arranged. Please give me your name, and a tell me why you need a detective so I can be prepared when you arrive."

"This is Mrs. Adrian Navarro, and I need photos to prove my grandson is a wastrel who doesn't deserve to inherit a cent of my fortune."

Joe loved the description of the boy. He'd seen wastrel in crossword puzzles, but never heard anyone use the term. Mrs. Navarro appeared to be an elderly lady intent upon safeguarding her wealth even from the grave.

"Thank you. Will eleven o'clock work for you?"

"I'll be there," she replied and abruptly hung up.

The office was as neat and clean as always, thanks to CC. Joe got up to straighten the landscape painting, and made certain his bulletin board was hidden from view behind his desk. He doubted Mrs. Navarro would want a cup of coffee, but just in case she did, he made a fresh pot and went downstairs to the drugstore counter to fetch cream and sugar and a handful of napkins. He already had clean spoons in his desk.

At precisely eleven o'clock, Mrs. Navarro's driver, in a chauffeur's navy blue suit and hat, opened the door for her. "Wait on the bench for me, Roger."

"Yes, ma'am, I'll be right here."

Joe stood to greet her. She was a tiny woman, barely five feet tall and dressed entirely in gently draped black silk. With fluffy white hair and sparkling blue eyes, she was very pretty. He saw she was comfortably seated, and offered coffee.

"No, thank you, but Roger might like some."

Impressed she would care about the chauffeur's comfort, Joe opened the door, and Roger leaped to his feet." Would you care for a cup of coffee while you wait?"

"Yes, thank you, if it's not too much trouble. Just black is fine."

"No trouble at all." Joe poured him a cup and handed it to him. He'd never had anyone wait for a client, and wished he had a magazine to offer. He'd buy one downstairs when he returned the cream and sugar.

"Can't keep good help if you don't treat them right," Mrs. Navarro whispered as Joe returned to his desk. "Constance Remson recommended you very highly."

"How nice of her." He had proven Constance's suspicions about Matteo, even if he'd yet to find who'd slain the cellist.

"My grandson, Timothy, has dropped out of more colleges than I can recall." She handed him a studio photo of him, and he was a handsome kid. "He blames his instructors, of course, rather than his own inability to concentrate. He cannot decide what to study, which exacerbates the matter. He began with engineering, and then went from math to architecture, and now art. He claims no one appreciates him, which is his parents' fault. They granted his every wish, and spoiled him terribly. They nearly ignored Teresa, his sister, and she's doing beautifully at Bryn Mawr."

"Have you considered leaving her the good portion of the inheritance?" he asked.

"That's precisely what I intend to do, but I want to be able to tell Timothy why she's receiving the greater share. It isn't only his lack of direction I find appalling, but his pastimes and companions. That's what I want you to document. Not that it will influence Timothy to reform his ways, but perhaps it will give him a moment's pause. I don't dislike the boy. I'm quite fond him, but I'll not fund the extension of his childhood forever."

"I understand," Joe sympathized. He got all the pertinent information from her, as well as a retainer, and opened the office door for her when she was ready to leave. Her chauffeur handed him the empty coffee cup, and held her arm as they made their way down the stairs. Physically, Mrs. Navarro might be becoming frail, but her mind was as sharp as a tack, and he liked her.

Joe returned the sugar and cream to the drug store, and perused the magazine rack for something that would appeal to everyone, and wouldn't have to be replaced each month.

It proved to be a nearly impossible challenge, but he finally settled on a magazine devoted to California history and the state's majestic scenery. It ought to be enough to keep someone entertained for as long as an office visit would take, and the reader might learn something in the bargain.

Dr. Raymond, the pharmacist who owned the building drew Joe aside after he had paid for the magazine. "CC told me someone may have broken into your office yesterday. None of the other offices was entered. Are you sure you didn't leave your door unlocked?"

"Yes, sir. I always lock my door, but only a few index cards I had pinned to a small bulletin board were missing. Whoever did it probably won't be back, and they would have no interest in any of your other tenants."

"Let's hope not, but I don't like that this happened to you. All day people come and go for appointments, and I'll have CC watch for anyone loitering in the hall. We certainly don't want another tragedy happening in the building."

A woman had been murdered in the hallway outside Joe's office, and he was grateful the pharmacist hadn't evicted him immediately. He left before Dr. Raymond could ask how the cards related to one of his cases, because he sure didn't want to discuss murder with the man.

Joe took the new index cards to Mary Margaret's that night. He brought ice cream for dessert, and she was still licking her spoon when he pulled the cards from his jacket pocket.

"I've cards for people who barely knew Matteo, as well as those who were close enough to have a reason to murder him." He put Lily Montell's card down to begin one stack, and Veronica da Milano's to begin the other. "Veronica was in New York, but she could still have conspired with another woman to kill her ex-husband."

Mary Margaret carried their empty bowls to the kitchen and called over her shoulder, "But why? Apparently they were still close if he left her everything in his will."

"She appears to be an unlikely suspect, that's true, but let's keep her in that pile for now. Constance Remson was the first to hire me to follow Matteo, but he died before I could give her a report. She has an alibi, but Detective Lynch suspected a tie between the women who'd hired me and Matteo's death. I thought he was nuts, but maybe his theory should be considered."

"That's a first," Mary Margaret commented under her breath. She slid into her place beside him at the table. "Who were the other women he believed to be involved?"

"An artist, Paloma Val Verde, and Lily Montell. Paloma loved Matteo far too much to want to harm him, and Lily didn't care enough about him to do him in." He lay Paloma's card with Lily's, but put Constance's card in the middle.

"You're not sure about Constance?"

"She's been very helpful, but if she's really behind the murder, she'd want to keep me close to keep track of what I've discovered."

"Is she dangerous?"

"If she killed Matteo, she certainly is. I met Suzanne Ritter in Matteo's building on La Peer. She's a fashion designer, a sophisticated woman with hair dyed a striking burgundy shade. She told me Matteo liked to make milkshakes after making love."

"Milkshakes? I thought he'd sip champagne all evening."

"So did I, that's why her story struck me as merely a distraction rather than the truth. I've read liars often add details to back up their story. That may be what Suzanne did. I'll make a few calls tomorrow and see if milkshakes were part of Matteo's usual routine."

"Yes, do. A fashion designer could have easily produced the fur coat and hat worn by the woman you saw leaving Matteo's building."

"Indeed she could have. When I met Suzanne, she was still dressed for work, but barefoot. She might have wanted out of her stilettos as soon as she got home."

"Put her in the pile with Constance," she suggested.

"My thoughts exactly." He drew Sean's card. "Sean is the only one who'd gain professionally from Matteo's death, and he's close to Veronica." He placed their cards together.

"Matteo wasn't above romancing the wives of the other men who played in the LA Philharmonic. One of them might have planned to leave her husband for Matteo, and been deeply hurt when she realized her feelings weren't returned."

"A woman scorned? It's a good theory, and I did suggest the woman in furs might be a married lover wearing a disguise."

"You did." He drew a new card. "Tanya Olson lives next door to Matteo, and recalled hearing classical music coming from his apartment, but claimed not to know him. I doubt Matteo would ignore such an attractive young neighbor. She was home at the time of the murder, and could have disguised herself with furs, whipped around the building and returned to her apartment via the backdoor. When I knocked on her door a few minutes later, she answered wearing a robe."

"Did Detective Lynch question her?"

"Yes, but she'd changed her clothes by then. She batted her eyelashes at Lynch, and he quickly let her go. She didn't strike me as a suspect either then, so I can't fault him for it. Now, I wonder if the fur coat and hat weren't stuffed into her hallway closet."

"She had the opportunity it seems, but could a young woman have become angry enough to kill? Murder seems more of a crime a woman would commit after suffering a lifetime of betrayals and disappointments."

"Which brings us back to Constance, who has an alibi, and Suzanne Ritter."

"Could they have known each other?"

"Constance wears beautiful clothes, so it's possible she's bought something from Suzanne Ritter."

He gathered the cards and returned them to his pocket. "We've spent enough time on this. Let's talk about something more entertaining."

"Wonderful idea. What about our wedding?"

As long as there was going to be one, he didn't care about the details, but he smiled as though nothing would interest him more.

CHAPTER 13

After playing golf Saturday morning, Joe drove by Timothy Navarro's home and found the young man working on a 1934 Ford Roadster coupe in the driveway. He parked up the street and watched Timothy greet a friend, who joined him working under the hood. The roadster looked as though it had seen better days, but lots of guys bought old cars to turn them into showy hot rods.

Timothy and his buddy were so intent on their work they didn't notice Joe walking by until he stopped and called to them, "That should be a great car when you're finished."

Both young men straightened up, and Timothy smiled with pride. A lanky, fair-haired young man with blue eyes, he came down to the sidewalk. "It's already a great car. It just needs a little more attention on the engine, some work on the body, a new paint job, and leather seats."

Joe laughed. "That's quite a list."

"I know, but it's worth it. I'll make a good profit when I sell it, and buy another old car and start over again."

"It could be a good business."

Timothy quickly agreed. "Sure is, but I should take a mechanic's course so I'd have some credentials to show. Many men came back from the war knowing everything there is to know about truck and jeep engines. I can't compete with them, but I don't expect to work as a mechanic except in my own driveway."

Joe gazed into the distance as though he were deep in thought. "Detroit must always be looking for people who can design new cars."

"Yeah, I've probably taken enough engineering and math classes to qualify, but for now, I'm concentrating on turning near junkers into hot rods."

"Good plan, but does it leave any time for girls?"

Timothy looked down at his scuffed shoes. "My girlfriend is a student at USC. She's a great girl, and loves cars as well as me."

"Perfect combination." Joe wished him luck and walked all the way around the block to return to his car. He picked up his camera, and got a good shot of Timothy working on his car without being noticed.

He needed to call Mrs. Navarro, but not yet. On a couple of other occasions, he'd switched loyalties from his client to the subject of his investigation. As he saw it, Timothy loved cars, and his grandmother couldn't abide such a frivolous pursuit. If he could adjust her thinking, everyone would come out ahead.

With plenty of time to spare, Joe drove to Matteo's apartment building on Altmont. He thought Veronica might be there sorting the cellist's belongings, and she was, along with Sean Dermot, and interior designer, Michael Campbell.

There was no longer any evidence of Matteo's murder, and the smell of fresh paint lingered in the entryway air. Georgia Dixon had been killed right outside Joe's office door, and a crew had been hired to remove all trace of her murder. Maybe the same company had come there. There were all sorts of ways to earn a living, but he thought cleaning up bloody crime scenes had to be among the worst.

"Come in and help," Veronica welcomed him with a frantic gesture. "Michael believes he can sell whatever I don't want, but I'm torn about what to keep."

Joe greeted the two men, and asked where she'd like him to begin. "First, did Matteo have a blender to make milkshakes, the kind they have at soda fountains? I'd sure like to have one."

"A blender?" Veronica looked sincerely puzzled. "There isn't one in the kitchen, here or on La Peer. I don't believe Matteo ever drank milkshakes, so why would he have one?"

"No reason at all," Joe responded. "I just thought I'd ask. Isn't art a good investment, Mr. Campbell?"

"Call me Michael, and yes, good art, which is the only type I promote, always appreciates in value. However, it's really a matter of personal taste."

"And mine isn't the same as Matteo's might have been," Veronica interjected. "I suppose I could leave paintings in their shipping crates and sell them ten years from now. That would work, wouldn't it, Michael?"

He shuddered at the thought. "Art is meant to be enjoyed, rather than hidden. It would be better to sell the work you wouldn't hang in your home. I'll cut my commission to twenty percent."

"You'd charge a widow that much?" Sean asked.

Deeply offended, Michael spoke slowly, as though he were addressing a small child. "Clearly you know nothing about the sale of art, but galleries often take fifty percent of the painting's price. Why don't you call one and ask what their commission is? I promise you'll regard my offer of twenty percent as a gift."

"Do you see why I can't make up my mind?" Veronica asked Joe. "I don't know what to do, and I'm afraid any choice I make will be the wrong one."

"It may be too soon to make decisions about art, or anything else," Sean suggested. "Why not give yourself more time?"

She sighed. "I doubt I'll feel any better about losing Matteo a year from now."

Out of the corner of his eye, Joe saw Sean flinch, apparently hurt by her fond mention of her late ex-husband. "Maybe you should begin with things you know you don't want, and work up to the art."

"Yes!" Michael cried. "That's what we should do. Let's start in the kitchen where there's nothing you want to keep."

Sean checked his watch. "I had planned to stop by for only a moment to see how you are doing, Veronica. I'll talk to you, or see you again soon." He started for the door, but Veronica overtook him, and whispered in his ear. Whatever it was, he left smiling.

Veronica returned to the project at hand. "I like your idea, Joe, but I don't want to keep you all afternoon."

"I hadn't meant to stay. I should have asked about Matteo's Stradivarius. Is it still here?"

"No, it's far too expensive to leave in an unguarded apartment. Gunnar Ingvild picked it up to store with the Philharmonic's instruments, where there is no chance it will be stolen."

"That's very wise."

By the time Joe bid them good-bye, Sean had already driven away, so he'd missed his chance for another talk with him. Still, it was plain he'd been hurt by Veronica's mention of Matteo. Maybe he loved her and had grown tired of waiting for her to get over her ex-husband. Love was a powerful motive for murder, but if not Veronica, who had been his accomplice?

Saturday afternoon, Joe visited Frederick's of Hollywood on Hollywood Blvd. to search for a source of murderous stiletto heels.

The owner, Frederick Mellinger, had designed the push-up bra. The store stocked them in multiple colors along with mere wisps of lingerie men would love to see their women wear. A voluptuous red-haired clerk in a tight low cut dress greeted Joe warmly.

"We have many men come in to buy gifts for their sweetheart or wife. Are you perhaps interested in a nightgown? We have a gorgeous selection."

"I'm a detective, working on a case, and heard you have stiletto heels."

"Indeed we do. A detective, I like that, but you needn't be embarrassed to shop here."

"I'm not embarrassed," he insisted with the cool detachment he'd cultivated for his work, but he purposely avoided glancing at the scantily clad mannequins on display.

"I understand," she responded. "You wish to be serious. We do have stiletto heels. Do you wish a particular size?"

Exasperated by the flirtatious clerk, Joe showed her the photo. "Do you by any chance recognize this women?"

She studied it carefully. "We don't sell furs, and it's impossible to tell who she is or if her stilettos came from here."

"Do you keep records of your sales?"

"We record them only to see what's selling, and most of our customers pay with cash. We are a discreet business, and don't share our customers' names with anyone. If something catches your eye, please let me know. Excuse me, I need to see another customer."

Joe left believing a search for the source of the mystery woman's furs or stiletto heels was only marginally less ridiculous than the hunt for a female hit woman.

On his way home, he stopped by the library and asked the librarian to recommend a book on planning weddings. Despite her quizzical expression, he chose not to elaborate on his request. She led him through the non-fiction stacks and pulled out the most popular volume.

"This is a good resource. It will be due in two weeks, but you may renew it if you need to."

"Thank you." The book was bigger and heavier that he'd expected, but there hadn't been any thin ones beside it on the shelf. He left before anyone coming up to the counter could see what he carried, and nearly ran to his car.

Mary Margaret wanted to go dancing that night. She loved dancing, and he was grateful for any excuse to hold her. He'd just finished polishing his dress shoes when he heard a soft rap at his door. He didn't care what the problem might be, he wouldn't be late for his date. He swung open the door, and couldn't believe his eyes.

It was the fur-clad woman again dressed as he'd photographed her coming out of Matteo's building. Her hat shadowed her eyes, but the light from his doorway gave her bright red lipstick a forbidding glare. She wore black gloves, and black suede low-heeled boots. She responded to Joe's startled appraisal with a low, throaty laugh.

She handed him his business card, and spoke in a suggestive whisper, "You're on the wrong track. Matteo was dead when I found him. When I had only one reason for being there, it would have badly embarrassed my husband had I remained to summon the police. Another woman wearing stilettos killed Matteo."

Her earnest comments sounded well-rehearsed. He'd not risk inviting her in and blocked the doorway with his body. "You claim to merely be a witness?"

"Yes, but I saw only poor Matteo, not the woman who killed him." She stepped away. "I've said all I wished to. Good night."

He'd passed out so many business cards, he couldn't be certain where she'd gotten the one she'd handed him. Dumbfounded by her surprise visit, he wasted precious seconds before following her down the stairs. He scanned the central courtyard, but she had already disappeared. Tail-lights would still be visible had she driven away down the alley behind the building, but it was dark. He raced out front, but there were no empty spaces between the cars parked along the curb. She'd disappeared just as swiftly as she had on the afternoon Matteo had died.

Cursing didn't even begin to touch his anger. He should have tackled her on the landing before she reached the stairs, but he'd been raised to respect women, and it hadn't even occurred to him.

Mary Margaret needed to sit down to hear the details of Joe's encounter with the fur-coated lady. "Did you get a good look at her?"

"No, she remained in the shadows. Even if she dared not disgrace her husband, it didn't prevent her from cheating on him."

"Do you believe she was telling the truth?"

He paced in front of her. "Why would she risk making an appearance at my apartment to lie?"

"To fool you, and throw you off the scent. Are you going to tell Detective Lynch?"

The thought held no appeal. "He hasn't kept me up to date on his investigation, so I don't see why I should relate mine."

"You're a bigger person than he is," she countered. "I don't like this, Joe. If she had murdered Matteo, she could have carried a gun and shot you when you first opened the door."

He'd had the same thought. "You're right, but I didn't sense any danger when I went to the door. I expected to find one of my neighbors asking for an ingredient for a recipe. Not that I'd have it, but my instincts completely failed me tonight."

She patted the sofa, and he sat beside her. "Is your home address on your business card?"

"No, just the office and my telephone number there. She must have followed me home tonight, or she could have any other night."

"That's truly frightening." She gripped his hands tightly. "Let's not tell my mother about this."

"Lord, no. She'd imagine marauders storming through your cottage every night."

"This is a safe neighborhood, but when the bell rings, I look out the front window to see who's there."

"Wise move. I was concentrating on our date tonight, and it didn't even cross my mind that she'd turn up."

"It doesn't sound as though she threatened you."

"No, she just told me I needed to focus my investigation elsewhere, which is what a clever murderess would say. She's either innocent and helpful, or a conniving killer who intended to spin me in the wrong direction."

"Which do you believe she truly is?"

He brought her fingertips to his mouth for a tender kiss. "I don't know, and that's a big problem."

"Did anything about her strike you as familiar, her perfume, or gestures?"

He'd gotten used to Constance's heady fragrance, but there was no identifying scent tonight. "No, I recognized her instantly from the fur coat and hat, but there was no other way to identify her. She remains as mysterious a figure as when I first saw her. You were the one who believed she might be a married woman wearing a disguise."

She stood and pulled him to his feet. "True, but it doesn't thrill me to be right. I still want to go dancing. How about you?"

There was nothing more he could do on the perplexing case tonight except brood over how foolish he'd been to let the fur draped woman escape. "Sure, we might as well enjoy ourselves. I drove the long way here and no one followed me, so she's not hanging around."

"Well, I hope not." She snuggled against him. "You lead such an exciting life, Joe."

"It's all in your point of view, but please don't say that to your mother."

She appeared horrified by the thought. "No, of course not. It's our secret."

* * *

The telephone rang as Joe entered his office Monday morning. "Discreet Investigations."

"Hi, Joe, it's Hal. Do you have time for a job for California West? One just crossed my desk that might interest you."

"I'll make time." He went downtown to the insurance firm's offices and was promptly shown into Hal's. "Is this another case of suspected fraud?" he asked.

"No, I don't believe so. It may look rather silly, but it's serious to our client. Liam Dolan claims expensive ceramic pots were stolen from his front porch. The thief yanked out the plants, which were also pricey, dumped them and the potting soil on the lawn, and made off with the empty pots. Here are photos. Do you know anything about pots or plants?" He handed Joe the Dolan folder.

"I can tell a rose bush from a palm tree, that's about it." Joe settled into his chair. "Was the client engaged in a feud with a neighbor?"

Hal referred to his notes. "Apparently not. Mr. Dolan's home was to have been part of a garden tour in the spring. He described it as a heated contest to win selection for the tour, and for the cash prizes. He's won in past years, and fears someone is holding a grudge against him, and the vandalism is meant to force him to withdraw from the tour."

"One of your usual investigators isn't able to handle the case?"

"I suppose one could, but it seemed more perfectly suited to a man of your unique talents."

Joe sincerely doubted it, but skepticism wouldn't pay his bills. "I'm flattered." He opened the file, and studied the photos. The five ceramic pots were in a variety of shapes and sizes, all with an aqua glaze ranging from pale to a deep turquoise. The largest held a massive Boston fern.

"Dolan claims the collection of pots were worth more than the plants," Hal said.

"Mrs. Dolan went out to bring in the newspaper last week, and began screaming when she found the plants withering on the lawn and the pots gone. She upset the whole neighborhood, but no one had heard anything during the night."

"Pots that size must be heavy," Joe observed. "Probably more than a single man could handle, unless he used a dolly. Are any of the neighbors missing pots or plants?"

"None have reported it to the police. Dolan is retired, so you should be able to catch him at home this morning."

"I'll go there now." Joe was tempted to tell Hal about his puzzling visitor, but afraid he'd sound like an idiot, he didn't risk it.

The Dolans lived on San Pasquel Street, near Cal Tech, in Pasadena. It was a lovely tree-lined neighborhood. Even to Joe's unpracticed eye, the front porch of the two-story Craftsman home looked oddly bereft without their cherished potted plants.

Liam Dolan answered Joe's knock at the door and stepped outside when he saw the detective's California West identity card. "Glad you're here. The police took the information, but the officer responding clearly thought he ought to be working on more serious crimes. This theft is serious to us. I've got the plants temporarily stored in buckets in the backyard. I'll replanted them when we get the pots back, or are forced to buy new ones."

"I'm glad you were able to salvage the plants. California West doesn't require receipts, but it would be helpful if you had kept them for the pots."

"We bought them before the war, and can't keep track of everything we buy. Who does?" Tall and deeply tanned, he gestured with a sinewy grace. "They cost more than I'd wanted to spend, but I wouldn't disappoint my wife and not buy them. Are you married?"

"I will be right after Christmas." Joe couldn't wait to make Mary Margaret his wife, but he also understood how greatly his life would soon change.

Liam lowered his voice, "My dad gave me the secret to a happy marriage. Just never refuse your wife anything. It doesn't matter if she wants to go to Paris, and you have less than a hundred dollars in the bank. Just smile and tell her it's a terrific idea and ask her to help you save for the trip."

"Thanks. I'll remember that." Mary Margaret was a level-headed young woman who wouldn't have to be tricked into thinking she'd gotten her way when she hadn't. Rather than discuss the joys of marriage, however, he redirected his attention to the front of the house.

Steps led up to the long cement porch, and the missing pots and plants had provided a lush green frame for the front door. Five pale circular rings showed where they had stood, three on one side and two on the other. Joe walked down the brick steps to the front walk to get a better view.

"It's difficult to imagine how someone could dump the plants, lift the pots off the porch, and drive away without alerting you or your neighbors."

"It has us stumped too, but our bedroom is upstairs in the back. When I bought the pots, I carried them empty to the porch, set them where we intended them to be, and filled them with potting soil. I never tried to lift them after I added the plants, and they didn't dance around. They stayed put until last week."

Joe opened the file he carried to study the photos. "Those were such striking pots, you should be able to recognize them if they turn up elsewhere."

"I've driven around, but whoever took them must not be from around here. We bought them at the Bellefontaine Nursery. They came from New Mexico, and the artist's name, Joseph Blue Feather, is signed on the bottom. Maybe that's why he was partial to the color. The nursery might keep their records longer than we do. You want to go there?"

When Joe had murder suspects knocking on his door, a trip to the quiet serenity of a nursery posed a welcome diversion. "Sure, give me the address, and I'll follow you there."

* * *

Located on Fair Oaks in Pasadena, the Bellefontaine Nursery had a wide array of flowers, plants, vines, and small trees along with clerks who gave excellent gardening advice. Joe and Liam parked in the lot and made their way to the pottery shed. Joe waved down one of the clerks, and showed him the photo of Liam's porch.

"We're looking for something similar to these pots you once sold. Do you have any?" Joe asked.

The gray-haired man needed only a quick glimpse of the photo. "We used to carry those several years ago, and it's funny you should ask about them. A man came in on Saturday with one, said his grandmother had died, and he was cleaning up her house and yard before he sold the place."

"Did you take it?" Liam asked.

"I told him I was interested, but needed to talk to the boss first. Completely forgot about him until now. You want the guy's number?"

Joe smiled. "We sure do."

When the clerk led the way to the office, Liam whispered, "This was too easy."

"Don't get excited. From my experience, nothing is as easy as it first appears."

Liam nodded thoughtfully. "Yeah, that's often true. If the man who came here is trying to sell my pots, what are we going to do?"

The plan came easily to Joe. "We'll ask him to bring all the pots here. He might recognize you, so you'll have to stay out of sight. I'll pretend to be a landscaper working for an eccentric woman who wants nothing but blue pots for her garden. Size and shape won't matter, they just have to be blue. I'll take my time, and if they are your pots, call the police and let them handle the arrest. There's no need for us to confront the man ourselves."

"If they keep the pots as evidence," Liam complained, "I still won't have them."

It was an unnecessary complication as far as Joe was concerned. "Let's tackle one problem at a time."

The clerk plucked a scrap of paper from the bulletin board behind the telephone. "Said his name was Bob Rasmussen. You want to call him, or should I?"

Joe reached for the note. "I'll call him." The telephone rang so many times, Joe was ready to hang up when Rasmussen finally answered.

"What!" he barked.

"Mr. Rasmussen, I'm at the Bellefontaine Nursery. I'm a landscaper, and heard you have a blue pot I might be interested in buying."

"It ain't cheap," he warned gruffly.

"The cost isn't the issue." Joe gave him the story about the woman who demanded blue pots for her garden.

"I've got a mess of them here."

"Really? Would you bring them to the Bellefontaine Nursery? The owner is interested in buying any I don't want."

"That's a whole lot of trouble. You sure that's what the owner said?"

"I'll probably buy them all, but he's interested too. It will be well-worth your while."

After a long pause, Rasmussen agreed. "All right, I'll be there in half an hour."

Joe hung up and smiled. "We've baited the trap, let's see if he takes a bite. There's a good view from here in the office of the parking lot, Liam, and I'll make sure you can see the pots clearly."

In twenty minutes, a dusty Chevy pickup rolled into the parking lot. Bob Rasmussen unfolded himself from behind the wheel. He stood six feet five inches tall, and weighed two hundred seventy pounds on a well-muscled frame. With dark hair and a close-cropped beard, he reminded Joe of Bluto from the Popeye cartoons. He wasn't going to fight the man over the pots, but wearing a helmet for his jobs seemed like an increasingly good idea.

"Mr. Rasmussen," Joe called.

"Yeah, that's me." He stuck out his hand, and Joe's nearly disappeared in his. A tattoo of a hula dancer on the inside of Bob's right forearm swayed when they shook hands. "Come around to the back of the truck. I figure there's no reason to take them all out if they're not what you want."

Joe leaned over the tailgate. "They look good. Let's start with the smallest one."

Rasmussen had stored the pots in cardboard boxes and easily freed it, showing off the strength he'd used to soundlessly sweep the pots from the Dolans' porch.

It was heavier than Joe had anticipated, but he got a firm hold on it before he turned it to read the name inscribed on the bottom. Joseph was carved into the clay, underlined with a drawn feather and a touch of blue glaze. He set it down carefully. "I like it. Let's see the others."

"First, let's talk about money. Don't you want to know how much each one costs?"

"Of course, I do, but my client isn't all that concerned about money. She just wants what she wants, and that's it."

Unable to wait another minute, Liam walked up wearing a clerk's straw hat pulled low and a green Bellefontaine apron. "I don't want a bidding war, but I'd like to see the pots too."

Intrigued, a woman carrying a philodendron to her car, called to them. "Are you having a pot sale?" she asked.

Liam waved her away. "Sorry, it's not open to the public. Come by next week and see what we have that's new."

"All right, I will."

Liam had thrust himself in the middle of their plan, so Joe had to use him. "I understood I'd have the first chance with the pots."

"Sure, I'm just looking now," Liam assured him. He peered into the bed of the pickup, and then stepped back. "I like these a lot, but I have work to handle in the office before I can offer a bid."

"You can bid on whatever I don't want," Joe shouted after him.

Liam waved. "Fine."

"Would you unload them all so I could walk around them?" Joe asked. "It's difficult to judge their size otherwise."

Rasmussen plucked the tallest from his truck, and carefully placed it on the asphalt. "That's the largest. These others are medium sized."

Joe checked to be certain they all had Joseph Blue Feather's signature. Stalling for the police to arrive, he arranged them in several ways. "These are too nice a grouping to leave any behind. How much do you want for them all?"

Rasmussen leaned back against his truck and folded his arms over his broad chest. "Thirty bucks for the smallest, and fifty each for the other four."

"I'll give you two hundred for the lot," Joe countered. He'd stalled as long as he could, and was greatly relieved when a police car turned into the lot and pulled up behind Rasmussen's truck to block its exit.

Liam had been waiting for them, and quickly ran from the office. He pulled a photo of his porch complete with the potted plants from his shirt pocket. "Those are my pots. I filed a report of the theft last week."

"What is this?" Rasmussen hands curved into ham-sized fists. He took a menacing step toward Joe.

Joe grabbed the smallest pot, and stood ready to swing it in a slow arc into the bigger man's head. He hoped it wouldn't break, but he needed more than bare fists to defend himself against this brute.

"Back away, Rasmussen," one of the officers shouted.

"You know him?" Liam asked.

"We do. He'll steal anything that isn't nailed down, but this is the first time he's taken a fancy to pottery."

Joe didn't place the pot on the ground until Rasmussen had been handcuffed and forced into the backseat of the squad car. He whispered to Liam, "They don't have enough room to transport the pots, why don't you offer to take them home where they belong? I have a camera to take photos they can use in court."

Liam removed the straw hat and apron, and after a quick discussion with the officers, he smiled and turned to Joe. "It's fine with them. Were you really going to defend yourself with the small pot? It's my wife's favorite."

"It was the only thing handy, and California West would have replaced it if it had been broken." He waited until the squad car had driven away to fetch the camera. He posed the pots with the nursery sign behind them, and the pickup's license plate in view. He took several photos and promised a set for Liam.

Once the pots were carefully stowed in the trunk and rear seat of Liam's Packard sedan, Joe shook his hand and counted his case closed. What he needed now was lunch, and for some reason, a large green salad sounded particularly appealing.

CHAPTER 14

Monday afternoon, Joe called Mrs. Navarro. She did not want a report over the telephone, and appeared in his office an hour later. Joe had coffee ready and the new magazine for her chauffeur. He smiled and hoped the visit would go better than he feared it would.

"You were interested in how your grandson spent his time," he began.

"I already know that," she responded with a quick flip of her wrist. "What evidence did you gather to prove he's amounted to nothing?"

After Constance had praised his work and given a referral, it would be unprofessional to return Mrs. Navarro's retainer and show her the door. However, he was sorely tempted. "I drove by your grandson's home and found him working on a car in his driveway."

"Did you take a photograph so I can show him I know all he does is waste his time?"

He handed her one of Timothy and his friend with their heads under the hood of the old jalopy. "I spoke with your grandson that afternoon. He's bright, and impressed me with his ambition. He's restoring old cars and selling them for a profit."

"That isn't a job for a well-educated man," she replied. She studied the photo, promptly dismissed it, and slapped it on Joe's desk.

"That's a matter of perception," Joe argued. "People will always do better when they are employed doing something they enjoy. Many veterans are using the GI Bill to pay for college, and younger men like your grandson may feel intimidated. It could be a factor in his uncertain focus."

"So what? He should work harder rather than repeatedly shift majors."

Joe rocked back in his chair. "He's young, and may need more time to mature than his sister. He did tell me he's dating a young woman who attends USC. She has to be a good influence."

Mrs. Navarro stared at him. "I'm paying for your time, why are you taking Timothy's side?"

She had him there. "It's an effort to help you resolve your differences. Timothy is a capable young man, and while he's not on the path you'd choose, it doesn't mean he won't be successful in life."

Her eyes narrowed as she swept his small office with a critical eye. "Are your parents proud of you?"

"They're no longer living, but yes, they were enormously proud of me and supportive of everything I wished to do."

She grabbed the photo, rose, and turned toward the door. "This has been a complete waste of my time and money."

Joe stood, took out his wallet, and handed her a refund. "I'm sorry not to have pleased you, Mrs. Navarro." He opened the door for her, and the chauffeur leaped to his feet.

"Excellent magazine," the man remarked. He handed it to Joe along with the empty cup.

"Thank you, I'm glad you liked it."

Mrs. Navarro shoved the cash Joe had given her into her purse, took the chauffeur's arm, and left without bothering to say good-bye.

Still on her nephew's side, Joe made a few notes in the Navarro file, counted the case closed, and filed it.

With that unpleasantness out of the way, he called Hal to relate his success with the Dolan case. "The police arrested the culprit, the Dolans have their pots, and Liam thought he might be able to reuse the original plants."

"You solved the case in a single day?" Hal asked.

Joe couldn't blame him for being incredulous. "It wasn't difficult. If you like, I'll take longer the next time you pass along a case."

"No, wrap them up as quickly as you can. I'll put your check in the afternoon mail to save you a trip downtown."

"Thank you, as always it's a pleasure to work for California West." It was certainly a lot more pleasant than dealing with Mrs. Navarro.

He checked his calendar. Thanksgiving was Thursday, and Mary Margaret was looking forward to celebrating the holiday with the other residents of the Chrysanthemum Court. He'd met them all working on Georgia Dixon's murder. He ought to bring something to the party, and he leaned back in his chair, propped his feet on his desk and wondered what he could possibly contribute.

A knock on the door brought him upright. "Come in."

Marty Streech peered in. "It was so quiet, I doubted you were here."

Joe had forgotten to turn on his new radio. "Come on in. What's new?"

"Someone has been following me." He took one of the chairs facing the desk. "I must have stepped on the wrong toes interviewing people for my stories, and I need you to discover who it is before they turn violent."

They weren't close friends, but Joe admired the reporter's perseverance. He picked up a pencil and yellow pad to take notes. "When did it begin?"

"Over the weekend. I'd been out running errands, and when I saw the same car, a gray four-door DeSoto, multiple times, I became suspicious."

"Did you see the driver?"

"No, and when I parked in the lot at the hardware store. I turned back, and saw he'd parked two spaces away. I watched from the front window, and after half an hour, no one had returned to the DeSoto. I left and drove around the block. The DeSoto was gone when I rolled through the parking lot the second time. On my way home, I saw it a couple of cars behind me. I pulled over, and he drove by me. He turned right at the corner, went around the block, and came up behind me again."

"Have you received any threatening letters in the mail?"

"I've gotten plenty over the years, but not lately. I've no idea who it could be, that's why I want you to follow him and discover who he is and what he wants. He followed me to the *LA Examiner* office this morning."

"Did he follow you here?" Joe asked.

"I didn't see him, but that doesn't mean he wasn't there. I've told everyone I've spoken to that I need information on the Black Dahlia's killer. If my questions have reached him, he might be following me."

Last January's gruesome murder of Elizabeth Short, called the Black Dahlia, had been the subject of many of their conversations. "He'd be dangerous in the extreme," Joe replied. "He'd attack you when you least expected it rather than follow you and risk being sighted. Have you considered going to the police?"

Marty brushed his hair off his forehead with splayed fingers. "I've criticized the police for not solving the crime, so they'd laugh at me. Which I'd probably deserve."

Joe got up to look out the window, and found a four-door gray DeSoto parked across the street. "Come here."

Marty came up behind him, and Joe moved out of his way. "Is that the car?"

"Sure looks like it. Maybe I should go out the back door and take the bus home."

"That shouldn't be necessary. I recently met a man who raises Doberman Pinschers. Have you considered owning a guard dog?"

Marty scoffed, "What would I do with him when I go out on interviews or work at the office?"

"Leave him at home. Have you considered whoever is driving the car might have information for a story? He could be building up the nerve to approach you."

"Or kill me." Marty returned his chair. "Is there any coffee in the pot?"

Joe poured him a cup. "Enjoy that, while I go across the street to see who the owner of the DeSoto might be."

"Just like that, go ask him?"

"Yeah, if he points a gun at me, I'll call the police on him. If he doesn't, I'll find out why he's there."

The telephone rang before he could step out of his office. "Discreet Investigations."

"It's Mary Margaret. We didn't have plans for tonight, but will you please come by for dinner? We've something important to discuss."

She sounded badly troubled, which worried him. "Do you want to give me a hint?"

"No, I don't dare. See you later."

Joe hung up, and shrugged. "Looks like my fiancée has a problem. I'll make short work of yours first." Without intending to, he'd looked fierce in *Arizona Sunrise*. If he were going to be called an actor, practice should help him refine his modicum of talent.

Marty got up to look out the window. "Get his license plate number so we can file a police report if we need to."

"Sure." Joe crossed the street with the light at the corner, pulled out the notebook and pen he carried and did just that before approaching the car. The driver was watching the drugstore in Joe's building and didn't notice him until he swung open the passenger side door and looked in.

Joe pitched his voice low, "You ought to keep your doors locked so strangers don't accost you on the street."

The driver was a husky fellow with an odd assortment of features, none of them handsome, which created a perfect face for a villainous cartoon character. As he spoke, his mouth twisted into a downward snarl. "Get out of here!"

"You're following a friend of mine, and he doesn't care for your company."

"Who are you, his secretary?"

"You might call me that. If you want to talk to Mr. Streech, he can be reached at the *LA Examiner*."

"Clacking typewriters give me headaches."

The man certainly didn't look delicate, and Joe pressed him further. "Why don't we go across the street and have a cup of coffee at the drugstore counter. I'll relay your message to Mr. Streech, and if he's interested, he'll set up a meeting."

"Do they have tea?"

Joe had seen women order it. "Yes, they do." This guy had proved to be as terrifying as a cream puff. Nothing is at it seems, he reminded himself, and didn't take his eyes off him as they crossed the street. The man was both tall and broad, the type his mother would have referred to as a galoot.

They took stools at the counter near the front windows. "How's the pie here?" the man asked.

"Very good," Joe answered, although he doubted he'd had more than a single slice.

The waitress at the counter approached them. "Did I hear someone mention pie? A pastry chef who sells only to us delivers fresh pies every morning. What's your pleasure, cherry, berry, or apple with a scoop of vanilla ice cream?"

"Cherry," the man answered. "With hot tea."

"You got it, hon. What can I bring you, Joe?"

"Just coffee, thanks." He waited for her to walk to the far end of the counter to fetch the pie. "Let's talk now, while we won't be overheard."

After a long hesitation, the man asked, "Have you heard of Howard Hughes?"

"Who hasn't? Did you see the Spruce Goose when he flew it?"

"November 2, this year, it was. I'll not forget the date. I helped to build it, and heard a lot of stories about Mr. Hughes. Stories I figure someone would pay to know, but I won't say my name and have Hughes fire me."

Joe couldn't fault his discretion. "I can't speak for Mr. Streech." He sat back when the waitress brought their orders. The pie did look awfully good, but he'd not spoil his appetite for Mary Margaret's always fine dinner. "How long have you worked for Hughes?"

"A couple of years." He paused to add sugar to his cup of tea and to savor the pie. "We aren't close buddies, but I saw and heard a lot that should interest curious people."

Howard Hughes being such a flamboyant figure, Joe understood completely. "If you'll stay right where you are, I'll contact Mr. Streech, and see if he's interested."

He raised his hand to promise. "I won't move."

Joe went up to his office and found Marty pacing. "The guy thinks you'd be interested in information about Howard Hughes, but he didn't want to go to your office."

"You're kidding me," Marty exclaimed.

"No, and that's not a story I'd even think of. He's eating a piece of cherry pie at the end of the drugstore counter. Want to come down and meet him?"

Marty didn't need to think long. "I should before he gives the story to someone else."

"I'll walk you downstairs, but I'm leaving you two there."

"Fine, lead the way. I won't forget this, Joe. Do I owe you something?"

"Not today, but the next time you need a detective, I'll give you a bill."

"Fair enough."

Joe left when Marty was seated beside the man. The fellow didn't want to be identified as the source of the story, but what would Hughes's reaction be should the *LA Examiner* publish it? Marty was smart enough to anticipate the problems even if he couldn't avoid them.

Worried Mary Margaret had received some disheartening news, Joe stopped by the flower shop close to his home and bought a bouquet of fresh flowers. It was a mere token, but he hoped it would raise her spirits. He smiled as he knocked on her door, but when it was opened by a red-haired woman rather than his beloved, he knew exactly who she must be.

"Mrs. McBride!" he exclaimed. She was as petite as her daughter, and he leaned down to kiss her cheek. "How wonderful it is to meet you."

She didn't move out of the doorway until her daughter took her arm to nudge her aside. "This is Joe, Mama. Do you want him to call you Matilda?"

"Mrs. McBride will do," she replied, with a mortician's lack of humor.

Joe ignored her icy mood, and kept smiling. "You'll be a great help to Mary Margaret with plans for the wedding." He handed his beloved the bouquet.

"I'll put these in a vase," she answered and made a quick dash for the kitchen.

Rather than make another effort at conversation, Joe waited for his future mother-in-law to speak. She looked more likely to growl. He gestured toward the sofa, and she sat at the end. He took the armchair opposite her.

"I didn't care for your movie. It was too violent for my tastes."

He'd had only a couple of lines and couldn't claim the film as his own. "I know exactly what you mean. Westerns often have too much gunplay. I prefer films with humor myself."

She nodded. "Well, at least you're better looking than I first thought."

"Thank you," he replied, uncertain if she'd actually paid him a compliment. "Did you come on the train?"

"Yes, with beautiful scenery along the way, it was a more pleasant trip than I had anticipated."

She seemed to always expect the worst, and with her husband's sudden death in 1945, he couldn't blame her. "I'm looking forward to seeing the coast when Mary Margaret and I travel to Seattle." After several minutes of strained conversation, he was relieved when Mary Margaret called them to dinner.

With her mother's attentive assistance, Mary Margaret had made meatloaf with mashed potatoes, and green beans. The dinner was delicious, but Joe struggled to swallow. Mrs. McBride's frosty gaze focused on him each time he raised his fork, as though he were displaying a shocking lack of manners. When he glanced down at his plate, there seemed to be more food waiting, and he feared dinner might never end.

"Will you be able to stay for Thanksgiving?" he asked.

"Of course. I'd not come this far and then turn right around and go home. My daughter, Rose, will have the rest of the family to her home for Thanksgiving dinner."

Joe's smile grew increasingly shaky, and his cheeks began to ache. "Wonderful. Being here will give you a chance to meet Mary Margaret's neighbors." He wondered if Patrick Wood, the widower in cottage three, could be persuaded to keep Matilda company. He might be a few years older, but it would be for only a single afternoon, not a lifetime.

There was ice cream for dessert, which Joe welcomed gladly, then as gracefully as he could manage, he bid them good night. "It was so nice to meet you, Mrs. McBride. I know Mary Margaret needs to be at work early, so I'll leave for home. I'm looking forward to Thursday. Is there something I can bring?"

Mary Margaret took his arm and ushered him toward the door. "I always forget the relishes, you know, carrots, celery, olives? Could you do that? I have a dish for them."

He owned a peeler, even if it had been awhile since he had used it. "Sure, I'll bring them." He pulled her out the door to kiss her goodnight.

"My mother can be a real pill. Was she too awful?" she whispered.

Another kiss answered her question. "As long as you love me, she can be a whole bottleful."

"Oh, Joe. I can always count on you to say the right thing." She slipped back inside, and Joe left without attempting to overhear when her mother might say something he wouldn't want to take in.

The lights were still on in Patrick Wood's cottage, and Joe knocked softly on the door. Quite naturally, Patrick was surprised to see him. A slender man with thick gray hair, he had a friendly smile. "Mr. Ezell, come in. What can I do for you this evening?"

A grandfather clock dominated the room, but Joe understood its chime comforted the watchmaker. "Mary Margaret's mother is visiting from Seattle for Thanksgiving. I wondered if you could make a point of speaking with her."

"It will be a pleasure. Are you asking everyone to do the same?"

Joe immediately saw the need to do so. "Your lights were on, and I'm beginning with you, but I'll certainly encourage everyone to be charming. Matilda is a widow, and clearly needs more attention than she receives at home. You needn't attach yourself to her, just be friendly."

Patrick straightened up. "I doubt I have much in the way of charm, but I'll give it a try for Mary Margaret's sake."

"Thank you so much."

Daniel and Patty Hill in cottage two had a new baby, and he bypassed their home to stop at number one. Phyllis and John Cameron, an elderly couple, were always eager to entertain.

"I'll take them some scones tomorrow morning," Phyllis volunteered. "If Mary Margaret is at work, I'll invite her mother to come visit with us."

"Thank you, that would be so kind." He left before they could ask him to stay awhile and went home feeling better about the prospects for Thanksgiving. He could count on Luke Hatcher to be friendly, and he'd introduce Matilda to the other two couples living on Chrysanthemum Courts on Thursday.

Once home, Joe kicked off his shoes and sat down in his only arm chair. Attempting to impress Matilda had completely worn him out, but he had fared better than he'd feared. When the telephone rang, he hoped it wouldn't be Mary Margaret in tears, but it was Constance Remson.

"I want to host a small cocktail party on Wednesday evening and invite anyone who could possibly be a suspect. I'll include some others from the symphony so our motive won't be obvious, other than to remember Matteo. We won't be following a movie script, but I really feel we should try to shake out the murderess."

After the night he'd had, he welcomed the diversion. "All right, I'll call the women I've spoken to about Matteo. Will you ask Sean Dermot to bring Veronica?"

"Yes, they're on my list. Bring your girlfriend. I'd like to meet her."

"Her mother is in town, so…."

"Bring her too, there's plenty of room, and we never run out of booze, which makes for the perfect party."

"Fine, I'll ask them both, and let the others I've spoken with know." As he hung up, he feared Matilda would refuse to attend a party full of strangers and make Mary Margaret feel so guilty about leaving her mother at home alone she wouldn't go either.

Tuesday evening, Joe told Mary Margaret about Constance's party. Her eyes lit with glee. "This is just what I wanted, a party like the one in *Song of the Thin Man*! This will be so exciting, Mother, and Joe might even unmask a murderess. You'll come with us, won't you?"

Matilda raked Joe with a skeptical glance, and then smiled. "I wouldn't miss it."

Wednesday evening, the stately Remson home was brightly lit with a welcoming party glow. Red-jacketed valets met those arriving, and Joe handed over his keys. He helped Matilda from the car, Mary Margaret had insisted her mother ride in the front seat. He'd expected them to be impressed by the Remson estate, but other than smile, they didn't react with astonishment or even mild surprise.

Constance stood just inside the front door in a stylish black dress, ready for an evening that would include a memorial to Matteo. Joe introduced his guests, and she responded with an enthusiastic grasp of their hands. "It's so nice to meet you two. Joe is such a resourceful detective, I've come to rely on him."

Mary Margaret reacted with a slightly raised brow. While Joe often told her about his cases, he withheld the names and descriptions of his clients. Perhaps he should have mentioned Constance was an attractive young woman before they'd arrived. It was too late to remedy the omission now. Instead, he led them into the living room, where twenty early guests were gathered. A string trio grouped by the baby grand piano were playing charming classical melodies.

Paloma Val Verde smiled as she approached them. She'd chosen a black dress, another from a Mexican boutique on Olvera Street. The bodice and sleeves were embroidered with colorful flowers. She'd piled her hair atop her head and added fresh roses in her customary tribute to her idol, Frida Kahlo.

Joe introduced Paloma as an artist, and was grateful when Matilda inquired about her work, because the young woman could talk about art for hours. A waiter came by to take drink orders, and another soon passed by with sumptuous hors d'oeuvres.

Gunnar Ingvild was easily the tallest man in the room. When the conductor turned away from the fireplace, an easel holding a large portrait of Matteo da Milano dominated the front of the room. Lily Montell stood beside it. In one of her lily-splashed dresses, she looked her elegant self. She caught Joe's eye and nodded a silent greeting.

Andrea Donovan, the pretty blonde from Mildred Street in Venice Beach, headed for Joe as soon as she stepped into the living room. In a tailored black suit, Joe bet her sister wore to the bank, and her roots newly bleached, she appeared to be a competent professional. He introduced her.

"Joe is the only one I know here. I wanted to come, but this isn't what I expected."

"How so?" Mary Margaret asked.

"It's a party, and I thought it would be a more respectful gathering. We're here to remember Matteo, aren't we?"

"Yes, but Miss Remson has her own way of doing things," Joe remarked, and Mary Margaret responded with a questioning glance. Andrea was cute, but he thought it must have been the mention of Constance that had bothered his fiancée. He anticipated a long conversation about the evening later, and he'd rely on truthful, innocent explanations.

"How are things going for you, Andrea?" he asked.

"Pretty good, actually. I've been to one interview at the bank where my sister works, and I go back for the second one next Tuesday. Once we had a reliable babysitter for Daniel, I didn't waste a minute sitting around at home." She turned to Paloma. "That is such a beautiful dress."

"Thank you, I'm an artist, and love colorful clothes."

Paloma drew Andrea into her conversation with Matilda, and Mary Margaret stepped to Joe's other side. "It looks as though there's a lot about your cases you aren't telling me," she whispered.

"I never bore you with tedious details." He hoped she'd let him off with that, and then Lily joined them.

She extended her hand to Mary Margaret. "I'm Lily Montell."

When she didn't add more, Joe introduced his fiancée. "The last time we spoke you mentioned possibly going to college."

"I did, but I still can't decide upon a major."

"Have you considered nursing?" Mary Margaret asked.

Lily certainly possessed the talent to cheer up patients as no other nurse would, and Joe left them to discuss the benefits of a nursing career. He edged his way around the increasingly crowded room. He thought the serious looking men were probably from the LA Philharmonic. He approached one such fellow and woman standing in the corner, introduced himself and asked how they knew Matteo.

"I play the oboe in the orchestra and knew him well," the man offered. His wife, an attractive brunette, rolled her eyes.

Joe remembered her from the tea, but she hadn't said much when he'd joined her table. "I've heard nothing but compliments for his talent as a cellist, but away from the Philharmonic, he appears to have been a different man."

"Not entirely," the oboist said. "Many talented men feel the world rotates around them, and Matteo was no exception."

"Men weren't jealous enough to kill him," his wife stressed. "One of his numerous affairs must have proven fatal."

"It looks that way." Joe excused himself to speak with others. He saw Suzanne Ritter across the room. He'd made a point of inviting her, and she'd come in a burgundy hued suit that nearly matched her hair, and black stiletto heels. He glanced over his shoulder to be certain Mary Margaret and Matilda remained in conversation with Paloma, Andrea, and Lily.

When he'd taken Mary Margaret to Sherry's, they hadn't seen Lily's striptease act, and he doubted Lily would reveal her current employment tonight. At least he hoped not when thick black smoke would surely spew from Matilda's cute little ears.

"Mr. Ezell." Suzanne had made her way to him before he could reach her. "People aren't speaking the truth about Matteo, unless they're whispering under their breath. Can't anyone bear to be honest about him?"

"Not at a memorial," Joe countered. "Since talking with you, I've often thought of his love of milkshakes. Were you the one who owned the blender?"

"Yes. Matteo had absolutely no talent in the kitchen." She smiled slyly. "No one held it against him though."

She took a sip of her drink and licked her lips. "Who is the tall fellow?"

"Gunnar Ingvild, a visiting conductor with the LA Philharmonic."

"Excuse me, I just developed a new interest in the orchestra, and should introduce myself."

She left him with a provocative sway. She'd been on the suspect list, but if she'd killed Matteo, she would be too preoccupied covering her own guilt to be drawn to another man at a memorial for the cellist. She was another woman he hoped Mary Margaret wouldn't meet.

Constance appeared, took his arm, and nodded toward the study. "Come with me."

He followed her into the book-lined room. She shut the door, and leaned back against it. "What do you think? Has anyone caught your interest who hadn't before tonight?"

"Not yet, but I'm doing my best. Only one young woman, Tanya Olson, who lives in Matteo's Almont building, said she really didn't know Matteo well enough to come tonight. She may have had the opportunity, but no motive, so she wasn't a serious suspect anyway. Is Veronica da Milano here? I need to speak with her."

"She arrived a few minutes ago with Sean Dermot. He's clearly in love with her, but she barely notices him. Poor guy. Do you suppose he has the patience to wait for her to get over Matteo?"

"He may, or may not, I don't make any predictions when it comes to love."

"That's very wise." Constance answered a soft knock at the door, and Gunnar looked in.

"Is anything wrong?" he asked.

"Of course, not, darling. Joe and I were just having a little chat." She left with the conductor, and Joe followed. They were a striking couple, and clearly Gunner was drawn to sophisticated women. Joe wondered how happy Constance would be in Norway, but she could certainly afford to purchase a lovely fur coat.

Veronica had told him she no longer owned the fur coat and hat similar to the mystery woman's. Now he was curious as to what she'd done with them. He had to wiggle through the guests to reach her. She stood at Matteo's portrait, regarding it with a fond glance, while Sean concentrated on the crowd.

Joe found an open place by her side. "This may seem to be a strange question, but you mentioned the fur coat and hat you no longer owned. Do you recall what you did with them?"

She wore a black jersey sheath dress that hugged her slender figure and complimented her fair hair. Even with exquisitely applied cosmetics, she appeared desperately sad.

"Well, yes and no. They were in my hall closet in this fall, and then they weren't. My maid has been with me for several years, and wouldn't steal my things, but if a burglar broke in, they were all he took."

Expensive clothing didn't just disappear, unless someone planned to use them, perhaps to trick Matteo into welcoming them into his home. "Do you remember when you last wore them?" Joe asked.

She turned to Sean. "When you were in New York in October, do you recall if I wore my sable coat and hat the day you took me to lunch?"

Sean closed his eyes a moment and rocked back on his heels. "I believe you did, and they were lovely with your fair coloring. Why do you ask?"

"Just following loose threads," Joe responded. Whoever had picked the lock on his office, could have gotten into Veronica's home just as easily and taken her fur coat and hat. Had Matteo's murder been planned a month ago?

"Have any of your New York friends moved to Los Angeles or come here to visit in the last month?" he asked.

Veronica took a sip of her drink. "No, my New York friends prefer the East coast to California. I don't have any friends here, other than you, Sean. I don't know what I'd do without you."

Sean blushed. "I'm so sorry for the reason you need me, but it's been a pleasure."

Joe couldn't bear to watch Sean drool over Veronica. "Excuse me, I need to check on my fiancée and her mother." Paloma was still entertaining them, and a cluster of others, with a description of a recent art exhibit at the gallery showing her birdhouse paintings.

Mary Margaret stepped close to Joe. "This is a most interesting crowd. Have you discovered anything promising?"

"If I have, I haven't figured it out yet."

The waiters brought in folding chairs, and with Constance's subtle urging, her guests found seats. Gunnar moved to Matteo's portrait. "I'll always remember Matteo's incredible talent. He seized each piece of music with a passion that will forever set him apart. He added to the great privilege I've enjoyed conducting the Los Angeles Philharmonic, where all the members are exceedingly fine musicians."

On the edge of the crowd, Joe eased from his chair to take a place where he could keep an eye on all the guests. It wouldn't matter if the killer did no more than twitch, he'd notice. Constance followed Gunnar and spoke for the Philharmonic board.

"We have so many talented musicians here tonight. I'd love to hear your stories about Matteo, as you would have known him best." After charming coaxing, the oboist spoke, and other members of the orchestra followed. Some shared amusing anecdotes, while others praised Matteo's generosity. Apparently the cellist had helped several men with loans when their family desperately needed one.

Sean held Veronica's hand, but he didn't rise to speak. He had not spoken at the reception after the funeral either. He'd described Matteo as a close friend, but being so devoted to Veronica, Joe wondered if any praise he might give the late cellist would sound insincere.

None of the women present praised Matteo for reasons other than his musical talent. It may have been discretion, or self-preservation. Joe could easily imagine a tacky scene with spitted insults as to whom Matteo had loved the most. Constance wouldn't abide such an unseemly display, but he could not help but smile at the thought.

At the end of the spoken memories, Constance again moved to the front of the room. "Thank you all for coming tonight. Please stay as long as you wish, and we'll call it an early Christmas party."

Gunnar moved to the piano to create a festive start and with the string trio began *Deck the Halls With Boughs of Holly.* Andrea and Paloma leaned on the baby grand and sang along. The waiters removed most of the folding chairs, and returned carrying trays with tiny cream puffs and crystal flutes of champagne.

Disappointed he'd learned nothing of real value, Joe focused again on Sean and Veronica. Despite the praise for her late ex-husband, she looked no happier than when she had arrived. Sean moved close, dipped his head to speak with her, and Joe was struck by how gracefully the man moved. They were both slender, and nearly the same height. With a sudden smack of the obvious, he knew who had murdered Matteo da Milano.

CHAPTER 15

Mary Margaret stood close by. Joe took her hand, and led her into the adjoining study. He closed the door to assure their privacy. "I have an idea, please hear me out before you comment."

She leaned against the desk, raised a finger to her lips, and nodded.

"We already knew Sean Dermot had powerful motives for murder. He's in love with Veronica, and if Matteo were out of the way, he may have believed she would fall into his arms. Matteo's Stradivarius cello would have sweetened their romance. He must also have expected to take Matteo's place with the Philharmonic.

"My mistake was in believing Sean must have had an accomplice if he were behind the murder. We all thought a woman had killed Matteo, but that's what the murderer planned for witnesses to see. Sean visited Veronica in October. He could have taken her fur coat and hat to use as a disguise. Matteo would have recognized them, and believed Veronica had come on a surprise visit. He would have welcomed his caller in, and death quickly followed."

"It's logical," Mary Margaret agreed softly, as though they were exchanging dangerous secrets. "But why would Sean attack with a stiletto heel rather than a knife or gun?"

"To make it look as though a woman had killed Matteo, so there would be so many suspects no one would consider him a threat. I noted the ungainly way the fur-swathed woman nearly ran in stilettos, but it didn't occur to me the murderer would be a man unused to wearing high heels. Sean would have tossed the bloody stilettos, but he kept Veronica's fur coat and hat and wore them to visit me."

"Why would he have kept them?"

"They belonged to the woman he adores, and probably still have the scent of her perfume. I'll ask Constance to keep Sean and Veronica here after everyone else leaves."

"What will you do? He'll never admit to killing Matteo."

"Something will occur to me."

She rested her hands on her hips. "We need a better plan than that."

"You're right, of course, but trust me. I can see it all coming together in my mind. Just keep your mother safe if the evening ends in a wild fist fight."

She straightened up. "Is there a risk of that happening?"

"I plan to corner the murderer, and he might fight back. Gunnar will be on our side, and that's a big plus."

"I'll say." She led the way from the study, reached for a champagne flute on a passing waiter's tray, and turned to toast him. "I know you'll make me proud."

Joe appreciated the encouragement, but she might be stretching it a bit.

Constance had produced a book of Christmas piano music for Gunnar, the strings followed along, and the holiday party lasted far longer than Joe had anticipated. He thought over what he wished to say, and analyzed how the clues he had strung together pointed directly to Sean Dermot. Accusing him of murder would again shatter Veronica's heart, but there was no way to shelter her from the truth. Sean had offered such tender sympathy, but it wasn't nearly enough to erase his guilt.

Near midnight, the waiters switched from serving champagne to hot chocolate and coffee. Matilda was yawning openly, but Mary Margaret urged her to stay awake just a little while longer.

Constance circled the room, first thanking the Philharmonic members, and then the women Joe had invited to come, guiding them toward the front door. With Gunnar's help, Veronica and Sean remained later than the others. They sat close together on the sofa, holding hands.

"I didn't think I could ever attend another party," Veronica murmured. "Maybe it was the Christmas music, but I feel better than I have in many days."

"How sweet of you to say so," Constance sat down beside her. Gunnar stood behind the sofa, close enough to lend Joe support if need be.

Mary Margaret and her mother found chairs, and perhaps hoping to be the last to leave, Paloma Val Verde sat near them. Despite the lateness of the hour, the roses in her hair were still fresh.

Joe pulled up a chair, closing the circle of remaining guests. "Thank you, Constance, this has been a wonderful evening, but your guests were invited under false pretenses."

"Weren't we here to remember Matteo?" Paloma asked.

"Yes, of course, you were," Joe replied. "But the real purpose of tonight, was to discover who wanted him dead."

Veronica gasped and sat forward. "You've discovered who she is?"

Joe nodded. "I believe I have, but the photograph I showed everyone of someone fleeing Matteo's apartment house convinced us all a woman had killed him. It was what the murderer wished us to believe. After a careful investigation, I've come to the conclusion it was a man wearing stilettos and your fur coat and hat."

"My furs?" Veronica appeared bewildered. She clutched Sean's hand. "How did they come to be here in Los Angeles rather than in my closet?"

"A man you knew visited New York. He took them while you were out, and brought them here. He also picked the lock on my office door. He took cards with suspects' names, which I quickly replaced, but in doing so, he gave himself away for the burglary at your home."

Sean's expression hadn't changed. He appeared interested in Joe's commentary, but if he felt threatened, he hid it well. "You're seeing all this in the photo you showed us?"

"Yes. It's like working a jigsaw puzzle when you lack the picture on the lid of the box. When you get enough of the pieces together, you recognize what it is."

"I'll never wear another fur," Veronica murmured.

"I don't blame you," Constance agreed. "What more have you discovered, Joe?"

He stood, and moved behind his chair. "Premeditated murders are committed for a variety of reasons, financial gain, or just plain greed. Sometimes it's to hide a dangerous secret. A fierce rivalry can erupt between former friends, let's say over whose name goes on a patent for an invention. A lust for revenge can lead to murder. Jealousy is also a powerful motive, especially in a contest for a woman's love."

"I hate to say this in front of you, Veronica," Sean began, "but Matteo was involved with so many women, there must be dozens of men who wanted to eliminate him as a rival for their sweetheart or wife's love."

"But how many had access to Veronica's coat and hat?" Matilda asked.

"Excellent question," Joe complimented. "Her furs were purposely used to fool Matteo. If he had any time to think after the first blow, he must have thought Veronica wished him dead."

"Oh no," Veronica cried. "I loved him dearly, and I'd never hurt him." A fresh flood of tears welled up in her eyes.

Joe waited for her to realize Sean had been in New York the last time she'd worn her furs, and whether it was professional jealousy, or a desperate love for her, he had multiple motives for murder. Instead, she went off on a tangent.

"I refuse to believe I'm in any way involved in my darling Matteo's death. Maybe someone stole my furs to trick him, but it couldn't have had anything to do with me. I don't care whether it was a man, or a woman in the photograph, I just want to go home."

Sean rose and offered Veronica his hand. "Thank you, Miss Remson, up until the last few minutes, this has been a wonderful evening. Thank you for inviting us."

Constance walked them to the door, and quickly returned to the living room. "Has Sean been in New York recently?"

"In October, when Veronica's furs went missing," Joe confirmed.

"Sean killed Matteo?" Paloma leaped from her chair. "Why didn't you keep him here and call the police?"

"They prefer evidence to theories, no matter how logical," Joe responded.

"Veronica may be oblivious, but if Sean still has her furs, he'll get rid of them tonight," Mary Margaret surmised.

"Constance, do you have home addresses for members of the Philharmonic?" Joe asked.

"As a matter of fact I do. Let me get them." She hurried into the study and returned with several neatly typed pages. "I have these to mail the board's holiday cards."

Joe thanked her. "Sean will take Veronica home first, so if we hurry, we can reach his place first. He won't be able to toss out any evidence tying him to the murder without our seeing him do so. Why don't you come with me, Gunnar? Mary Margaret, will you please call a taxi to take you and your mother home. How did you get here, Paloma?"

"In a taxi, but I don't want to be left out."

Constance stepped forward. "I don't want to be left out either. If Paloma comes with me, we can also watch Sean's apartment building. We can take the front entrance while you and Gunnar watch the back."

"I don't want to go home now the evening has gotten so exciting," Matilda declared. "Let's go with them, Mary Margaret."

"I don't need to be asked twice," she answered.

"Yes, do come with us," Constance invited.

Joe shook his head. "That's a really bad idea, but I don't have time to argue with you. Sean's address looks like an apartment building. When we get there, we can decide who parks where and what signals we might use."

"We understand," Mary Margaret promised. "What if Sean carries out a bag, puts it in his car trunk, and drives off? Shouldn't we all follow him?"

"Let's work on our strategy once we get there," Joe stressed.

Constance took another look at the address list. "I know the street, and we're only a few minutes away."

One of the valets was still working, and he brought Joe's car to the front right away. Joe tipped him and got behind the wheel.

"I'd really hoped the evening would end differently."

Gunnar moved back the front passenger seat to allow room for his long legs. "I've found people tend to be unpredictable. That's why we rehearse every piece of music until we can nearly play it backwards. Sean may have had a motive," he added, "but he's such a mild-mannered man, it's difficult to imagine him pulling off a murder. How do you know the furs the murderer wore were Veronica's?"

"I've no facts to back it up, but when I showed people the photo, those who knew Veronica thought it was her. So Matteo must have too."

"Clearly the murder was no sudden impulse."

"No, indeed. That's Sean's apartment building on the corner, and it has a parking lot. I'll park across the street where we'll have a good view of it and the rear entrance."

"Which apartment is his?"

"Number 3. If I can get in, I'll check where it is."

"Better hurry."

"Sean would stay a while at Veronica's to console her, so there should be time to scout the place."

Joe found the front door of the brick building unlatched. Perhaps a careless resident had left, or come home, without making certain the door was locked. Whichever, it worked to his advantage. Apartment three was at the rear corner facing the parking lot. There was a rear door, but before he could reach it, he heard the front door swing open. It could have been any of the building's residents coming home, but the way his luck was running that night, it had to be Sean.

The stairway to the second floor occupied the center of the building, and Joe quickly stepped around it to hide in front of apartment four. His navy blue suit blended into the shadows cast by the dim hallway lights.

A woman giggled, and as she and her male companion made their way up the stairs, he whispered an urgent plea for silence. Joe waited until the sound of their footsteps receded in the upstairs hallway. The backdoor was nearest to apartment three, and he wondered whether Sean routinely used it when he came home. Even if he did, there would be more places to hide outdoors than there were in the shadowy hallway.

The backdoor opened with a gentle touch to insure a safe emergency exit. Before Joe could run across the street to his Chevy, bright headlights swept across the building as a car pulled into the parking lot. Joe ducked, and afraid of being seen, he hurried down the alley to a conveniently placed row of trashcans. He breathed deeply to slow his thundering heart, and waited in the dark while a man used his key to open the rear door, and entered. Recognizing Sean, Joe straightened up, and after several more steadying breaths, he hurried back to his car.

Mary Margaret was crouched behind his Chevy. She whispered, "You scared me to death! I thought Sean would catch you."

The lights came on in apartment three. Joe had been scared too, but would never admit it. "I managed to avoid him. Where is Constance parked?"

"Down the way where we can see the front entrance."

Joe gave her quick kiss. "From here, we'll be able to see Sean leave his apartment and go to his car. If he drives away, we'll follow him. Let us handle this. You all don't need to stay."

"Are you kidding?" she asked. "This is too exciting to leave. We'll stay as long as you do."

Joe glanced at Gunnar, who shook his head. "Fine, but you must promise to follow us at a distance. If Sean notices two cars following him, he'll turn around and go back home, and our whole effort will be wasted."

"I understand, and so will the others. Be careful." She squeezed his hand, and hurried back to Constance's convertible.

Joe slid into his Chevy. "If Sean plans to unload evidence, he should do it soon."

"Even if he doesn't hurry," Gunnar posed, "let's still wait."

"That's fine with me." Joe took his camera from the glove compartment and added the flash attachment. He had extra bulbs, and slid them into his coat pockets. "If Sean does anything suspicious, I want a photo of it."

He'd had only a taste of the champagne at the party, and his senses were so sharp they nearly crackled. The lights soon went out in apartment three, and he used the flashlight he kept in the car to check his watch.

"Sean barely had time to get into his pajamas and brush his teeth."

Gunnar whispered, "Wouldn't hideous dreams of Matteo's death keep him awake long into the night?"

"Look, a man just came out the back door." Joe reached for his car keys, but the fellow disappeared down the alley rather than enter the parking lot for his car. "He looks like Sean, but he doesn't appear to be carrying anything. Let's follow him anyway."

Disregarding the possible danger, Gunnar and Joe darted between the shadows as they pursued Sean down the alley. He turned left at the first street, then right down the next alley. At the next street, he again turned left, and right down the alley. When he reached the large trashcans behind a twenty-four hour café, he opened one, and pulled a small sack from under his jacket.

Joe crept close enough to get a good photo. As Sean dropped the bag into the can, he got a great shot. The flash blinded Sean, and Gunnar lurched across the distance separating them, caught his arm and shoved it behind his back to hold him with a strong grip.

Gunnar had carried the flashlight, and shone it in Sean's face. "You're a long way from your apartment to dump your trash."

Joe placed his camera on the ground, pulled the bag out of the can, held it up to the flashlight, and found a pair of black stilettos, one with blood smeared up the heel. He fought down a wave of nausea, and showed Gunnar what they'd found.

"I'm surprised you kept these, Sean, but the police will be overjoyed that you did." Joe held the paper bag with two fingers as though it were contaminated, and picked up his camera.

Rather than struggle to get away, or make any denial or excuse, Sean remained silent, and stared at them with a cold, menacing gaze.

"Let's go into the café, call the police, and have a cup of coffee while we wait for them to arrive," Joe suggested.

Gunnar marched Sean through the back door, and into the nearest booth. Joe called the police from the public telephone in the hallway. His hands were shaking so badly, he needed a couple of tries. It was a shame Detective Lynch wouldn't be on duty at that late hour, but he'd hear about the arrest tomorrow, a Thanksgiving present.

Joe didn't recognize either of the officers who arrived with their siren blaring, but they were well-aware of the search for Matteo da Milano's killer. After a quick glance at the deadly pair of stilettos, they arrested Sean and handcuffed him. They searched him and found what appeared to be a multiple blade pocketknife, until opened.

"Aren't these lock picks?" one officer asked.

"They sure are," his partner replied. "Are you a locksmith? We sure don't want you escaping a cell tonight."

Sean ignored their attempt at humor.

Joe and Gunnar stood on the sidewalk and watched them drive away with Sean, and the gruesome bag of evidence, again with a siren accompaniment.

"What will happen next?" the Norwegian asked.

"Sean owns a very expensive cello, so he should be able to make bail, if a judge grants one. However, I doubt he'll turn up for rehearsal on Friday."

"He wouldn't dare, and now the Philharmonic is short two cellists," the conductor remarked with a frustrated sigh. "Veronica gave me Matteo's Stradivarius for safekeeping, and I'd hoped to find someone worthy of it. I don't suppose you play the cello?"

Joe turned for the return walk to his car, and they'd use the streets rather than alleys. "No, sorry, I don't. Aren't there excellent cellists clamoring to be in the orchestra?"

"Of course, a great many, but none will ever be as fine at Matteo da Milano."

"They'll still be able to play the right notes, won't they?"

"Yes, but that is the minimum expected. Do you suppose the women gave up and went home?"

"I sincerely doubt it." He was right.

"We heard sirens, and when we found no one in your car, we were afraid you two had been arrested," Mary Margaret exclaimed.

Joe took her hand to pull her close. "If you'll promise to listen without interrupting, we'll give you the news."

Constance, Paloma, Mary Margaret, and her mother all regarded him with an impatience stare. Rather than tease them with a long-winded version, he came right to the point.

"We caught Sean dumping the bloody stilettos in a trashcan behind an all-night café. He's been arrested, and with a bag of gory evidence, he can't deny any knowledge of the crime. He also had a set of lock picks on him, which answers how he took Veronica's furs."

"Now I understand what Mary Margaret sees in you, Joe," Matilda enthused. "I'm very impressed as well."

Joe didn't know which was more exciting, catching a murderer, or being praised by his future mother-in-law. "Thank you, Mrs. McBride."

"Please call me Matilda."

"Thank you, Matilda, I will."

"What about Veronica?" Paloma asked. "That Sean killed her beloved husband will be doubly difficult to bear. What's going to happen to her?"

"I'll call on her early tomorrow morning," Constance offered. "I'll bring her home to celebrate Thanksgiving with us so she won't be alone."

"That's very kind of you," Gunnar complimented. "Morning will come soon, why don't we switch cars and go home."

Mary Margaret, Matilda and Paloma climbed into Joe's car, and Gunnar left with Constance. The women were still so excited they talked all at once, but Joe didn't mind at all. He drove Paloma home, and then headed for the Chrysanthemum Court.

Thanksgiving morning, Joe got up early to dress and make coffee. He fully expected Detective Lynch to come pounding on his door before nine. He was there at eight thirty.

"I've just made coffee. Would you like some?"

"No, of course not. Yesterday, we found a fur coat and hat at a Salvation Army thrift shop. Veronica da Milano's initials were embroidered on the satin lining. I'd planned to call her in today, but now that Sean Dermot has been arrested, I'll wait until he confesses to speak with her."

Joe waited to hear a word of thanks for his part in Sean's arrest, but Lynch ended his report without issuing a single particle of gratitude. "Sean isn't the talkative sort, and you may have a long wait. I have a photo I'll have developed tomorrow and send over."

"Bring it with you when you come in to write a statement."

"I'll include every detail," Joe promised. He'd type it up in his office while Pete developed the film.

"Be sure you do."

Joe opened the door for him. "Happy Thanksgiving." He loved the way the detective flinched as though he'd cursed him, and wished he'd gotten a photo of that.

The residents of Chrysanthemum Court divided up the tasks for holidays. Phyllis and John Cameron baked the Thanksgiving turkey and made gravy. Daniel and Polly Hill, parents of a new baby girl, made mashed potatoes. Patrick Wood provided the cranberry sauce. Mary Margaret and her mother baked pumpkin and mincemeat pies. Luke Hatcher brought sweet potatoes. The bankers, Tim and Barbara Garcia in cottage six, brought freshly baked rolls, and butter. Joe arrived with the olives, carrot and celery sticks Mary Margaret had not wanted forgotten.

Blessed with warm weather that afternoon, tables and chairs were set up on the lawn in the center of the facing cottages. The edges of the tablecloths stirred lightly in the gentle breeze. John had carved the turkey in their cottage kitchen, and brought it to the table ready to serve. The tables were soon filled with the other flavorful dishes. Luke gave a brief blessing, and everyone whispered so as not to wake the baby, Catherine Elizabeth. She slept through the whole delicious meal.

Joe was still running on last night's adrenaline, and had to remind himself to slow down rather than choke on a carrot and embarrass himself as well as Mary Margaret. Matilda smiled each time she looked his way. Patrick Wood had taken the chair beside her, and they found much in common to discuss. In many ways, it was a perfect day.

"You're awfully quiet." Mary Margaret leaned close. "Did you get any sleep last night?"

"Not much, but I'm fine. How about you?"

"Mother and I were too excited to sleep more than a few hours. I can't help but worry about Veronica. She was already so deeply unhappy, I doubt she could feel any worse, but she was close to Sean, and must feel doubly betrayed."

"Constance said she'd take care of her. Let's trust her to do so."

"Ah yes, Constance. We still need to have a long talk about her."

Not feeling a bit of guilt, Joe shrugged slightly. "She apparently has near limitless wealth, and energy, and wears a ghastly perfume. That's the whole story," he swore.

"That's unlikely," Mary Margaret countered.

"It's the absolutely truth. Would you please pass the mashed potatoes?"

She passed the bowl. "I can't help but feel you owe me a lot more."

Joe had been waiting for this moment and responded with a warm smile. "I have an autographed photo of Thalia Dupré for you."

"You don't!"

"Yes, I do."

She hugged him, and he hoped to keep her in such a happy mood until their wedding, and then, long afterward. They'd take Matilda to Union Station tomorrow morning, and wish her a pleasant train trip home. Life would be back to normal then.

He hoped for a busy, but uneventful December. He'd finish studying the wedding book, and do his best to avoid getting a black eye right before their wedding. How difficult could that be?

THE
DETECTIVE JOE EZELL MYSTERY
SERIES

MURDER ME TWICE
STAIRWAY TO MURDER
MURDER ON ICE
MURDER ON STILETTOS
EYE FOR MURDER

*Turn the page for an
excerpt from*

EYE

FOR

MURDER

A Detective Joe Ezell Mystery
Book Five

P.J. Conn

Los Angeles, December 1947

Joe Ezell whistled *Santa Claus Is Coming To Town*, as he left Discreet Investigations for the day. He loved the joy of the holiday season, and waved to the clerk placing a sprig of holly in the corner drug store window. He waited for the light to cross the street, and smiled at the young woman cradling a baby in her arms standing beside him.

"This will be his first Christmas," she said. "That's obvious, isn't it?"

Joe laughed with her. As the light changed, she stepped off the curb into the crosswalk just ahead of him. He turned at the sound of a revving engine, saw a Studebaker about to blaze through the red light, and grabbed for her. All he caught was the blanket wrapped infant before she was struck with a sickening thud and tossed like a ragdoll into the air.

The man driving the gray Studebaker roared through the intersection and was gone as fast as he'd appeared. Jerked from his mother's arms, the terrified baby looked up at Joe, began to scream, and it was all the detective could do not to scream with him.

Dr. William Raymond, the pharmacist from the drug store rushed to the battered young woman's aid. Cars entering the intersection screeched to a halt, with more than one hit from behind by a driver who was unaware of the horror laying just ahead.

Badly shaken, Joe carried the frightened baby into the drug store and sat down on a stool at the counter to rock him. The clerks had left their posts to go out on the sidewalk, and many were crying. An ambulance's wailing siren could be heard approaching, but Joe doubted the young mother could possibly have survived.

Sick clear through, he went to the pay telephone to call his fiancée, Mary Margaret McBride. "I need you to take the bus and come down to my office right away. I'll tell you why when you get here."

"I can hear a baby crying, has there been an accident?"

Joe knew what he'd seen. The driver of the Studebaker had plowed through the intersection, his head down, his shoulders hunched, and his intent clear.

"No, there's been a murder."

EYE FOR MURDER

available in print and ebook

ABOUT P.J. CONN

Always a passionate lover of books, this New York Times bestselling author first answered a call to write in the 1980s and swiftly embarked on her own mythic journey. MURDER ON STILETTOS, the fourth book in her Joe Ezell Mystery series, written as P. J., is her forty-sixth release. With more than seven million copies in print of her historical, contemporary and futuristic books written under her own name as well as her pseudonyms, Cinnamon Burke, and P. J. Conn, she is as enthusiastic as ever about writing.

A native Californian, Phoebe attended the University of Arizona and California State University at Los Angeles where she earned a BA in Art History and an MA in Education. Her books have won Romantic Times Reviewer's Choice Awards and a nomination for Storyteller of the Year. Her futuristic, STARFIRE RISING, won a RomCom award as best Futuristic Romance of the year. She is a member of Romance Writers of America, Novelists Inc. and Sisters in Crime.

She is the proud mother of two grown sons and two adorable grandchildren, who love to have her read to them.

You can contact Phoebe through her publisher at PhoebeConn@epublishingworks.com

www.ingramcontent.com/pod-product-compliance
Lightning Source LLC
Chambersburg PA
CBHW020833260626
47169CB00003B/962